Home Before Midnight

"Sexy and suspenseful . . . A really good read."
—Karen Robards, *New York Times* bestselling author

"Virginia Kantra is a sensitive writer with a warm sense of humor, a fine sense of sexual tension, and an unerring sense of place."
—*BookPage*

Close Up

"Holy moly, action/adventure/romance fans! You are going to *love* this book! I highly, highly recommend it."
—Suzanne Brockmann, *New York Times* bestselling author

"Kantra's first foray into single-title fiction is fast-paced, engrossing, and full of nail-biting suspense."
—Sabrina Jeffries, *New York Times* bestselling author

"Honest, intelligent romance." —*Romance: B(u)y the Book*

MORE PRAISE FOR VIRGINIA KANTRA AND HER BESTSELLING NOVELS

"Smart, sexy, and sophisticated—another winner."
—Lori Foster, *New York Times* bestselling author

"An involving, three-dimensional story that is scary, intriguing, and sexy." —*All About Romance*

"Kantra creates powerfully memorable characters."
—*Midwest Book Review*

"Virginia Kantra is an autobuy . . . Her books are keepers and her heroes are to die for!"
—Suzanne Brockmann, *New York Times* bestselling author

"Packs a wallop!"
—Elizabeth Bevarly, *New York Times* bestselling author

Immortal Sea

VIRGINIA KANTRA

BERKLEY SENSATION, NEW YORK

THE BERKLEY PUBLISHING GROUP
Published by the Penguin Group
Penguin Group (USA) Inc.
375 Hudson Street, New York, New York 10014, USA
Penguin Group (Canada), 90 Eglinton Avenue East, Suite 700, Toronto, Ontario M4P 2Y3, Canada
(a division of Pearson Penguin Canada Inc.)
Penguin Books Ltd., 80 Strand, London WC2R 0RL, England
Penguin Group Ireland, 25 St. Stephen's Green, Dublin 2, Ireland (a division of Penguin Books Ltd.)
Penguin Group (Australia), 250 Camberwell Road, Camberwell, Victoria 3124, Australia
(a division of Pearson Australia Group Pty. Ltd.)
Penguin Books India Pvt. Ltd., 11 Community Centre, Panchsheel Park, New Delhi—110 017, India
Penguin Group (NZ), 67 Apollo Drive, Rosedale, North Shore 0632, New Zealand
(a division of Pearson New Zealand Ltd.)
Penguin Books (South Africa) (Pty.) Ltd., 24 Sturdee Avenue, Rosebank, Johannesburg 2196,
South Africa

Penguin Books Ltd., Registered Offices: 80 Strand, London WC2R 0RL, England

This is a work of fiction. Names, characters, places, and incidents either are the product of the author's
imagination or are used fictitiously, and any resemblance to actual persons, living or dead, business
establishments, events, or locales is entirely coincidental. The publisher does not have any control
over and does not assume any responsibility for author or third-party websites or their content.

IMMORTAL SEA

A Berkley Sensation Book / published by arrangement with the author

PRINTING HISTORY
Berkley Sensation mass-market edition / September 2010

Copyright © 2010 by Virginia Kantra.
Excerpt from *Forgotten Sea* by Virginia Kantra copyright © by Virginia Kantra.
Cover art by Tony Mauro.
Cover design by Rita Frangie.
Interior text design by Laura K. Corless.

ISBN: 978-0-425-23747-2

BERKLEY® SENSATION
Berkley Sensation Books are published by The Berkley Publishing Group,
a division of Penguin Group (USA) Inc.,
375 Hudson Street, New York, New York 10014.
BERKLEY® SENSATION and the "B" design are trademarks of Penguin Group (USA) Inc.

PRINTED IN THE UNITED STATES OF AMERICA

10   9   8   7   6   5   4   3   2   1

To my readers.
Thank you.

And for my children.
You have my heart.

Hence in a season of calm weather
Though inland far we be,
Our souls have sight of that immortal sea
Which brought us hither,
Can in a moment travel thither
And see the children sport upon the shore,
And hear the mighty waters rolling evermore.

—WILLIAM WORDSWORTH

As fair art thou, my bonie lass,
So deep in luve am I:
And I will luve thee still, my dear,
Till a' the seas gang dry.

Till a' the seas gang dry, my dear,
And the rocks melt wi' the sun:
I will luve thee still, my dear,
While the sands o' life shall run.

—ROBERT BURNS

Foreword

IN THE TIME BEFORE TIME, WHEN THE DOMAINS of earth, sea, and sky were formed and fire was called into being, the elementals took shape, each with their element: the children of earth, the children of the sea, the children of air, and the children of fire.

After earth had flowered and life crawled from the sea, humankind was born.

The children of fire rebelled against this new creation, declaring war on the children of air and humankind. Forced to cohabit with the mortals, the other elementals withdrew: the fair folk to the hills and wild places of earth and the merfolk—selkie and finfolk—to the depths of the sea.

Over the centuries, the children of fire grew strong, while the children of the sea declined in numbers and in magic. Now the very survival of the merfolk hangs in the balance. A closer alliance with humankind might save the children of the sea. Or destroy them.

Yet all acknowledge that some contact is inevitable

between the elementals and mortal men and women. From such encounters, souls are redeemed and lost, wars are waged, great art is created, empires are raised.

Of such meetings, legends—and children—are born . . .

1

THE TRIP OF A LIFETIME, THE TOUR BROCHURE had promised. *Culture, nightlife, adventure, and romance in Europe's most swinging capital.*

Twenty-two-year-old Elizabeth Ramsey tightened her grip on her purse strap. Getting accosted outside a dance club in Copenhagen might qualify as adventure.

But *romance*?

She looked at the men blocking her way back inside the club. Three of them—she counted—with pockmarked skin, bad hair, and crappy attitudes.

Not a chance.

She bit her lip, betrayed by the travel company's PR and her own expectations. Her cheeks were hot. Her head still pounded from the techno beat vibrating down the grimy steps.

The skinny guy in the middle called an invitation, thrusting his hips forward suggestively. The red neon sign over the club's entrance illuminated the line of his underwear and a slice of hairy stomach.

Oh, no.

She glanced again at the club door, hoping for rescue. A couple of women maybe, or another American. If Allyson had only stuck by their buddy arrangement . . . But her roommate had ditched her earlier that evening for a Swedish graduate student, Gunnar or Gondor or whatever his name was. Sooner or later, Liz would have to make her way back to their hotel alone.

She looked around for a cab. Or a cop. Copenhagen was safe, everyone said, even at three in the morning. But she didn't speak the language. She wasn't in control of the situation. She hated that.

Plus it would totally suck if the first time ever she flouted her parents' wishes, they turned out to be right after all.

Liz shifted her weight in her platform sandals. Better to walk away, she reasoned, than get into a wrestling match with the Grunge Triplets. She was only a block or two from the square. Plenty of taxis there.

She anchored her tiny purse under her arm and picked her way along the cracked, uneven sidewalk, scanning for a cab.

Mistake. She realized it almost at once. Because instead of abandoning her for more willing game inside, the three men followed. Skin prickled on her upper arms, exposed by her skimpy halter top. She needed a jacket.

She needed to get the hell away.

She heard them behind her, scuffling feet and whistles that required no translation. Her breathing hitched. She quickened her step, her gaze darting in search of a lit window, an open door, the lights and bustle of Nørrebrogade.

Nothing. Just the flat, black waters of a canal and a row of small, shuttered shops, their bright facades faded to gray by the night.

Nerves scraped under her skin. Had she turned the wrong way? Should she turn back? But they were right behind her, heavy footsteps, coming closer, coming faster, almost—

Her neck wrenched. Her head jerked back.

Ow ow ow.

Pain and panic flared. Tears stung her eyes. The guy following her had grabbed her hair, yanking her to a halt.

She whirled in self-defense, striking out, striking back. Her clenched fist connected with something hard and moist. Her knuckles burned.

She'd hit the bald guy. The big one. Snatching back her hand, she watched, appalled, as blood bloomed in his mouth.

His companions laughed. Violence thickened the air.

Oh, God. Oh, shit. What had she done?

Slowly, her attacker dragged the back of his arm across his cut lip. He stared down at his wrist; up into her eyes. And smiled, his teeth stained with blood.

Fear tightened her chest. She sucked in her breath to scream. Before the sound escaped, movement flashed in her peripheral vision. Something big, something fast, flowing out of the darkness behind her.

She flinched from this new threat.

But the thing—*shadow*—man—brushed by her like a shark in the water, knocking her flat on her ass. She landed hard, jarring her wrists, scraping her palms.

Darkness swirled in the narrow street. Dazed, she heard a thud, a crunch, choked sounds of pain or surprise. *Fighting.* Her insides roiled with fear and relief. They were fighting. She grabbed her purse, fumbling for the whistle she carried on campus.

Two sets of footsteps pounded against the pavement, leaving her attacker splayed in the gutter on the other side of the street and one man standing in a puddle of moonlight.

Shadow Man. Her rescuer.

She blinked. From her position on the ground, he looked larger than life, tall and leanly muscled in a long black leather coat.

He turned, the coat flaring around his ankles, and her heart jumped into her throat. His face was angled, cold, and pale, his hair the color of moonlight.

Liz swallowed hard, her gaze sliding up that long, powerful body to his face. His features were too strong to be
really handsome, his nose too broad, his jaw too sharp.
His upper lip was narrow, the lower one full, curved, and
compelling.

She shivered with fear and something else. Just because
he was cleaner and better dressed than the punks who
had followed her from the club didn't make him any less
dangerous.

She snuck a glance at her attacker lying motionless in
the gutter.

Okay, more dangerous.

She couldn't see her rescuer's eyes, shadowed by the
line of his brow. He stood a moment longer, watching her,
waiting for . . . What? Thanks? Tears? Hysterics?

And then he turned away.

An unreasoning urgency gripped her, sharper than fear.
"Wait."

He paused. Her heart hammered. Did he even speak
English?

She scrambled to her feet, wiping her palms on the
thighs of her jeans. "I . . . Thank you for, uh, helping me."

He ignored her, dropping on his haunches by the body in
the gutter. She watched him pat down her attacker, searching for a pulse.

Or maybe his wallet.

She gripped her purse tighter. "Why did you?"

He glanced briefly over his shoulder. "It was hardly a fair
fight. I do not usually interfere in the affairs of your kind."

Liz's eyes narrowed. *Her kind?*

Okay. She forced herself to consider the situation from
his point of view, the dark street, her scanty club wear. He
didn't know her. She could have been anyone. Anything. A
hooker on the run from her pimp.

"You're English," she said.

"No." He did not elaborate.

"But your accent . . ." Not English, not exactly. But he
definitely wasn't American.

He straightened and walked away.

"Wait."

He turned, silhouetted by the moon, impatience in every hard line of his body.

She swallowed. "We can't just leave."

"I can."

"But . . ." She hugged her elbows, torn between her instinct for self-preservation and her sense of what was right. "Shouldn't we notify the police?"

"I have no desire to be detained by your police."

Which made her wonder uneasily what, exactly, he was doing alone on this deserted street at night.

Unfair, she thought. She didn't want to stick around either. Not that she expected the very polite Danes to lock her in some foreign cell for being stupid enough to walk alone at night. But what if they contacted the embassy? Or her parents?

Her gaze skittered to the body stretched out in the gutter. "What about him?"

"You wish him punished further?"

"No." The suggestion horrified her. "But he . . . Look, if he dies, you could be in trouble."

His eyes widened slightly, as if she had surprised him. His pupils were large and very dark, banded with a pale rim of color. Not blue, Liz thought, despite that white blond hair.

And she had no business puzzling over his eye color when there was an unconscious man lying practically at her feet.

Steeling herself to approach him—to approach them both—she knelt in the street, grateful for the thin protection of her jeans. She was uncomfortably conscious of her rescuer standing over them. His heat. His height.

"He will not die," he said quietly.

Awareness tightened the back of her neck. Nerves sharpened her voice. "How would you know?"

"I could ask the same of you."

She overcame her distaste of the body before her, forcing

herself to conduct a patient assessment. *Airway, breathing, circulation* . . .

"I'm going to be a doctor." Not for another seven years or so, but merely saying the words gave her a measure of confidence, a portion of control.

She took a deep breath. A sour smell leaked upward from the gutter. Stale sweat maybe, or unwashed feet. Or Shaved Head Guy could have been popping nitrates. She'd seen plenty of little glass vials crushed on the sidewalk outside the club.

He sprawled on his back, in danger of swallowing his tongue. She felt gingerly for neck or spine injuries before tilting his head to clear his airway. He groaned, making her start.

Her rescuer's voice dropped out of the darkness. "Unless your compassion extends to being here when he wakes, I suggest you leave now."

She gulped. "Right. Good idea." She rocked back on her heels and stood, her legs trembling slightly in reaction.

Above the jagged rooftops, the sky was heavy purple, pregnant with early dawn. There was nothing to tell her what to do or which way to go, only dirty windows, darkened doors, and stinking puddles. Shadows lay across the street like bars, collected in drifts between the buildings like garbage.

She glanced nervously at her companion, his face etched in black and white perfection by the moon. With his broad shoulders and long black coat, he looked dark and solid. She wanted to burrow under his coat.

She cleared her throat. "Would you mind walking me as far as Nørrebrogade?"

Those strange, pale eyes fixed on her face, the pupils widening like a chasm at her feet, reflecting nothing, revealing nothing. They pulled at her like gravity. She imagined herself sinking into his eyes, falling *down, down, down*.

"I will take you." In that voice, his low, deep, mocking voice, the words sounded almost sexual. "Since you ask."

Her cheeks flushed as she snatched herself back from the edge of . . . *what?*

"Just to the main street," she clarified.

He inclined his head in an oddly formal gesture. Foreign. "As far as you wish."

Her heart bumped against her ribs. He had saved her, she reminded herself. She could trust him.

She was less sure if she should trust her own judgment. She got A's in all her classes and—according to Allyson—a C minus in men.

This one stood like a bulwark in the moonlight, blocking the stench of the puddles, the reek from the alleys. His scent teased at her senses, fresh and wild as the sea.

She released her breath. "I'd appreciate it."

His gaze skimmed her face again. "Would you, I wonder," he murmured.

His words barely registered over the pounding in her ears. He was so close. If she stood on tiptoe, she thought dizzily, she could kiss him.

Not that she would. Not that she wanted to.

He turned and strode away. Her knees sagged with disappointment and relief. She felt his absence like a chill against the front of her body.

But at least he seemed to know where he was going. He moved as surely as a cat in the dark.

She hurried after him, envying both his confidence and his shoes. Her open-toed sandals were fine on the dance floor. Not so great on these uneven streets.

She stumbled on the curb, grabbing for his arm. The leather was smooth beneath her fingers, his muscles hard as iron.

At her touch, he froze.

*   *   *

Morgan looked down, arrested, at the woman clinging to his arm. Was she aware what she invited? His kind did not touch. Only to fight or to mate.

His blood rushed like water under ice. Perhaps tonight he would do both.

He had not come ashore to rut. He was not as abstemious as his prince, Conn, but he had standards. Unlike his sister Morwenna and others among the mer, he did not often waste his seed on humankind.

The woman's throat moved as she swallowed. "Sorry," she said and dropped his arm.

She was very young, he observed. Attractive, with healthy skin and glossy brown hair. Her face was a strong oval, her jaw slightly squared, her unfettered breasts high and pleasing. There was even a gleam that might be intelligence in those brown eyes.

It would be no great privation to indulge her and himself.

"Do not apologize." Grasping her hand, he replaced it on his sleeve. Her nails were clean and unpolished, her fingers tapered.

He imagined those short nails pressing into his flesh, and the rush in his blood became a roar. *No privation at all.*

He glanced around the narrow buildings fronting the street. He would not take her here, in this filthy human warren. But there were other places less noxious and nearby. Adjusting his stride to hers, he led her away, seeking green ways and open water.

The lights and noise of the city at night eddied and ebbed around them, the amber pool of a street light, the green glow of a bar sign, a lamp in a second-floor window.

At the next intersection, she hesitated, her gaze darting down the street toward a café where trees strung with tiny lights canopied a cluster of empty tables. "Don't we want to go that way?"

She did possess intelligence, then. Or at least a sense of direction.

"If you like." Morgan shrugged. "It is quieter toward the harbor."

Her brow pleated. Her eyes were big and dark. He

watched the silent battle between feminine caution and female desire, felt the moment of acquiescence when her hand relaxed on his forearm. He fought to keep his flare of triumph from his face.

"Quieter," she repeated.

"More . . . scenic," he said, searching for a word that might appeal to her.

"Oh." Her tongue touched her lower lip in doubt or invitation. "I haven't seen the harbor yet. This is my first visit to Copenhagen."

"Indeed." Warmth radiated from her hand up his arm. Anticipation flowed thick and urgent through his veins. She was not part of his purpose here. But she was a respite, a recompense of a sort, for long years of trial and frustration.

Her bare shoulders gleamed in the moonlight, sweetly curved as the curl of a shell. The night swirled around them like seaweed caught in the tide, the smell of beer and piss and car exhaust, a waft from a flowerbox, a breeze from the sea.

"I almost didn't come," she continued, as if he had expressed an interest. "Not part of The Plan, you know?"

He did not know and cared even less. But her voice was low pitched and pleasant. To hear it again, he asked, "There is a plan?"

She nodded, touching the ends of her hair where it brushed her smooth shoulders. He observed the small, betraying gesture with satisfaction. Consciously or not, she was signaling her awareness of him as a male.

"I start med school in the fall," she said. "My dad wanted me to stay home and do a post-bacc program, get a leg up on the competition. My mother wanted one more summer of tennis and Junior League before I slip her grasp forever."

He had no idea what she was talking about. "And what do you want?"

Her eyes crinkled. "A break," she said with such rueful honesty that he almost smiled back. "Everything always revolves around school. Like I don't live my own life, I *prepare* for it. I wanted . . . something different. An adventure, I guess."

He could give her something different, he thought. He would even make sure she enjoyed it.

The barred storefronts ceded ground to cobblestone streets and narrow houses with cramped garden plots. The scent of standing water and of lilies carried on the breeze. *Not much farther now*, he thought.

"What about you?" she asked with friendly interest.

He glanced down in surprise.

"What brings you here?"

His purpose was bitter as brine in his mouth, deep and cold as the sea.

For Morgan was warden of the northern deeps, charged by a lost king to fight a losing battle.

For a thousand years he had served the sea king's son, battling demons in the deep, defending his demesne from the sly encroachments of the *sidhe*. But his powers had proved useless against the depredations of humankind. For more than a century, the overflow from this city's streets and canals had polluted the sound and the sea, turning the port into a shit house. Only now, when the humans had finally learned to curb their waste, could Morgan begin the slow process of repair. Recovery of the seabed would take centuries.

He did not blame this girl—much—for what her kind had done. She was here and female and willing. Under the circumstances, he was prepared to overlook a great deal.

"Business," he said.

Her deep brown eyes assessed him. "You don't dress like a businessman."

He wore the black and silver of the finfolk, subtly altered so he could pass for a man of this place and time. "No?"

"No."

He did not respond. The sky was thick with moisture, glowing with the lights of the city and the promise of dawn. The moon wore golden vapor like a veil.

"You don't want to talk about it," she guessed.

He smiled, showing the edge of his teeth. "You did not seek my company for my conversation."

She stopped on the sidewalk, her chin tilted at a challenging angle. Despite her earlier signals, he had been too blunt. Women, human women, required some preliminaries. Or perhaps her female pride was offended. "Really? What is it you think I want from you?"

Her cheeks were flushed. Her scent filled his nostrils. Beneath the sharp notes of her annoyance, he could smell the sweetness of her body readying itself for his. His shaft went hard as stone.

"My protection," he offered.

She nodded once, her eyes big and wary. "Yeah," she admitted. "Okay."

He stepped closer, watching her face carefully. "And perhaps . . . an adventure?"

He heard the betraying intake of her breath. Her small round breasts rose. And suddenly he wanted this, wanted *her*, beyond habit or reason, instinct or expedience. The intensity of his lust surprised him.

She was only human, after all.

* * *

Liz inhaled, her breathing no longer under her control, her heart thrumming with nerves and longing. She shouldn't . . . She never . . .

Oh, but she wanted to.

He was right in front of her, adventure personified in moonlight and black leather. Those strange, pale eyes were dark with promise, his mouth curved in a knowing smile.

She moistened her lips. "I don't even know your name."

He lowered his head, stoking her senses with the heat of his body, the flavor of his breath. "Morgan."

"Liz." He was going to kiss her, she realized. And she was going to let him. "Elizabeth Ramsey."

"Elizabeth," he repeated, a whisper of flame against her mouth.

Her bones melted. She was tingly and melting all over. Her lids drifted shut in anticipation.

A cold draft replaced the warmth where he had been.

"Come with me," Morgan said.

Her eyes popped open. "What?"

He stood several feet away, the dark sky haloing his silver hair. Behind him she could see a bridge stretching over a zigzag moat and the needle of a church spire rising like a scene from some romantic movie.

Except in the movies, the girl always got kissed.

She wrapped her arms around her waist. "Where?"

"Come."

She trailed after him under the trees and on to the flat narrow bridge; glanced uncertainly down at the water and then to the end of the bridge where the walkway ended in an arched gatehouse and a short white wall with steep grassy banks on either side.

"What's that?"

"Kastellet."

A little shiver of pleasure and excitement ran up her arms. "A castle?"

"Citadel. Yes."

Elaborate iron sconces flanked the archway, reflected on the water. "It looks really old."

He shrugged. "A few centuries, no more."

She wandered closer, peering through the iron gate with disappointment. "It's closed."

She hadn't planned on sightseeing at four in the morning. She should get back to her hotel. Yet now that the way was barred, the citadel took on the lovely lure of the forbidden. The moonlight transformed the smooth stone walls and tiled roofs to a fairy fortress full of magic, just beyond her reach.

Morgan's teeth gleamed. "Then we will be undisturbed."

Her pulse fluttered. "But the gate . . ."

In one smooth move, he crouched on the railing of the bridge, balancing on the balls of his feet. "Is not the only way inside."

He leaped for the bank.

Her stomach catapulted into her throat. "Oh, be careful!"

He landed without a slip, without a splash. Turning, he held out his arms to her. "Jump."

She shook her head. "I am not the kind of girl who jumps into things."

Ever. The thought made her vaguely resentful.

"What kind of girl are you?" His deep voice was cool and amused.

She swallowed. "I'm more the look-before-you-leap, watch-your-step type."

"I could change that," he said.

She inhaled sharply. Her gaze swung from the three-foot railing to the eight-foot drop to the yards of swirling water between her and the bank. Her hands clutched the railing. "It's too far."

"I will catch you."

"It's too dangerous."

He didn't reply.

He didn't need to. She stood restlessly on the bridge, on the brink, on the edge, suspended in place and time.

"*I don't live my life,*" she'd told him in truth. "*I prepare for it.*"

Morgan waited below her in the dark, her personal adventure. She felt him in the beat of her blood like every rule she'd never broken, every risk she hadn't taken, every impulse she'd denied.

Every man her mother had warned her about.

The water chuckled and flowed.

Gripping the top rail with both hands, she swung one leg over, feeling for a toehold on the other side. Her palms were damp. Her heart thundered. She was about to commit trespass and God knew what else.

She hesitated. "What if someone sees us?"

"No one will see. Jump now. *Jump.*"

The sky had lightened enough for her to see the pale blur of his face in the dark. With a breathless gasp, she let go, launching herself across the moat and into his arms.

Sky and water whirled. Her ears rushed, her stomach churned, her breathing stopped as she fell—dropped—*smacked*—into something hard and unyielding. Into him. His chest. He seized her, hauling her safely onto the bank, against his body.

Dizzy with her own daring, she tipped back her head, laughing in reaction and relief. "I did it."

His eyes gleamed. "Not yet," he said. "But we will."

Her jaw dropped.

He kissed her open mouth, hard and leisurely, as if he had every right and all the time in the world. He tasted wild and salty sweet as the sea, and she felt the surge kick in her blood, washing away her doubts, weakening her knees. She staggered, sliding her hands into the slippery coolness of his hair, holding on for balance and dear life while his hot mouth ravaged hers.

His tongue stroked, probed, plunged, distracting her from the play of his hands, the heel of his palm on the exposed side of her breast, his fingers splaying on her naked back. She arched closer, wanting more. Demanding more. He murmured encouragement, molding her hips to his, his erection pressing long and thick against her stomach. She forgot to breathe.

He released her, turned her, so that she faced the slope, and gave her a little push. "Up."

She stumbled, dazed. He steadied her, urging her up the steep grass bank, supporting her with a touch at her back, even boosting her with a firm hand on her butt when she slipped.

At the top of the embankment, she drew breath. Below, the long, low barracks gleamed through the cover of night and the trees. The sky above was suffused with dawn and possibilities. She filled her lungs, holding the moment inside her until a cold wind skipped from the harbor, making her shiver.

What was she doing here?

Morgan wrapped an arm around her waist. "This way."

He led her to the shelter of a low stone wall and a dappled hollow under the trees. *No turning back.* Where could she go? She'd never make it over the moat again.

He stopped and cupped her face in his hands, drawing her close. She was aware of him all along her front, the places their bodies brushed and even where they didn't. Breasts, belly, thighs. With the pad of his thumb, he traced her eyebrows and the line of her cheek before resting his hands lightly, easily, around her neck.

Liz swallowed against the faint pressure of his fingers, her breathing loud in her ears.

He stroked his thumb lazily up the side of her throat to the sensitive hollow just below her jaw. Her pulse throbbed under his touch. "You are nervous," he murmured.

"This is nuts," she said. "I don't even know you."

"You know what you want." He watched her with those odd, pale eyes, those deep, dark centers swallowing her up. "Take what you need. You are starving for life. How long will you ration yourself, tasting life in tiny sips, in careful bites? Always hungry." He laid warm lips against her neck, his silken hair brushing from her chin to her collarbone. "Never satisfied."

His voice moved like a drug through her veins. Her head fell back in heavy acquiescence as he nibbled his way up her throat, making her lips want and wait, making her breasts ache for his touch. She squeezed her thighs together to ease the awful emptiness there.

He rubbed a kiss against her mouth.

"I could satisfy you," he whispered and bit her lip.

She moaned and shuddered against him, falling helplessly into his kiss, under his spell, against his body. He slid his palms down to cup her buttocks and ground slowly against her, stoking her hunger. Feeding it. Grabbing his shoulders, she kissed him back, tangling her fingers in his hair, sucking on his tongue.

His hands clamped on her hips before he pushed her gently away.

Her breath rasped like a drowning woman's. "What?" she demanded, frustrated. Embarrassed. Bereft. "Too pushy? I'm just supposed to stand here and take it?"

"Take it, yes. But not standing." He stripped off his coat and tossed it on the ground.

Her eyes widened. He wasn't wearing any shirt. Just pants and some kind of necklace, a textured disk on a silver chain. He should have looked ridiculous. He did not. Above the black pants, against the dark trees, his body looked white and smooth and very strong. His shoulders were knotted, his chest heavy with muscle.

She gasped as he swept her off her feet, laying her on his open coat under the spangled sky.

He loomed over her, on his knees, between her legs. In moments, he had his pants undone, her top ruched up, and her jeans shoved down around her ankles. She blushed and squirmed. His cock reared up against his stomach. No shirt. No underwear either.

She reached out—to cover herself? to push him away?— and her hand brushed his stomach and then the broad, smooth head of his penis. It jerked at her touch. Morgan made a sound between his teeth and covered her hand with his, holding her palm against him. He felt wonderful, thick and hard. She wiggled closer, fluid and restless as water, running her free hand over his chest, his thighs. He caressed her stomach, making the muscles there contract, before he pushed her legs wide. Crouching over her, he rubbed himself slowly up and down her slit.

She arched toward him; twisted away. "Wait."

"Why?" He thrust one long finger inside her, then two. "You are ready."

Before she could say "condom," he slammed inside.

She convulsed in shock. *Too much*, her mind cried. Too soon. Too . . . perfect.

She had not known that she had been so empty, that she could feel so full. She felt him everywhere, in her breasts, between her legs, and deep, deep inside. He didn't do anything fancy or fumbling, none of the tricks she'd tried with her few boyfriends. She was glad. She didn't need technique, only this, only him, his hot skin, his overwhelming size, the violent grace of his body in hers. He pinned her down and pulsed inside her, pounded inside her, slippery and strong, while the cold ground dug into her shoulders and the sky wheeled and changed colors behind his head. She cried and clawed and came, again and again.

He stiffened above her, his back rigid, his lips pulling back in a snarl. She couldn't help him. She was stretched too full to do anything clever with her muscles. It didn't seem to matter. With a growl, with a groan, he erupted inside her, pressing deep, setting her off again.

She trembled as he lowered his weight onto her, his body hard and slick with sweat, cradled between her thighs.

She closed her eyes, stunned. Numb. Her body quivered with aftershocks as her brain struggled to process what had just happened. What *could* happen as a result.

Oh, dear God.

Something brushed briefly across her forehead before he withdrew, his shaft dragging from her wet and swollen flesh. She concentrated on breathing, in and out. The light of dawn pressed against her eyelids. She heard a scrape as he rolled to his feet, a rustle as he adjusted his clothing.

She opened her eyes.

He stood half-naked in the blue shadow of the trees, his back to her. She regarded the strong indentation of his spine, the faint scratch marks on his shoulder blades, and wanted to weep.

He turned, his face calm, composed, polite, and offered her something. His hand? She blinked sudden moisture from her eyes. A handkerchief. An absurd bubble of laughter rose in her throat. No shirt or underwear, she thought, but he carried a fucking handkerchief.

She managed to sit up and take it, pleased to notice her hand was steady. Evidence of her awesome self-control, she thought, and winced.

"You are all right." His voice was deep and without expression. She couldn't tell if he was asking her or telling her.

"Fine, thanks." She finished with the handkerchief and, after a brief internal debate, wadded it up and stuffed it in her pocket.

"We can leave now," he said.

A hollow opened in the pit of her stomach. She stared at him blankly. His eyes weren't blue at all, she noted inconsequentially, but tarnished gold.

"The gates unlock at six," he explained. "The bridge will be open."

"Oh. That's . . ." She struggled to force words past the constriction in her throat. "Convenient."

"You will wish to return to your place of lodging." Another statement.

"I guess." She got a grip. "Yes."

"I will accompany you."

She wanted to tell him she didn't need his charity or his company. But that was stupid and unfair. He hadn't promised her anything. Only his protection, which she'd been plenty grateful for. Face it, anything could happen to her wandering around the streets of a foreign city in the early morning hours.

She looked at his brutally handsome face, her insides aching and her heart sore. *Anything at all.*

"Thank you," she said.

They walked through the open gate without incident and across the bridge to a strip of park. The waterfront was waking up with chugging boats and rumbling busses and early morning joggers. Liz finger-combed her hair, uncomfortably aware of her bare shoulders and her companion's naked chest, magnificently visible in his open leather coat. Oddly, though, no one seemed to notice. Maybe the Danes were inured to tourists stumbling home at sunrise.

Golden clouds streaked the sky. Sunlight sparkled on the blue waters of the harbor. The buildings were flat and bright as dollhouses or images on a postcard.

Liz raised her head, momentarily roused from her funk by the scene. "That's the Little Mermaid."

Morgan spared a glance for the rocky shore and the life-size statue gazing out to sea. "A facsimile."

She stopped. This was still her trip of a lifetime. She might never get another chance to see the iconic statue, its bronze warmed to blush by the rising sun. "She looks sad."

"She was a fool," Morgan said.

"Excuse me?"

He looked down his brawler's nose at her. "To sacrifice the sea."

"Well, but she had a good reason, didn't she? She fell in love. With a prince."

"Another fool."

She was not going to let him ruin her fairy tale. "The point is, she chose love."

"She chose death."

Liz looked at him wryly. "I take it you're not a believer in the Disney princess version."

He looked blank.

"You know, Ariel and the happily-ever-after ending?"

"Ah. No," he said. "I am not a believer in happy endings. Not when there is such . . . difference between two people."

Which pretty much said it all, didn't it? They were too different.

So she wasn't surprised when he dropped her off at the hotel without asking for her cell phone number. Or when he didn't drop by the next day or the next to see how she was doing or invite her out for a beer and a hot dog. She asked the concierge. He didn't even leave a message.

It was just another one-night stand, she told herself.

Just a summer romance.

Just the best sex of her life.

And like her vacation, when it was over, it was over.

Boy, was she wrong.

2

~≈~

"YOU *SAID* WE COULD GO TO THE BEACH TODAY."
Seven-year-old Emily bounced on the sofa, her doll Molly
clutched in her arms.

Dr. Elizabeth Ramsey Rodriguez glanced up, distracted,
from unpacking the last of the moving cartons. The box had
traveled with them for nine hundred miles, crammed into
the back of the CRV with Zack's Xbox, Emily's American
Girl doll, and Liz's laptop—items too precious, too necessary to living, to trust to a stranger's care.

"We will," she promised. "Just as soon as I . . ."

"Finish," Emily said for her and grinned.

Liz smiled back, love and guilt weighting her chest,
tightening her throat. The whole point of this move was to
spend more time with her children.

Today was Sunday, her first official day off. The clinic
was closed today. Of course, as the island's new and only
doctor, she was still on call. In an emergency—fish hooks,
boating accidents, strokes, earaches—she was all that stood

between the residents of World's End and a hasty trip to the hospital on the mainland.

But today was for Zack and Emily.

Liz glanced at the clock. Almost noon. At home in North Carolina, fifteen-year-old Zachary rarely emerged from his room before lunchtime. Yet ever since their arrival on World's End, he'd roused himself from bed to watch Emily while Liz saw her morning patients. His behavior was hardly extraordinary on World's End, where other boys his age got up at dawn to haul lobster traps.

But the change gave Liz hope. Maybe this move was just what her son needed.

"Don't you want to wait for your brother?" she asked.

Emily fiddled with Molly's braids, so different from her own halo of soft, dark curls. The doll's pale, stiff complexion contrasted sharply against Emily's warm, honey-colored skin. But they were dressed alike for the beach in bathing suits, flip-flops, and shorts. "Zack doesn't like the beach."

"Of course he does," Liz said automatically and then stopped.

When he was a little boy, Zack had loved the water. From the time he could hold a pole until Ben's illness four years ago, their annual fishing trip to the pier at Holden Beach had been the highlight of Zack's summers. Now he wouldn't swim, wouldn't even walk barefoot on the beach, and wore big, black, laced-up combat boots all the time. He had spent the ferry ride from Rockland buried below deck, ears plugged and eyes glued to his iTouch. Liz didn't know what her son liked anymore. What he wanted. What he was doing all those hours alone in his room.

"Why don't you grab a sweatshirt," she suggested. "We'll take our walk now, and when Zack gets up, I'll make us all some pancakes."

"Cool." Emily scrambled off the couch and bolted for the hall as if afraid her mother would change her mind. Her flip-flops slapped up the stairs.

Liz smiled and reached for the bottom of the box.

Ah.

Her hand froze.

Her heart clenched.

She recognized the swaddled lump at once by the weight, the feel of it in her hand. Her doves. Ben's doves. She lifted the package carefully from the carton. With trembling fingers, she pulled at the bubble wrap to expose the heavy sculpture: two birds blown of lead crystal, joined at the base and their beaks, Ben's gift to her on their first wedding anniversary, an unexpected and utterly romantic gesture from her normally prosaic husband. *"One heart,"* he had written on the card.

Sudden, hot tears flooded her eyes.

Bernardo Rodriguez had been dead three years. Long enough for his scent to fade from his pillows and their closet, long enough for her grief and rage to recede to a faint throbbing like an aching tooth.

She stroked a finger along the smooth crystal breast of a dove. They nestled together in their plastic wrapping, their perfection undimmed by time. Beautiful. Complete. Whole.

Emily clattered on the stairs. "Hey, Mom."

Liz blinked. She didn't want her daughter to catch her crying. Not now. Not here, where they were making a fresh start.

She swiped at her eyes, reaching blindly to set the doves on the mantle. The crystal slipped through her fingers.

Crash.

Splinters shimmered on the cold stone hearth. The heavy base rolled on its side.

Oh, God. Oh, no.

"Mom?"

Liz fell to her knees on the carpet, her mouth opening in a silent cry. Not broken, please, not . . .

Cracked.

Upstairs, a door creaked. Footsteps shuffled in the hall.

Zack's voice, rough with sleep and adolescence, drifted down. "What happened?"

Liz lifted the doves from the hearth, ignoring the glittering dust of tiny shards. The fall had knocked off a chunk of tail, a corner of the base. A crack ran through the crystal's heart like a flaw in ice.

"Shit," Emily said in a small, awed voice, and Liz couldn't even find the words to correct her.

Her children stood in the door to the living room. Zack towered at his sister's back, a black T-shirt hanging off his broad, bony shoulders, his dull black hair sticking up in every direction.

Liz pulled herself together. "Stay back. You'll cut your feet."

Zack scowled. "You'll cut your hands."

"You're *bleeding*," Emily squeaked in distress.

Liz glanced down. Sure enough, a thin red line welled on her finger. She pressed on it hastily, offering her daughter a shaky smile. "It's okay. I'm okay. It doesn't hurt."

Emily frowned, unconvinced. "But . . ."

"You heard her, she's fine." Zack poked his sister's shoulder. "Come on, let's get out of here so she can clean up."

Em tipped up her face. "Will you take me to the beach?"

"No, but I'll buy you ice cream." Zack's gaze, deep black rimmed with gold, met Liz's. Were his pupils a little too dilated? But he'd just woken up, she reminded herself.

"You want a broom?" he asked.

This was the boy she remembered, thoughtful, responsible, compassionate. Like Ben.

She swallowed, cradling the broken doves in her lap. "No, you go. I'll get it."

He nodded once, his shaggy dark hair flopping over his forehead. With his face free from powder and fresh from sleep, he could have been any average teenage boy stumbling out of bed.

Assuming the average teenage boy would be caught dead wearing black nail polish.

"There's money in my purse," Liz said. "For the ice cream."

Zack's mouth flattened. Did he remember the last bitter fight they'd had before leaving North Carolina, when she'd accused him of taking money from her purse to buy drugs?

Of course he did. Zack—sensitive, observant, intelligent—remembered everything.

A fresh start, she reminded herself. For all of them.

She held his gaze.

"Sweet," he said at last. "Thanks."

Liz expelled a shaky breath.

They would be all right, she thought as she listened to the front door click shut behind them. The sound of their footsteps thumped down the steps and faded away. Everything was going to be all right.

In time.

She regarded the fractured crystal in her hands, the furled and frozen wings, the fault line running through its pedestal like a bolt of buried lightning, and a storm of grief shook her heart.

She closed her eyes. A tear oozed beneath her shut lids and rolled unchecked down her cheek.

*   *   *

Zack shot a glance at the girl behind the cash register. His age, maybe a year older. With girls sometimes it was hard to tell. She was pretty, with purple eye shadow and a silver lip ring at the corner of her mouth. She was reading some thick book, but as he approached, she closed the black-and-white cover and shoved it beside the register.

Zack put his purchases on the counter without making eye contact. The Invisible Man.

The girl picked up the box of hair color with one hand. "This yours?"

Zack gave her his walled-off look. The store—WILEY'S GROCERY, announced the painted sign out front in big, old-fashioned letters—was practically empty. Who did she think he was buying it for?

"Because the other brand is better," she said, as if he'd

asked. "Not as harsh. And it comes with this little conditioning tube—"

"This is fine," he interrupted. "And an ice cream bar, please."

"Self-serve," she told him. "In the freezer."

"I know." He dug in his front jeans pocket for his wallet. "It's for my sister."

The cashier glanced toward the front of the store where a freezer case sat next to a bunch of store displays. Sunscreen. Bug spray. Charcoal briquettes. Emily propped the door open, shivering in the fog that rolled off the bags of ice.

The girl behind the cash register arched her eyebrows. "That's her? That's your sister?"

His mom was always going on about people in small towns, how everybody knew everybody and looked out for each other. He couldn't explain he didn't want people to know him without going into the reasons why, so he just nodded.

Emily selected an ice cream bar, letting the freezer door thump shut. Zack watched her peel back the paper.

"She doesn't look like you," observed the cashier.

No, she didn't. Emily took after their father, Ben: warm brown eyes, warm brown skin, warm, wide smile.

"I'm adopted."

"You're kidding."

Zack lifted one shoulder in a shrug. He didn't care if she believed him or not.

She blinked her purple-lidded eyes. "Seriously? Because some days I wish I was adopted. I used to pretend that my parents, my *real* parents, my fabulously wealthy real parents who lived in, like, the Bahamas or New York City or someplace . . . Anyway, I used to imagine that one day they'd show up and take me away and give me everything I ever wanted. A pony. A canopy bed. A scholarship to Harvard."

He bet nobody in this crappy town on this godforsaken rock in the middle of the ocean ever went to Harvard.

"You want a pony," he repeated.

"I want to get off World's End," she said frankly. "I want *choices* in my life."

Her gaze met his and something sparked. Attraction. Recognition.

He didn't have any choices either.

"It's fine if you're a guy," the girl added. She nodded toward the snack aisle, where a couple of dudes in flannel shirts loaded up on corn chips and meat byproducts. "Guys work stern for their fathers until they make enough dough to go out on their own. But if you're a girl, there's nothing to do here but raise babies or clean houses."

"You could still work for your father," Zack said. His mom was big on equal opportunity shit.

"I do. I'm Stephanie Wiley." In response to his blank look, she added, "Wiley's Grocery? George Wiley is my dad."

"Zack Rodriguez."

"I know. Your mom's the new doctor, right? You're a . . . senior?"

"Sophomore."

"I'm a junior." She studied him a moment, making him conscious of his big nose and his awkward height and his lack of a driver's license. She smiled. "Close enough."

He stared back, his heart pounding. Close enough for what?

An elbow jabbed him hard in the back. "Whatever you're selling, Stephanie, faggot boy isn't buying."

Shit.

Just . . . Shit.

Zack turned to face the two guys from the snack aisle, crowding behind him.

The girl sighed. "Jesus, Todd. Could you be a bigger prick?"

"Why don't you look and find out?" he invited.

His companion snickered.

Stephanie rolled her eyes. "Ignore these morons. They

have limited intelligence and even smaller . . . vocabularies."

They didn't need a big vocabulary to get their message across. Zack read it in their hostile looks, their fat, freckled faces, clear as a posted warning: *No Trespassing. Keep Out.*

Fine by him. He wasn't here to make friends.

He dropped a ten on the counter.

"Summer people," sneered the shorter of the two guys. "Throwing your money around."

"Shut up, Doug," the girl said. "He's one of us."

But he wasn't. He couldn't ever be one of them. That was his problem.

The familiar bubble of panic swelled in his chest, squeezing his lungs until he couldn't breathe.

He pocketed his change and left.

*   *   *

Morgan of the finfolk leaned against a pillar at the back of the small dark church, chafing against his human form and the need that drove him here. He was still stretched thin from the long sea crossing, his blood cold, his bones fluid, his very essence draining away through the stones at his feet, dissipating with each exhalation.

He filled his lungs painfully. He belonged on Sanctuary supervising the work of reconstruction. He should not have to abandon his duty and his people to chase their errant lord across the ocean.

But the sea lord, Conn ap Llyr, had bowed to his consort's desire to attend the birth of her niece on the humans' island of World's End.

Morgan had been forced to follow.

Which was how he found himself in this human house of God, an unwilling witness to a baptism.

He stirred restively, stifled by the stink of humanity and the atmosphere inside the church.

The air was thick with angels. He could not breathe.

The children of air pressed close around him like the brush of wings against his face, like a weight on his chest, like a blade at his throat.

He drew another painful breath as the priest fumbled with his book. "What name do you give this child?"

"Grace Anne," her parents answered together.

Morgan's eyes narrowed. He knew the infant's father, the selkie Dylan Hunter, newly created warden of this island. The dark-haired woman beside him with the cross around her neck must be the child's mother.

"And what do you ask of God's church for Grace Anne?"

"Baptism."

Morgan curled his lip. The children of the sea did not require the sacraments of men. They were one with the First Creation, elemental, immortal.

Or they had been immortal.

They were dying now. His sister, dead. His people, dying while the sea lord dallied on shore.

Morgan's hand clenched on the cold stone pillar. A silent howl tore through his chest, strong as anger, bleak as the winter wind through caves of ice. Yet his face remained calm, his gaze fixed on the font. He had not let himself feel anything, even despair, in a very long time.

His gaze flickered over the family in the front pew; narrowed in recognition on the selkie Margred, standing beside her human mate, a big man with a strong jaw and a short haircut. Margred had chosen to live as a human. Age as a human. Die as a human.

Yet she appeared content and even more beautiful than Morgan remembered, secure within the circle of her mate's arm, her belly swollen with his whelp.

Morgan wondered if their child would be born human or shifter. There was simply no way of knowing until it reached the age of puberty, the time of Change.

"*Hope for the future,*" Conn called these half-blood off-spring.

Perhaps. Morgan shifted his weight, uncomfortable in

his own skin, as restive in his own body as a cat tied in a sack, as a shark confined to a tank.

At the dawn of creation, the children of the sea had lived in balance with their fellow elementals, the children of earth, air, and fire. In recent centuries, however, the seas had sickened and the merfolk had declined. As their numbers and their power dwindled, every birth, every loss, assumed deeper significance. When three of their youngest had disappeared last year, even Morgan had winced at the loss.

Perhaps Conn was right. Maybe a closer alliance with humankind would ensure their survival.

His lips tightened as the infant at the front of the church was signed with water and the cross.

And perhaps it would destroy them.

He turned and stalked from the church.

At least outside he could breathe. The shadowed porch was cool and dim. He staggered like a sailor who had been too long at sea. The smell of grass and decay rose from the church yard, carried on a fresh breeze from the sea. To steady himself, he focused on the things of earth, leaning headstones, blowing grass, a tree.

A pair of children, an older boy and a little girl, turned off the main street, ambling along the crumbling asphalt at the side of the road. Something about the boy, the shape of his head or the set of his shoulders, snagged Morgan's attention. He narrowed his gaze.

Really, the boy seemed almost familiar, tall and wiry, a mop of hair above a lean, watchful face. Morgan had not known many children. Only the whelps on Sanctuary. Perhaps boys, like puppies, were all the same. This one had yet to fill out, to grow into his hands or his wrists, his feet or his nose. But he looked like . . .

Morgan's pulse quickened.

Almost exactly like . . .

"*Iestyn?*" Morgan whispered.

But as soon as the name escaped his lips, he damned himself for a fool. This was no missing selkie youth. This boy was bony where Iestyn was lean, black-haired while Iestyn was fair.

And human, the most insurmountable difference of all.

Morgan settled back into the shadows of the porch, ignoring the drumming of his pulse, the tug of instinct or recognition. Obviously, the sea crossing had addled his brain.

Two more boys in faded flannel and jeans turned the corner. They called up the hill, loud as crows. Morgan was too far away to distinguish the words, but the first boy stiffened.

"Faggot." This time Morgan heard the taunt clearly.

The black-haired boy bent and whispered to the girl, giving her a little push. She cast a quick look over her shoulder and ran, her pink sandals slapping the gravel.

Straightening, the boy turned to face his tormentors.

No coward, then, Morgan thought with approval.

The girl pelted past the church, her small face pink with exertion and excitement. Morgan barely noticed her as he assessed the boy's chances. Two against one. Not good.

This would be over quickly.

Red Plaid Shirt muscled in like a bull seal on a beach, all weight and noise. The black-haired boy defended himself with knees and elbows. The lad had height, Morgan thought disparagingly, but no real training. His stance was all wrong, his hands open like a child's.

The ensuing scuffle was too vicious to be called horseplay, too lacking in technique to be termed a fight. The two principals exchanged pushes, jabs, and jibes, while the third boy circled like a runt in a dogfight.

Red Shirt threw a shoulder into the dark boy's ribs. He staggered back a step, raised both hands, and shoved. Hard.

His attacker flew five feet through the air and crashed on the grassy strip beside the dreaming churchyard.

Well.

The black-haired boy stood breathing hard, spots of color burning in his pale face.

Morgan raised his eyebrows. He had not guessed the skinny lad had such strength in him.

Neither had his assailant, apparently. Red Shirt sprawled on his ass in the weeds, expression stunned, belligerence temporarily knocked out of him. His companion hurried to extend a hand.

Red Shirt waved him off.

The smaller boy frowned. "Todd? Aren't you gonna . . ."

Todd climbed painfully to his feet.

The black-haired boy braced.

"Nah. He's not worth it," Todd declared and spat on the ground. "Pussy."

They slouched off in the direction they came from. The boy stood and watched them go before resuming his climb, his shoulders hunched, his boots scuffing the road.

Morgan frowned as the lad drew even with the porch. He did not walk like a victor.

"Not bad." Morgan spoke from the shadows. "But when you fight, you should fight to finish."

The boy's shoulders jerked in a defensive shrug. "Whatever. It's over."

"Over, but not done." Morgan strolled to the top of the steps, once more in command of his body, the sea song in his head fading to a manageable roar. "The one you fought will try again."

"What do you care?" The boy raised his chin, his gaze blazing. His eyes were the color of tarnished gold.

Recognition hit Morgan like a rock.

Finfolk eyes. Iestyn's eyes. Morgan's eyes, in a mortal's face.

His breath hissed between his teeth. "Who are you?"

3

≈

THE STRANGER'S GAZE PINNED ZACK TO THE
sidewalk. "Who are you?"

Zack swallowed, taking in the hard jaw, the hard eyes,
the long, black leather jacket. The guy was tall, taller even
than Zack, and his arms were as big around as Emily's
head. No way was Zack going to be able to outrun him.
"Who wants to know?"

The man didn't seem to register his rudeness, which set
off all kinds of alarm bells in Zack's head. "My name is
Morgan."

No last name.

When grown-ups did that, they were usually trying to
be friendly. This dude didn't look friendly. He looked seriously badass.

"Zack. Zachary," he mumbled, the extra syllables
dragged out of him by the man's hard stare.

His hair was really blond, Zack saw. Almost white, like
his own hair before he dyed it. The thought gave him a
funny feeling in his stomach.

"You live here," the man said.

"Um . . ." Zack's mom was always going on about giving out personal information to strangers. For once, her warnings made sense. "Yeah."

"Where?"

The uh-oh feeling spread. "None of your business."

The man's mouth compressed. "What is your family?"

Not, *Who are your parents?* Not, *What do they do?*

"I have to go," Zack said.

"Wait."

Zack started walking. A dark blue, late model Honda CRV rumbled over the top of the hill. His mom's CRV with his mom driving and—Zack squinted to see through the glass—his sister in the backseat.

Relief, embarrassment, and annoyance churned inside him as the vehicle braked by the curb.

The window rolled down.

"Zack?" His mom's smile held a hint of apology, as if she knew she was babying him but couldn't help herself. She'd worn that smile a lot lately, which made Zack feel guilty and irritated him at the same time. "Em said you might need a ride home."

The back of Zack's neck crawled. Without turning, he knew the guy was behind him.

"Who is this?" the man asked.

His mother's gaze slid past him. Her smile faded completely. Her face turned white. "Get in the car."

Zack's gaze bounced between the man and his mom. "What's going on?"

"Get in the car, Zack. Now."

Out of instinct, out of habit, Zack obeyed. He hopped around to the passenger side and opened the door.

"I know you," the stranger said slowly.

"No, you don't." His mother's tone was fierce. Firm. But Zack heard the underlying high note, almost like she was scared. Like that time he hitchhiked to the beach without telling her.

"I have seen you before."

*   *   *

That voice, that well-remembered voice, stroked Liz like a hand and clutched her heart.

"I have seen you before."

Only for a couple of hours in the dark sixteen years ago. He couldn't possibly recognize her.

The passenger door slammed as Zack got in the car.

She had recognized *him* right away, Liz thought. Morgan. The white-blond hair, the brutally handsome face, the strange yellow eyes were the same. He looked exactly the same. While she . . .

She took a deep breath. Well, she'd changed, hadn't she? She was no longer a dewy, perky, naïve college student.

She was thirty-seven years old, for God's sake. A mother. A doctor. She had borne two children and buried her husband, and her face and body carried the lines and scars of laughter and of sleepless nights, of grief and resolve.

Liz gripped the steering wheel with sweaty palms. No, he hadn't recognized her.

"Who is this?" he had asked.

Anger caught her unprepared like a cramp, sharp and unexpected. She was what life had made her. She was the woman she had made herself, and she would protect that life, that woman, any way she could.

"Fasten your seatbelt," she ordered Zack.

At the click of the buckle, she threw the car in gear and punched the gas. She did not look in the rearview mirror as she drove away.

"Who was that?" Emily asked from the backseat.

Zack's father.

No, he wasn't. Bernardo Rodriguez was the only father her son had ever known or needed.

Zack's sperm donor?

She couldn't say that either.

"His name's Morgan," Zack said.

Emily leaned forward between the front seats. "Do you know him?"

"Sit back," Liz instructed, nerves snapping in her voice. She concentrated on turning the corner, struggling to keep the wheels and her tone even. "Not really."

"He said you did," Zack said.

Back in North Carolina, she'd been desperate for her son to communicate. She'd tried card games and car trips, nonverbal communication strategies and active listening techniques without success. She'd prayed this move would shake him from his self-imposed silence. But why did he have to start talking now?

"We've met," Liz admitted. "I meet lots of people. Doctors, patients, drug salesmen . . ." She was rambling. She shut up.

"Was he a patient?" Zack asked.

Oh, God.

She and Ben had agreed never to lie to Zack. He knew Ben wasn't his biological father. Liz's parents had cut off all emotional and financial support when she told them she was pregnant and wanted to keep her child. Ben had married her while they were both still in med school and adopted Zack a few months later. She would not impinge on her grieving son's bond with his dead father because of a chance encounter on the street with a virtual stranger.

If this was a chance encounter. Her heart raced as if she'd injected epinephrine. What if Morgan had sought Zack out?

She drew a deep breath. She was overreacting. Morgan never even knew of Zack's existence.

"It was a long time ago," she answered vaguely. "What did he say to you?"

Zack slouched in his seat, staring out the window at the dark pines bordering the road. "Nothing."

"He must have said something," she persisted.

"He asked where we lived."

"Did you tell him?"

"Mom." A staccato burst of impatience.

She waited.

Zack scowled. "No, I didn't, okay? Christ, I'm not a baby."

He was, though. He was her baby boy, no matter how tall he grew or what kind of language, dress, or attitude he affected. "I just wanted to be sure he didn't say anything to . . . to upset you," Liz said carefully.

"Well, he didn't." Zack shot her a quick, penetrating glance from beneath his fringe of black hair. "What's some guy you used to know doing here anyway?"

"I have no idea," Liz said coolly. "Maybe he's on vacation."

The other possibilities tightened her throat.

Zack slumped, staring out the window. "Yeah, because everybody wants to come to freakin' Maine."

She drove past the clinic and turned into their driveway, marked by an aggressively new lamp post and a clump of orange daylilies. The house was a renovated Victorian cottage with traditional New England charm and new, double-paned windows, dumped on the market when the previous owners tired of the Maine winters or the second mortgage. No sea views, but the property was convenient to Liz's work, and Emily could walk to school.

Liz pulled into the garage with relief. "We're home," she announced.

Safe.

As if there had been no interruption to their lives or their morning and everything could return to normal.

She turned to her children with a smile, determined to restore the security they had lost along with their father. "Who wants pancakes?"

Emily bounced. "I do."

Zack's face closed. "No, thanks."

"Don't you want lunch? Breakfast?"

"I'm not hungry."

She watched her son shuffle to the house, his head ducked between his shoulders, and her heart sank.

Everything back to normal.

* * *

Morgan stood with his back to the wall of Antonia's Ristorante, as aloof from the action around him as the cat drowsing in the restaurant window. Eating, chattering humans, all ages, both sexes, every size, filled the vinyl booths. Spires of pink, white, and purple flowers decorated the tables. Sunlight streamed through the red awning outside, suffusing the air with a rosy glow. The sound of laughter and conversation mingled with the aromas of red sauce and freshly baked bread. Noise, smells, and colors blurred together in his head, almost drowning out the persistent song of the sea and the lingering pulse of sexual arousal quickened by the woman in the car.

Her eyes were wide, deep brown, with shadows swaying in their depths. For a moment, falling into those eyes, he had wanted to breathe her, bite her, fuck her. Memory stirred, elusive as the night *or the scent of bruised grass as she cried and clawed and came under him, again and again.*

"I know you."

Her gaze had iced over before she turned away. *"No, you don't."*

He pressed his shoulders into the wall, absorbing the solid support of the plaster at his back. He did not trust his memories. His normally sharp mind was blurred with exhaustion, his head filled with the shifting world beneath the waves.

But he trusted his instincts. His gut recognized his kind. That boy . . .

His suspicions stirred and circled, mouthing over possibilities, drawn like sharks to the scent of blood.

"Cake?"

A skinny, dark-eyed boy thrust a plate under his nose.

Morgan almost recoiled. He eyed the pink and white confection cautiously. Perhaps he should eat. Food would anchor his body, would ground him in the here-and-now. He had not paused to hunt on the long sea crossing. His stretched, depleted body required nourishment now.

He took the plate. "Thank you."

On the other side of the room, Conn and his consort stood with her brothers and their families. Morgan's lips flattened. There was something he never thought to see, four selkies fussing over a human baby.

Bleakness settled in his bones, deeper than cold, sharper than hunger.

The world, his world, was changing around him, the ice caps melting, the oceans warming, the finfolk fading forever beneath the wave. He had pledged himself and his people to the selkie lord, convinced they must unite to survive. But now the selkie were allying with humans, breeding with humans, becoming more human in every way.

How could the children of the sea possibly survive that?

"Nick, your mother wants you for pictures." Margred stood before him, full and radiant as the moon.

"Okay." The boy darted off, threading his way through the crowded tables.

Morgan realized he was still holding a plate and set it down. "Margred. You look . . ."

Pregnant, was all he could think. With a human's child. Margred had chosen to forsake her nature and abandon her people for the privilege of rutting with one man.

He felt an ache like an old wound in bitter weather. His sister, his twin, had chosen the same. He had never forgiven her.

Margred's lips curved. "Round?" she suggested.

"Well," Morgan concluded. "You look very well."

Her gaze wandered over him, frank, female, assessing. "I wish I could say the same of you."

He bared his teeth in a shark's smile. "I will survive."

"No doubt." She touched the sleeve of the man beside her. "My husband, Caleb."

Lucy and Dylan's brother, Morgan remembered, the human son of the sea witch Atargatis.

The man stuck out his hand, human fashion. Morgan steeled himself to accept his touch.

Caleb's grip was firm, his gaze sharp and steady. "Will you be here long?"

"No longer than I must."

"Caleb is the island's police chief," Margred said.

Ah. That accounted for the warrior's eyes, the interest disguised as courtesy.

"You didn't come for the christening," Caleb said. "You want to see Conn."

"Yes," Morgan admitted shortly. How much did he know of their affairs?

Caleb nodded once and then jerked his head toward the swinging kitchen door at the back of the dining room. "I'll let him know. Give me five minutes. I'll have him meet you out back."

Morgan stiffened. He was not a servant to be ordered about or a rat to scurry through kitchens and skulk in alleys. But pride must bow to expedience.

"Five minutes," he said and left.

* * *

The alley behind the restaurant was sharp with shadows and broken glass. A whiff of clamshells and lobster carcasses carried from a hulking iron bin across the graveled strip. Scoured into the corner of the building, incongruous against the bricks and mortar, was a warden's mark: three interconnected spirals representing the domains of earth, sea, and sky.

Dylan's work, Morgan assumed.

He wore the same sign on a chain around his neck, the symbol of his power and his pledge, binding him to the service of the sea king's son.

"I smell rotting fish." Conn's deep voice carried a hint of humor. "If crossing the sea affects you so, you should have stayed on Sanctuary."

Morgan turned. The selkie prince regarded him from the shadow of the kitchen doorway, a tall man with eyes the color of rain.

Morgan was in no mood for joking. "Your concern

overwhelms me, lord. Or it would, had it moved you to remain on Sanctuary."

"I promised Lucy we would visit her family when her brother's child was born."

"And your consort's whims take precedence over all other claims to your attention."

The prince's gaze cooled to frost. "Have a care, Morgan. Lucy is the *targair inghean*."

The *targair inghean*, the daughter of the prophecy. She might yet prove to be the salvation of the sea folk—or she might be the biggest mistake Conn had ever made.

"No one doubts your consort's powers, lord. Only her priorities." He was too tired to be subtle, too frustrated to guard his tongue or weigh his words. "This is not the first time she has put her ties to her family above her duty to our people."

"Her people, too."

"Then let her act to save them," Morgan snapped. "Before there is nothing left to save. The children of the sea are being lost, our people disappearing beneath the wave, our pure blood being diluted by this flood of humankind. We need her on Sanctuary. We need you both on Sanctuary."

"I left you in charge."

"You left Griff in charge." Another slight, another sting.

"He is warden of Caer Subai," Conn pointed out with cool logic. "But you were in command of the work party."

"'In command.'" Failure was bitter as brine in his mouth. "Tell me to command the sea foam or issue orders to mackerel. I'd have better luck."

Conn's brows raised. "They do not obey you."

"They *obey*," Morgan said savagely. He could enforce obedience. "They do not *stay*. We are not day laborers. We are the children of the sea. We flow as the sea flows. I cannot explain to them, I cannot inspire them, to break their hands and their hearts hauling stone. Day after day, they are confined to one place, one task, and each other's company. And every night more slip away to sea."

"You cannot fault them for that. Not if they come back."

"Most come back," Morgan said. "Most of the time. The greatest loss is among the finfolk. We are not anchored to the land as selkies are."

The finfolk had no sealskins. They were true shape-shifters, able to take the form of any creature of the sea. But their fluid nature made them even more susceptible to the pull of the deep.

"I do not have the patience—Griff does not have the power—to hold them," Morgan confessed.

Conn drew a breath and loosed it. In his eyes, Morgan saw the burden of his kingship. Morgan had been trapped for months on Sanctuary. The selkie prince had ruled alone from his tower for nine centuries.

Alone, until Lucy.

"Then we will return," Conn said quietly.

"When?"

"Tomorrow."

Morgan bowed his head, hiding his exhaustion. "I will be ready."

"You do not come with us."

The simple command shook Morgan to a rare apology. "My lord, if I spoke out of turn . . ."

Conn sighed. "You spoke the truth. But you are in no shape to face another crossing so soon. You need time to recover."

"I am well enough."

"We cannot afford to lose another of your line."

Morgan's body went rigid. His temples throbbed. He did not need the selkie prince to remind him he was the last blood born of his kind.

Unbidden, the boy popped back into his head, the sullen mouth, the glinting eyes.

Morgan opened his mouth. Shut it. His suspicions were

too new to voice to Conn, his ambition too raw, his hope too fragile.

He cleared his throat. "It might do me good to stay."

Conn nodded in apparent approval. "Take as long as you need. There is magic on this island, in the place and in the people. You should get to know them, Morgan. As much as you dismiss them, our future is linked with theirs."

"Yes," Morgan said slowly. He thought again of the boy on the sidewalk. He remembered the woman in the car with the pale face and fierce voice.

I know you, he thought.

"Perhaps you are right," he said.

4

MORGAN SLIPPED FROM THE SUN-DAPPLED ROAD into the parking lot, avoiding the clinic's front entrance. The morning mist had burned away, leaving the air as bright and cool as crystal. Here he could not rely on vibrations in the water or the plumes of scent that trailed his prey. But his hunting instincts were the same on land or in the sea.

Find a base of operations.

Focus on a single target.

Observe from a distance.

And when the victim was vulnerable, strike.

The dark blue vehicle sat in the shade behind the building. Locked. Morgan considered the sealed windows, the crumpled yellow box with its protruding plastic straw on the floor of the back seat. He glanced toward the quiet street.

He might have enlisted Dylan in his search. But he disdained to ask the younger warden's help, especially for what might be a fool's errand.

Besides, he hunted alone.

He had located her vehicle. Now he must find her.

He selected a heavy rock from the line edging the parking lot and smashed it into the left rear window. Glass cracked and gave, a white spiderweb fracture spreading from the point of impact. A horn blared. Blared. Again.

Carefully, Morgan replaced the rock in the stone border. Dusting his hands, he walked around the building and through the steel and glass doors.

A human stench compounded of age and disease, blood and antiseptic, rose from the carpet and slapped him like a rogue wave. He froze. He had not considered his quarry could be sick. The thought caused an unexpected quiver in his belly.

His gaze passed over the rows of chairs, an old man with wrinkled hands and thick spectacles, a young woman with a child on the floor and another in her lap.

His mouth compressed. He did not see *her*. The woman in the car. The one he was searching for.

He approached the counter, where a female in soft, pink, shapeless clothes with a soft, pink, shapeless face peered at a screen. "Pardon me."

She glanced up, her eyes widening. Her color deepened. He stood patiently, well aware of his effect on her sex and willing to let it work for him.

"I, um. Can I help you?"

"Yes, I am looking for the owner of a dark blue vehicle parked behind this building."

Her face creased. "A dark blue . . . The Honda? Why?"

"The window is broken," he explained smoothly. "I noticed it as I walked by."

"Oh, dear." The faint suspicion vanished. Her frown cleared. "I'll let Liz know."

"Liz," he repeated, not quite making it a question.

"Dr. Rodriguez."

Not sick, Morgan thought. Muscles he was not aware of tensing suddenly relaxed. She was a doctor.

"*I start med school in the fall,*" he thought he heard or remembered. "*Part of the plan.*"

"I would like to tell her myself," he said.

"We-ll, I don't know . . ."

He held her gaze, granted her a smile. "Please."

She looked away, flustered. "I'll, um, see if she has a minute."

Picking up a folder marked with brightly colored stickers—HOP, he read—she bustled past a bank of metal cabinets into the building's bowels.

Silently, Morgan opened the door that led from the waiting room and followed her down the hall.

"Liz?" The woman in pink stood in a doorway at the end of the hall, her back blocking his view. "There's a man here to see you."

"He'll have to make an appointment." He recognized her voice. Strong and smooth, without a trace of the local accent. "Is that the Hopkins file?"

The woman in the doorway shifted to hand off the folder, and Morgan got a look past her into the room. Big desk, small chair, stacks and stacks of paper.

And her. Liz. Dr. Rodriguez.

She was sitting in a small, armless chair, her legs crossed, her hair caught up in a clip, her hands busy with the file. He thought her body deserved better than those straight, dull trousers, that loose white coat.

He knew her, though. His pulse quickened. He *remembered*.

Elizabeth.

No longer young, despite the slim shape of her and that shiny hair. Her eyes were still deep brown and intelligent, her face a smooth oval, her jaw slightly squared. But the creases in her neck and the lines at the corners of her eyes were a subtle reminder of time passed and years lived. Beneath a swipe of color, her lips were pale and firm.

He moved so she could see him, so she would be forced to acknowledge him. "Hello, Elizabeth."

His sudden reappearance had an effect on her, too, if not the one he hoped for.

Her chin rose as she looked him over. She set the file on

her knee, her movements sharp and compact. "What are you doing here?"

"There's been an accident," the woman in pink answered for him.

Elizabeth's face drained of color. "Oh, God. Zack?"

Seeing the genuine fear in her eyes, Morgan felt an unexpected pang of remorse. But his ruse had gotten him past her first line of defense. Any means was acceptable to the appropriate end.

"Zack is fine," he said. He assumed. "It's your car."

Her white-knuckled grip on the folder eased. "My car."

"In the parking lot." He strolled forward, taking possession of her space, subtly crowding the other woman from the room. "The window is broken. I noticed it as I was walking by."

Brown eyes narrowed in suspicion. "And you thought you would force your way back here and tell me."

He flashed his teeth. "I have never found it necessary to use force."

The female behind him gasped in excitement. The one before him was made of sterner stuff.

"All right, you've told me. Thank you. Nancy, can you get Chief Hunter on the phone? I need to file an accident report."

He admired her self-possession. But he would not be deterred. "We need to talk."

"No, we don't." She stood, reclaiming her space. The movement brought her closer to him. He could smell hints of lemon in her hair and on her skin. Fresh. Astringent. It suited her. "Chief Hunter can get in touch with you if he wants your statement."

"About Zachary," he said.

She froze for a small, betraying instant. He watched as her pulse throbbed in her throat.

Her gaze flicked behind him. "Nancy? Chief Hunter, please."

Her assistant retreated down the hall.

Elizabeth's jaw set, strong and square in her otherwise delicate face. "I can't talk to you now. I'm working."

"This is more important."

"Not to my patients."

He leaned a shoulder against the door jamb, blocking her in. "I will wait."

"No."

"Or I could come by your house," he suggested.

"No."

Their gazes locked. Fear and frustration warred in her eyes. But he had left her no choice. He did not think she would risk having this first confrontation within earshot of her family.

"All right." She conceded with surprising dignity. "I get off at four. I'll meet you someplace."

"I am staying at the inn. You could join me for dinner."

"I can't. I have to get home."

He wondered suddenly if she had a man at home, expecting her.

"You are married."

Her firm lips pressed together. Parted reluctantly. "Widowed."

Ah. "Recently?"

"Three years ago."

He was aware of a faint satisfaction, almost relief. Not that the existence of a husband would have mattered. The boy was his. "Then there is nothing to prevent you from joining me."

She sucked in her breath.

"Dr. Rodriguez, I've got Caleb on line three," her assistant called.

"Thank you, Nancy." She took a step forward.

Morgan did not budge from the doorway.

Her gaze held his for one heartbeat. Two. Beneath the lemon fragrance on her skin, he caught a subtler, salty note like panic or desire.

"Drinks," she snapped. "Four-thirty. I'll meet you in the bar at the inn."

Morgan shifted out of her way. "I look forward to seeing you."

It was true, he thought as she stalked past him without a word.

Not simply because their meeting would bring him another step closer to his goal. He was . . . intrigued by her. Attracted by warm brown eyes and a cool smile, by strong shoulders and delicate hands.

The years between were nothing to him. He had not changed.

Yet as he watched her walk away, her hips barely suggested by the shape of her coat, her dark hair bundled at the base of her neck, he was aware of the passage of time like the beating of his blood or the rush of angel wings.

She was grown, changed, different. Better armored and more interesting than the girl who had sex with him sixteen years ago.

Deep in his belly, he felt a tug of curiosity, a quick, hot coil of lust. How else was she changed? And what would it take to persuade her to have sex with him again?

* * *

Liz adjusted the rearview mirror, smoothing on her lipstick with a trembling hand.

Oh, God. She met her overbright eyes in the mirror. What was she doing? She was *not* fussing with her face like a twenty-one-year-old primping for the first date they'd never had.

She wasn't that stupid. Not anymore.

Even if he was the most compelling man she'd laid eyes on then or in all the long years since.

She jammed the top on her lipstick and zipped her purse shut. She just wanted to look presentable, that was all. Put together. In control.

Satisfied with her rationalization and her appearance, she slid out of the car and locked the doors, ignoring her broken back window.

The Inn at World's End was a sprawling white Victorian perched on the bluffs north of the harbor. Neglected gardens and old, storm-weathered trees surrounded the spindled porch and rolling green lawn. The owners, Caroline and Walter Begley, were transplants from Boston. Liz had already noticed that they catered more to the yacht crowd than to the islanders.

Which suited her just fine. She didn't need the entire island speculating about the new doctor's after-hours rendezvous with some hot stranger in the bar.

The Reef Bar had a separate entrance off the crumbling parking lot. Liz tugged on the heavy wooden door, grateful for the room's low lighting.

The Reef's walls were decorated with fishing nets and neon beer signs. At the bar, a couple of lobstermen in flannel shirts and faded ball caps provided additional local color. The rest of the scattered clientele was a mix of pastel stripes and plaids, a blur of tans and topsiders. The women wore white denim skirts and capris, the men salt-faded polos from L.L. Bean.

Alone in a corner booth facing the door, Morgan sat, his black shirt blending with the shadows, his pale hair capturing the light.

Liz met that gold-rimmed gaze and sucked in her stomach.

She threaded through the tables, head high. In control. "What do you want?"

He raised his brows at her bluntness. His lips curled in a thin smile. "You used to prefer some preliminaries. Sit down."

Her cheeks burned. Her hand tightened on the strap of her purse. She didn't let men—she didn't let anyone—boss her around. But she was attracting attention, standing here. She dropped onto the bench and lowered her voice. "How did you find me?"

"I recognized your vehicle. Drink?"

She glanced up as the waitress appeared beside their table, a fresh-faced college student who looked too young to serve alcohol. The girl smiled hopefully at Morgan, clearly ready to give him whatever he wanted.

Like Liz sixteen years ago.

She winced. "I don't need anything." This wasn't a date. And she wanted a clear head.

"You look like you do. Another whiskey," he instructed the waitress.

"Wine." She didn't have to drink it. "A glass of pinot grigio," she ordered, and tried to hide her annoyance when the girl waited for Morgan's nod before moving away.

Liz cleared her throat, the edge of her determination blunted. "Well."

"Yes."

"Here we are."

"Indeed."

The faint mockery in his voice made her fist her hands in frustration. "What are you doing here? What do you want?" she repeated.

"To see you."

"You haven't seen me in sixteen years," she said baldly.

"To meet my son."

Her stomach jumped. For one wild moment, she was tempted to deny he was Zack's father. He couldn't know. He had no proof. But the impulse died stillborn.

He wasn't stupid either.

"Is this some midlife crisis thing?" she asked.

"I beg your pardon."

She pressed her clammy hands together in her lap. "You didn't care about the possibility of fathering a child sixteen years ago. It's a little late for you to come forward claiming . . ."

He raised his eyebrows. "Paternity?"

"Concern." Their eyes locked. She leaned forward across the table. "Which makes me wonder what happened to change your mind. Life-threatening illness?"

"I don't get sick."

"Divorce?"

He held her gaze. "I never married."

Her heart gave an inconvenient kick. Oh, damn. He could have added, "*No one could ever compare with you.*" Or, "*I was waiting to find you again.*"

But he didn't, so she couldn't even accuse him of lying.

The young waitress returned to set a glass of wine in front of Liz and lingered. "Anything else? Another Scotch?"

Morgan shook his head without glancing up.

She pouted freshly glossed lips, twirling the ends of her blond hair around her finger. Morgan didn't seem to notice. "Well, let me know if you change your mind."

"We will," Liz said. "Thank you."

The girl smiled quickly, uncertainly, and left.

Liz sighed. Had she ever been that young? That hopeful and unguarded?

Yes.

She looked across the table again into Morgan's eyes, dark and bright as a night full of stars, a night sixteen years ago when she was young and foolish and aching with possibilities.

He looked exactly the same. Broad nose, sharp jaw, lean cheeks. His upper lip was still narrow, the lower one full, curved, and compelling.

She yanked her mind back. Okay, this was bad.

"I don't even know your name." Had she said that before, sixteen years ago?

"Morgan."

Another memory, of sitting upright in her hospital bed, staring blankly at the application form for Zachary's birth certificate. FATHER'S NAME.

Unknown, she had written, the point of her pen gouging the paper.

"Last name," she said.

He hesitated. "Bressay."

His accent, faint and indefinable, roughened on the word. She cocked her head. "What is that, French?"

"Scottish."

She waited. Sometimes listening encouraged patients to talk better than asking questions.

"Bressay is an island north of Scotland. Settled by the Viking longships."

He looked a bit like a Viking, big and brutally handsome with his hair like foam.

Like Zack's.

He was Zack's *father*. The implications made her head pound.

She drew a painful breath. "How did you find us?"

"I didn't," he said so simply she almost believed him. "Until I saw the boy yesterday, I was unaware of his existence."

She would have told him. If she'd ever had the chance. But he never came, he never called, he never contacted her.

He never tried to find them. Her.

The realization was like peeling adhesive back from an old wound. "So you're telling me your being here is, what? Coincidence? An accident."

"Or destiny," he said. "Fate has brought us together. Twice."

As if their one-night stand was more than lust on his part, stupidity on hers.

"I don't believe in fate. Bad luck, maybe."

Those pale gold eyes assessed her. "You consider the boy a misfortune."

"Of course not." She pressed her fingers to her throbbing temples. "When I found out I was pregnant . . . My parents didn't want me to have the baby. They said if I went through with the pregnancy, I'd have to take full responsibility for my choices and my child. So I did. I put myself through med school. I kept my baby." She raised her head, the old resolve burning in her breast. "And you can't just show up sixteen years later and take any of that away from me."

"No female among my people would choose as you did," he said quietly. "I honor your choice."

The sincerity in his voice, the admiration in his eyes, caught her off guard. Since Ben's death, she was used to getting through the days and the nights and the years on her own. There were rewards, sure. But precious few compliments.

She blinked back sudden tears. "Thank you."

"But the choice is not yours any longer," he continued inexorably.

She stiffened, on the alert again. "Zack is my son."

Morgan regarded her steadily beneath hooded lids. "He is almost a man. He must make his own choices."

"You don't know him. You don't know anything about him. He's fifteen years old and going through a very difficult time." So difficult she had given up her practice and moved her family nine hundred miles to provide them with a fresh start. "You have no right to tell me how to raise my son."

"What about his rights?" Morgan asked.

She stared at him blankly, attracted. Unsettled. Afraid. "What are you talking about?"

"He has the right to know his father."

She didn't want to consider the truth of his words. Without moving a muscle, he had managed to threaten everything she valued, her life, her family, her control. "Bernardo Rodriguez was his father."

"Your dead husband."

Anger shook her. Anger at Ben, for leaving. Fury at Morgan, for making her feel, for making her face that loss again.

She curled her fingers around the wineglass. "Ben loved Zack. He was there for him all of his life."

Morgan's gaze collided with hers. "But not at the beginning of it."

The air whooshed from her lungs, sucked away by heat and memory. *Only this, only him, his hot gaze, his overwhelming size, the violent grace of his body in hers as he pinned her down and pounded inside her, as the sky wheeled and the world changed around them . . .*

She sucked in her breath, gripping the stem of her wineglass. "Ben was there when it mattered. Zack is still adjusting to his loss. He doesn't need another disruption or another disappointment in his life. He doesn't need you."

"What of your needs?" Morgan asked. "This cannot be the life you envisioned for yourself."

She gulped her wine to dispel the faint bitterness in her mouth. "My life is none of your business."

"Look around you. You cannot be satisfied with this place." His gaze flickered over the bar's clientele, his lip curling. "By these people."

She set her glass down with a snap. "I have work I love and children who need me. What do you have?"

He looked back at her, his eyes dark. Menacing. Sexual. "I can have whatever I want whenever I want it. Can you say the same?"

His face was so cold, his body throwing off heat. Despite herself, she was shaken and attracted, her own body warming and softening in response.

She must be out of her mind.

"You mean the waitress," she said in a thin attempt at scorn.

"I mean sex." His deep voice taunted her, plucking at her nerve endings. She trembled like a violin to the pull of the bow, raw and roused, angry and achingly alive.

And that was absolutely unacceptable. She was not his instrument or his tool. He would not get to her child through her. Or the lure of . . .

"Sex," she repeated slowly, drawing the word out, testing it, tasting it in her mouth.

She felt the force of his attention, full-blown and intense. She smiled and slipped her foot from its shoe. "I can have sex with whomever I want."

With her bare foot, she touched his ankle, traced a line up his calf to his knee. His chest rose with one rapid breath, but he did not move, did not shake his gaze from hers. Her heart pattered wildly.

In control, she reminded herself.

She pressed her arch to his thigh. His leg was hard as iron, his thigh heavy with muscle. She meant to turn him on. To turn on him. But she was caught up in her sensual exploration, swept away by a quick surge of need, as riveted by this journey into new territory as he.

She moistened her lips, her toes casting higher. His eyes

blazed. He was . . . Oh, God, he was *there*, hot and hard under her foot. Her toes curled.

"Whenever I want," she said huskily.

His face was harsh. Focused. "My room is upstairs."

His invitation jolted her. Temptation—to go with the flow, to follow the current of desire—tugged deep in her belly. Oh, she wanted to. She wanted him.

Dropping her foot from his lap, she forced it into her shoe. She slid from the booth and stood looking down on him.

"But that's the difference between us." She was amazed her voice could sound so cool, so steady, when she was boiling and shaking inside. "I don't take something just because I want it," she said and walked out.

5

PERHAPS THE SEA LORD WAS RIGHT, MORGAN mused as he strolled down the inn steps late the next morning. Perhaps there was some magic on World's End.

Trees framed the view, the long green lawn falling away to a crescent of beach bordered by sea and stone.

It felt good to be away from the tensions on Sanctuary, from the sweaty labor of hauling rocks and the frustration of wrangling his work crew from the water. The children of the sea were hunters, not builders. They did not make or mine, plow or spin. Sanctuary had been furnished with the plunder of centuries, Viking gold and Spanish iron, French silks and Italian pottery. All gone now, all lost beneath the waves from which they had been recovered. Two days of hot meals and hot showers, soft linens and uninterrupted sleep had given Morgan a newfound appreciation for human comforts and surroundings. His mind was clear, his body alert, his spirits lighter than they had been in months. Years.

He squinted against the sun sparkling on the blue water below, free as the gulls soaring against the pale sky.

Of course, his current satisfaction might have had another source.

Elizabeth.

Anticipation hummed in his blood and low in his throat. He thought about her body braced in challenge, her cool control, that flash of heat. He'd thought about her quite a lot, in that quiet white room at the inn where he slept alone.

He enjoyed a test of wills almost as much as he enjoyed sex. With her, it would be a pleasure to indulge in both.

He wanted her again, more now than sixteen years ago. And unlike her, he had no hesitation taking what he wanted.

The road from the inn curved uphill and inland past weathered gray houses and small, bright gardens. Following the innkeeper's directions, he found the police department housed in the town hall, a modest brick building overlooking the harbor.

He went inside. The air was acrid with dust and ink and burned coffee.

The steely-haired woman behind the counter wore her eyeglasses around her neck like a badge of office and looked older than the building itself. Morgan glanced at the name plate on her desk. EDITH PAINE, TOWN CLERK.

"Chief Caleb Hunter," he said.

She continued to poke at her keyboard. "In his office," she said without looking up. "Take a seat."

Caleb had called Morgan with a request to drop by the police station. Possibly the policeman was following up on the report of the broken window. More likely, he wanted to keep tabs on the finfolk lord while he was on human turf. Morgan was willing to oblige in either case. He needed Elizabeth's address.

"He is expecting me," Morgan said.

"Maybe he is."

"You will tell him I am here."

The clerk raised her glasses to her nose and looked at him for a moment. As if, Morgan thought, he were a shark on her fishing line, unworthy of her bait or effort.

He bit back a grin.

"Maybe I will," Edith Paine said. "When he's free. Chairs are behind you if you want to wait."

He supposed he could wait.

Turning, he surveyed the row of uncomfortable-looking chairs. The one in the middle was already occupied. A small girl with a halo of soft black curls huddled on the wooden seat clutching a large, pale doll. A candy bar sat on the chair beside her, unwrapped. Uneaten.

Someone's attempt at comfort, Morgan deduced. It was none of his business. Clearly, the child was being cared for after a fashion. Children had survived on Sanctuary for centuries with less.

She looked up at him, her wide, dark eyes swimming with moisture, and stuck out her chin.

Something stirred in his gut. His memory.

"She seems rather young for a felon," he said to the woman behind the counter.

She sniffed and tapped the keyboard on her desk.

Morgan glanced back at the child. Her lips trembled. Something about that face . . . That chin . . . He narrowed his gaze.

Pink sandals.

Hell and buggering angels.

He ground his teeth together. "Where," he said very precisely, "is your mother?"

Edith Paine paused her tapping. "I called the clinic. She's on the way."

So that was all right, then, Morgan thought. He really had no responsibility here at all.

He frowned. "And your brother?" he asked the child.

Those wide brown eyes fixed on his face with a desperate, completely misplaced hope. "He had to go with the policeman."

"Where?" Morgan asked sharply.

One grubby hand released the doll. The girl pointed one small, nail-bitten finger to a closed door.

"He said he wanted to talk to Zack." She drew a shaky

breath. Hiccupped. "We had to get in his car. I had to wait out here, he said."

Morgan's cold blood boiled. He strode across the lobby.

"You can't go in there," Edith objected.

He ignored her. The little girl scrambled off her chair and after him.

Morgan opened the door.

Police Chief Caleb Hunter leaned back behind his desk, big and imposing in a wrinkled blue uniform. The boy—Zachary—hunched in a chair before him, face sullen and eyes miserable.

The chief shot a look at the open door, mild annoyance drawing his brows together. "Morgan. I have to ask you to wait outside."

Morgan felt a pressure against his leg and glanced down. The little girl had attached herself to him, one arm clinging to his knee, the other gripping the doll. Shaking her loose would be undignified and time-consuming, Morgan decided. He could tolerate her touch for the time it would take him to sort things out.

He locked eyes with the policeman. "What are you doing with him?"

"None of your business," Caleb replied evenly. "Edith! I told you no interruptions."

"You want a linebacker out here, call the Patriots."

Morgan looked at Zachary. The boy slouched deeper in his chair, his mouth sulky, his gaze defiant. Beneath the kiss-my-ass attitude, he stank of fear and shame, his muscles coiled with animal tension.

"What happened?" he asked the boy.

"That's what I'm trying to find out," Caleb said. "Now unless you're his mother or his lawyer, get the hell out."

"I'm his father."

Silence crashed over the room like a wave.

The police chief rubbed his face with his hand. "Well, shit. That puts a different spin on things. Let's see what his mother has to say."

* * *

Her son had been picked up for questioning.

Her daughter was in the care of strangers at the police station.

It was Liz's worst nightmare.

Well, not the worst. She'd survived the worst three years ago, watching Ben lose his hair, his strength, his voice . . . his life.

But the feeling she was wading through a bad dream, the sick helplessness in the pit of her stomach, the struggle to make sense of the unacceptable, those were the same.

"*There's been some trouble.*" Edith Paine's brusque Yankee voice replayed in her head. "*Chief picked up that boy of yours down by the ferry . . . Need to answer some questions before you take him home.*"

No one was hurt, Liz told herself. That was the important thing. Whatever else had happened, they would deal with it. That's what she did. Deal with things. She instructed Nancy to reschedule her afternoon appointments and drove to the police station, a hard ball of panic pounding in her chest.

She was the mommy. She was a doctor. She could fix this, whatever it was.

She parked the car and bypassed the required ramp to march up the town hall steps. In another mood, at another time, she might have been charmed or at least reassured by the small town vibe of the place, the old-fashioned wooden counter and modern fluorescent lights, the community bulletin board papered with wanted posters and bake sale flyers, city regulations and hand-lettered signs: HOUSE CLEANING. PET SITTING. DEEP SEA FISHING. ORGANIC JAM.

Her gaze swept the lobby. A small room housed a coffeepot and a copy machine. A row of straight-backed chairs lined up against one wall, a discarded candy bar on one seat.

But no Zack.

No Emily.

Taking a deep breath, she approached the counter. She

had met Edith Paine before. The town clerk had served on the search committee responsible for hiring the new island doctor.

Liz struggled to paste on a professional smile, but her lips refused to cooperate. Her hand trembled on the strap of her purse. "Edith, can you tell me—"

Edith's eyes glinted behind her glasses. "The party's in there."

Liz followed her gaze down the hall, and her wildly beating heart stopped, frozen in her chest. The blood drained from her head.

Morgan. She recognized the strong flow of his back, the muscled curve of his shoulders. Above his black jeans and black T-shirt, his hair looked almost white. His voice was deep, cool, annoyed.

And clinging to the long, black line of his leg was her daughter, Emily.

Trouble, Edith had said on the phone.

Oh, yes.

Liz rolled forward, propelled by a surge of protective fury. "What are you doing here?"

Morgan turned, his expression unreadable. "I was looking for you."

Her heart jumped. She ignored it. "I want you to stay away from my children."

Morgan cocked an eyebrow. "Then you will have to remove this one from my leg."

Hot blood swept into her face. "Emily, come here."

Her daughter loosened her grip on Morgan's pant leg. Liz pulled her close, steadied by the sharp, delicate bones beneath her palm.

"Maybe we should all sit down," Caleb Hunter suggested.

The police chief sat behind a battered desk covered with short stacks of paper and neatly aligned pens. Zack slouched in a chair on the other side, gaze fixed on his dirty black combat boots. He did not, would not, meet her eyes.

Liz's mouth dried. Her pulse pounded in her temples.

What had Morgan said to him? What was he thinking? Why was he here?

She turned to Caleb. She'd met the policeman a week ago at his wife's prenatal appointment. He'd struck her then as a clear-eyed, thoughtful man with big hands and a slow smile. He wasn't smiling now.

She moistened her lips. "There's no reason for him to be here."

"No reason," Morgan shot back. "But every right."

Oh, God.

Zack raised his head. His pale gold eyes blazed, hard and curiously adult. Morgan's eyes, in their son's white face.

The accusation in his gaze hit her like a punch in the gut. Liz's heart plummeted to her stomach.

He knew, she thought sickly. Or he suspected, and his suspicions were ripping him apart. Tearing them apart.

She ached to go to him, to take him in her arms. But in this mood, in this setting, she knew the teen would never tolerate her touch.

She crossed the small office to him and stood as close as she dared, Emily a warm weight against her side. "Zack . . ."

"I'll just get another chair," Caleb murmured and left the room.

"You lied," Zack said bitterly.

She clenched her hands together. "No, I—"

"When were you going to tell me?"

Liz sighed. "I don't know. I was trying to find the right time to—"

"Liar."

Morgan's rebuke cracked like winter ice. "You will not speak to your mother that way."

"Fuck off." Zack's head whipped around as Caleb reentered the room carrying one of the wooden chairs from the lobby. "I want him to leave," he said to the police chief. His voice wobbled around the edges. "I want them both to leave."

Liz's heart broke. She raised her chin. "He's only fif-teen. You can't question him without an adult present."

Caleb set the chair for her and shut the door. "That would be true if he was facing charges. However—"

"I won't talk unless they go," Zack said.

"According to Chief Hunter, you did not talk before we came," Morgan said coolly. "Now shut your mouth and listen."

Liz bristled in defense of her son.

"That sounds like a father," Caleb said dryly.

She opened her mouth to deny it. Shut it again.

Caleb moved behind his desk. "Why don't we sit down. See if we can clear this up."

She recognized the order beneath his mild tone. She unlocked her knees enough to perch on the edge of the chair.

"I will stand," Morgan said.

Caleb shrugged. "Suit yourself." He dropped onto his chair. "Look, your family situation is none of my business. But what happens on this island is. People here depend on the sea. The sea and their neighbors. Anybody interferes with that, they take it seriously."

Liz's face felt stiff. "I don't understand."

"There have been reports in the past week of lobster traps coming up empty." Caleb spoke to her, but his eyes were on Zack. "Most infractions around here, the fishermen handle themselves with a warning. Knot a line, bust a trap. If that doesn't work, they'll send a call out over the radio, sometimes a gunshot across the bows. With the economy so bad and lobster prices down, feelings are running pretty high. Poaching is the Marine Patrol's responsibility. But keeping the peace is mine."

She didn't need a lesson on the island economy or police jurisdiction. "What does any of this have to do with Zack?"

"Your boy here met the ten-thirty ferry with a cooler full of lobsters. He was selling them to tourists for four bucks apiece."

She'd been braced for something else. Drugs. Alcohol. Those would fit the pattern. Shoplifting, to support her son's suspected habit. Fighting, because they were new in town and Zack looked different, was different, from other boys. But . . .

"Lobsters?" Incredulity strained her voice. "Where would he get lobsters?"

"That's what I asked him," Caleb said.

"Zack?"

He jerked a shoulder, eyes on his boots.

"Did someone give you the lobsters to sell?"

He was silent.

"Because if you're protecting someone, they don't deserve your loyalty."

Something flickered across his face and was gone, too quickly to be identified. He didn't look up.

Frustration tightened her jaw. "He's not a poacher," she said, wanting to believe it. "We don't even have a boat."

"I wondered about that," Caleb said.

"He would not necessarily need a boat," Morgan murmured.

The two men exchanged a long look.

"I wondered about that, too," Caleb said. "He one of yours?"

"The evidence would seem to point that way."

Incomprehension swam in her head. She narrowed her eyes. "*One* of yours? How many children do you have?"

He flashed his teeth at her. "Only one. And I do not intend to lose him again."

*   *   *

Zachary watched from under his lashes while they talked about him as if he wasn't there. His stomach churned with a combination of guilt and greasy panic. His eyes burned.

They couldn't prove anything. It's not like lobsters came painted with lobster serial numbers.

But maybe Big Cop would lock him up anyway. Maybe it would be a relief. Ever since they'd come to this stupid island, Zack was finding it harder and harder to control himself. If they threw him in jail, at least he could stop trying.

His mom was in full doctor mode, pressing, prodding, trying to get at the root of the problem. But she couldn't fix this. She couldn't fix him. Nothing in her medical books, no online diagnosis Zack had ever found, offered him any help, any hope at all.

So he kept his mouth shut and prayed Em would do the same.

She was just a baby. Too young to be charged, too young to be believed. Too young, he thought with another lurch of guilt, to be mixed up in his shit. To her, the furtive trip to the beach had been a game, an adventure. Anyway, he'd been careful not to let her see anything that would scare her. She'd been a hit with the tourists, too. Grown-ups who wouldn't give Zack the time of day had stopped to talk with Emily, charmed by her big brown eyes and that stupid doll she carried everywhere.

His gaze slipped past her to the man who claimed to be his biological father. Big Bad Ass in black. Zack sneered. He hadn't looked so tough with Emily clinging to his leg.

The man turned his head. His eyes pierced Zack, skewered and held him in his chair like a bug pinned to a piece of Styrofoam.

Zack's heart pounded. Like the man could read his thoughts, like he could see inside his head.

Shit.

He dropped his gaze hastily, his blood drumming in his ears.

Through the roaring in his head, he heard the man say, "The boy is not under your authority. This is not your concern."

"It is if he's stealing," Big Cop replied.

"He's not your responsibility either," his mom said to the man in black. "Zack is my son. Let me talk to him."

The cop leaned back in his chair. "Maybe it would be best if you both talked to him."

His mother sucked in her breath like she did before she launched into a lecture. Emily ducked her head, hiding her face in her doll's hair.

Zack couldn't stand it.

"Okay," he said.

Silence descended on the room. He fought not to squirm.

"Zack . . ." His mother's voice was brittle and unhappy.

His hands tightened on the arms of the chair. He knew she was only trying to help. But she didn't understand. Nobody understood.

But just for a second, meeting the eyes of the man who claimed to be his father, he'd felt a flicker of something. Not hope. Recognition.

He swallowed hard and looked at the cop. "If I promise to talk to them, can we go?"

The cop regarded him until Zack's mouth went dry and his palms stuck to the arms of the chair.

"For now," the cop said at last. "I've got no cause to hold you. I'm going to ask around, see whose catch is missing. We're not finished with this by a long shot."

"No," the man in black agreed softly. "I would say we were just beginning."

6

~≈~

THEY WALKED OUT OF THE POLICE STATION TO-
gether, Liz holding on to Emily's hand and Zack with his
shoulders up around his ears and Morgan stalking behind.
Like a unit. Like a family.

Liz hated it.

He was crowding her. She felt him on the back of her
neck and in the pit of her stomach, a tickle like lust or
alarm. She stopped abruptly and turned.

Her breath caught. Too damn close. "You're not coming
with us."

Morgan looked down at her, his face as cool and unim-
pressionable as marble, and a chill chased the tickle up
her spine. He was not a man she could boss around, which
made him dangerous. And far too attractive.

She shook her head to rid it of that thought. "I need to
talk to Zack alone."

"So must I."

"Not alone."

"Very well," he agreed so promptly she wondered if
she'd been set up. "Then we will talk to him together."

She frowned. "No, I . . ." She couldn't think with him standing so close. She took a step back, still gripping Emily's hand, and bumped into her car. "It's my responsibility."

"And you are always responsible."

Was he mocking her?

Her lips set. "Yes."

"Responsible and . . ." The pad of his thumb hovered at the corner of her eye where the skin was thin and sensitive. "Tired. Let me help."

The unexpectedness of his feather contact robbed her of breath. Of speech. He traced a line from cheek to jaw, making her throat constrict. For one weak moment, she was tempted to close her eyes and lean into his hand, to absorb the warmth and strength of his touch.

Self-preservation straightened her spine. She was not a woman who leaned on anybody.

"I'm not tired," she said, ice in her voice. "I'm frustrated."

Unholy laughter gleamed in his eyes. "I could help you with that, too."

Her jaw cracked. She was not swapping innuendos with this man in full view of the town and within earshot of her kids. "No, you can't. Go away."

"After I talk with the boy."

"Not here. Not now. When you talk to my son, it will be on my terms and my turf."

"Fine. When and where?"

"I . . ."

Their eyes locked.

Trapped, she realized, her heart knocking against her ribs. Emily leaned into her side, watching them with wide, anxious eyes. Zack scowled from the other side of the car.

For her children's sake, it was important she maintain a pretense of civility. A semblance of control.

"You can come to dinner," she decided.

"Tonight."

She pressed her lips together in annoyance. "Fine. Six o'clock. Eighteen Juniper Road."

"I will see you then." He nodded across the car at Zack. "All of you."

Liz's gaze darted between them. They were nothing alike, one big, blond, commanding, the other bony and dark.

And yet something about the shape of their lips, the cant of their shoulders, those weird, pale, golden eyes proclaimed them father and son. Her stomach sank.

"Maybe it would be best if you both talked to him," the police chief had said.

Maybe.

Liz bit her lip. And maybe she was making a big mistake.

*   *   *

Morgan stood half-naked at the pedestal sink in his room, scraping the blade of his knife over his face to remove three days of stubble. The finfolk's skin was almost smooth, but to pass as a human, he must groom as a human.

The door to his hotel room banged open.

His hand checked and then continued carefully along his jaw.

Dylan Hunter, dark and furious, blew into the room behind him. "What the hell are you playing at?"

"Next time, knock."

"Why? You were expecting me." Dylan tossed an armload of clothes onto the wide, white bed.

Morgan put down his knife and reached for a towel. "I would prefer not to cut myself."

"I don't care if you slit your throat," Dylan said.

Morgan met his gaze in the mirror. "I take it you spoke with your brother."

"Yeah. He calls me into his office to find out what's going on, and I have to tell him I don't have a damn clue."

"I do not answer to him. Or to you."

A flush stained the younger warden's cheekbones. "This is still my territory. My charge. We've had enough demon activity around here that anything out of the ordinary makes my brother twitchy. You need to keep me informed."

Morgan crossed to the bed and pulled a couple of shirts from the pile. Fortunately, he and Dylan were almost the same size, though Morgan's frame was heavier. "The prince ordered me to stay."

"To recuperate."

"Yes." He held up a white shirt with buttons. "Linen?"

"Cotton. Natural fibers anyway, like you said. Read the damn label."

He did not need a label to know it would chafe. He tossed it back on the bed.

"So what's this bullshit story about a long lost son?" Dylan asked.

Morgan found a thin sweater in soft black, cashmere or silk. "Not bullshit. The boy is mine."

"*You* have a kid." Disbelief scored Dylan's voice.

"You question my ability to father a child?"

"No, but . . . You, with a human woman?"

Morgan raised his eyebrows. "It is not only selkies who can fuck with humankind."

He half expected Dylan to take offense. His mother had taken a human husband; Dylan, a human wife.

But the selkie only pursed his lips thoughtfully. "Still, that's some coincidence you finding him now. Here. On World's End."

"I sired him sixteen years ago in Copenhagen."

"Which makes him a teenager, right? Past the age of Change."

"So was your sister when she first came into her powers."

"You think he's finfolk."

"I suspect." Morgan tugged the black shirt over his head. "Tonight I will know."

"Then what?"

"You do not need me to explain to you the importance of offspring." Not when the sea lord himself had come to celebrate the birth of Dylan's half-blood daughter. "Our people are dying. The finfolk are going beneath the wave in even greater numbers than the selkie. Children are survival and power."

"Children are children. What if the boy isn't finfolk?"

Morgan shrugged. "Then I have no use for him, and he has no need of me."

A memory of Elizabeth's taut, white face flared in his mind. *"Ben was there when it mattered. Zack is still adjusting to his loss. He doesn't need another disruption or another disappointment in his life. He doesn't need you."*

Morgan's teeth clenched.

"And if he is?" Dylan prodded. "What will you do then?"

Morgan regarded him blankly.

Do?

Their kind flowed as the sea flowed. If fate had given him a child, he would take it, as he accepted the bounty of the oceans or the gifts of the tide.

"I will take him," Morgan said.

"To Sanctuary."

A trickle of unease rolled between Morgan's shoulder blades. "Why not?"

"In the first place, Lucy won't stand for you taking the kid anywhere without his consent."

"I do not answer to your sister."

"Conn, then. He listens to her. And the kid is only fifteen."

"You were younger."

"I was miserable," Dylan said frankly. "And I did my damnedest to make everyone around me miserable, too. Kids have feelings, you know. The situation on Sanctuary is difficult enough. Do you really think you can run the work crew if you're baby-sitting some misfit teen with a bad attitude?"

The prospect appalled him. "I do not intend to baby-sit anyone."

"Then before you take this kid from the only family he's ever known, you better figure out what you *are* going to do with him," Dylan said.

Morgan regarded Dylan with dislike. All he wanted was a chance to secure his posterity and engage in a mutually pleasurable seduction. He did not need this half-blood selkie muddying the emotional waters with his talk of feelings.

"The boy will survive," he said shortly.

They all would survive. Conn would see to that. Would agree to it.

Survival was all that mattered.

*   *   *

The hearty scent of chicken asopao—garlic and onions, pepper and chorizo—rolled from the kitchen and followed Zack's mom up the stairs and into his room. "*Puerto Rican comfort food,*" his dad Ben used to say whenever Mom made one of his family's recipes.

Zack sniffed. Mom was really pulling out all the stops tonight. Because she thought he needed comfort? Or because that guy was coming to dinner? Morgan. His biological father.

She sat on the end of Zack's bed, watching him with a sad, patient expression that made him feel about two years old and two inches high.

"You know you can tell me anything," she said like she believed it.

Zack wanted to believe it, too.

But he knew better. He couldn't tell her what was really wrong with him. And so he couldn't say anything at all.

They'd already gone a couple of rounds, his mom hitting him with a combination of concern and sneaky open-ended questions she'd picked up from the counselor she'd dragged him to see back home. "*Tell me what happened.*" "*How are you feeling?*" "*What do you want to happen next?*"

Zack stared down at his hands. He didn't want to discuss his feelings, for Christ's sake. Or what happened next. He wanted to be left alone. The pressure—to speak or keep silent—built in his head and chest like a scream.

In sheer desperation, in self-defense, he went for his mom's weak spot. "So how well did you know this guy Morgan before you slept with him?"

His mother's face turned white and then red. "Not as well as I should have," she said calmly. "We've talked before about choices. I made some bad ones. But I've never regretted having you."

Guilt pressed his ribs like a five-hundred-pound gorilla. "Until today."

"Today was not a good day," Liz agreed. "But you're still my son, Zack. I love you."

"I'm his son, too," he said, hoping for . . . what? Reassurance, confirmation, denial?

Her eyes met his, straight on. "Yes."

His sneer slipped. He wrenched it back into place. "So what am I supposed to call him? Dad?"

She couldn't quite hide her wince. "You'll have to decide that for yourself."

A knock, sharp and imperative, sounded from the front door.

Zack swallowed the lump of nerves in his throat. Like this guy never heard of a doorbell.

His mother stood, wiping her palms on her slacks. "That's probably him now. Why don't you answer the door while I add peas to the asopao?"

*　　*　　*

Liz looked around the dining room table, trying to snatch satisfaction from the jaws of impending doom.

Dinner so far was not a disaster. The chicken was good, not as good as Ben's mother's, but with the same desirable soupy texture. Emily was spooning up rice with the concentration of a starving child. Zack hunched over his plate, sullen and silent.

On Liz's right, Morgan was dressed all in black, fitted black pants, slim black sweater. Like a jewel thief or an assassin. Like . . . Zack, she realized. An older, *Esquire* version of Zack. He leaned back in his chair, a glint in his eye she didn't trust.

Not a problem. All she had to do was stick to neutral subjects, satisfy whatever curiosity Zack harbored about his biological father, and then shove him out the door.

"I hear it's supposed to be warmer tomorrow," she said.

The glint sharpened.

She cleared her throat. "Of course, if it's overcast, that will make a difference."

"No doubt."

Okay, so Morgan didn't share most Mainers' ability to talk for hours on end about fog and rain.

Emily raised her gaze from her plate and fixed it on Morgan. "I want a kitten."

Morgan frowned as if she'd announced she could grow two heads. "I beg your pardon."

Liz fought a grin.

"There was a sign. At the police station," Emily explained. "Free kittens. I want one."

As if she expected him to go out and get it for her.

Liz's smile faded. "The kittens aren't really free, Emily."

"The sign said they were."

"Yes, but there are costs involved in owning a pet. Shots and food and—"

"You could take the money out of my allowance."

Liz was no longer remotely amused. "Honey, we talked about this. This is a bad time for us to take on another responsibility."

And a worse time to discuss it, she thought.

"But—"

"Later, Em," she said firmly and turned to Morgan. "Thank you for bringing the wine."

A very nice Tuscan red, a Barolo. She used to like a glass of wine with dinner. It was another thing she'd given up when Ben died. She didn't want to drink alone, to finish the bottle after the children went to bed.

He shrugged. "Dylan said it would be appropriate."

She ran through her mental file of patients. "Dylan Hunter?"

"You know him."

This was an island. Eventually, she would know everyone. It was one of the reasons she'd moved her family here.

"He brought in his daughter for her three-month checkup last week," she said.

"Ah." Morgan turned his attention to his plate.

He ate with controlled appreciation, she noticed, an almost animal grace and focus. She watched the movement of his mouth, the flex of his hands on knife and fork, and felt herself flush.

She stabbed at the chicken thigh on her plate. "How did you two meet?"

"Dylan is a colleague."

"I thought he helped his wife in the restaurant."

"On occasion. He is also involved in . . . I suppose you would call it environmental protection."

"And that's what you do?"

"Yes. Marine protection, exploration, and salvage." Morgan's eyes gleamed. "Amazing the things one finds underwater."

Zack's fork clattered.

Liz felt control of the conversation slipping and grabbed for the serving dish. "More chicken?"

"Thank you." He took another leg, some rice, the last length of sausage.

Even Ben, before his health failed, hadn't attacked his food like this.

Liz watched Morgan heap food on his plate, aware she hadn't cooked for an adult man in a long time.

Morgan looked up and smiled, his teeth very white. "You have stirred my appetite."

Her breath snagged in her throat. She was light-headed. Dizzy. Dismayed.

This man was not Ben. And the hunger he stirred in her wasn't anything she should feel. Certainly nothing she could satisfy.

"This was one of Ben's favorite dishes. My husband, Ben." She grabbed her wine to steady herself.

"Then I am honored you prepared it for me. I expected you to serve seafood. Lobster."

Liz choked.

While she reached for water and a napkin, Morgan turned to Zack. "What did you do with them?"

Zack jerked his shoulder. "He took them. The cop."

"Frustrating," Morgan observed.

"Whatever."

"Unless you can get more."

Liz stopped her frantic blotting of the tablecloth. Zack regarded Morgan through his lashes and said nothing.

"Where did you find the lobster?" Morgan asked.

Liz held her breath.

"In the water," Zack muttered.

"Four meters down? Forty?"

"What difference does it make?"

"None to me," Morgan said blandly. "Though I am interested to know how you brought them to the surface."

He was questioning her son at her dining room table. That was wrong. But she wanted answers. She was tired of battering herself against the wall of her son's silence. There was a certain guilty relief in letting Morgan bear the burden of interrogation and the weight of Zack's resentment.

At least he hadn't stomped off to his room. Yet.

"What does it matter?" Zack shot back. "It's over."

Morgan's shoulders lifted in elegant imitation of Zack's shrug. "Until you do it again. Once you give in to it, that kind of thrill is hard to resist."

"What thrill?" Liz asked. "Stealing? Zack doesn't need to—"

"The sea," Morgan said. "It's in his blood now."

Zack's pale face flushed. "It's not. I'm not . . . I did it for the money."

Nerves roiled Liz's stomach. She crumpled her napkin in her lap. "Zack?"

He wouldn't look at her.

"If you needed money, all you had to do was—"

"I'm too old to run to you every time I want something," he flashed.

Liz lifted her chin. "I was going to say, 'Get a job.'"

Morgan laughed shortly.

Zack's face sagged before he shaped it into his usual scowl. "I can't. I have to watch Em."

"I think today proved you and Emily would both be better off with some other arrangement," Liz said as calmly as she could. "Tomorrow I'll look into options for her. You can walk into town and see if any of the stores are hiring."

Zack's chair scraped as he thrust to his feet. "That's bullshit."

"Sit down," Morgan ordered.

"She can't tell me what to do."

"Of course she can." Scorn edged Morgan's voice. "She feeds you, clothes you, shelters you like a child. Sit."

Zack flopped onto his chair.

Liz frowned. Not that she didn't appreciate the support, but she was responsible for discipline in this house. "I don't need you to stand up for me."

Morgan gave her a long, cool look. "You are female. This is between men."

"I'm his mother," she said, indignant.

He held her gaze. "Precisely."

She felt naked, all her weaknesses, all her failings as a parent, exposed.

An image sprang into her mind of Morgan, standing in the police station like a black-clad guardian angel, Emily clinging to his leg.

At the table, Zack watched them with the focused

attention he usually reserved for his video games. On any other evening, after any other fight, he would be in his room with the door shut and music shaking the walls.

Liz drew a deep, careful breath.

"Can I speak with you?" she said to Morgan. "In the kitchen."

His teeth flashed. "I am at your service."

7

MORGAN FOLLOWED ELIZABETH FROM THE DIN-
ing room, a buzz in his blood. Amusement or annoyance
or lust. She walked with long, smooth strides, hips rolling,
shoulders braced for battle.

If she was looking for a fight, he could give her one. He
ran his tongue over his teeth. He was prepared to give her
any number of things.

She turned to face him, the yellow light from above the
sink gleaming on her sleek mahogany hair. The pads of his
fingers tingled.

Anticipation, he realized. That accounted for the hum in
his blood, the tightening in his belly.

He was immortal, but she made him feel alive.

She crossed her arms over her breasts. "You can't just
stroll into Zack's life and start acting like his father."

"I am his father. He is my seed."

"He's not some test tube baby," she snapped. "He's a
person. He's my son."

"My son, too."

"Which means nothing without some kind of commitment."

It meant everything if the boy were finfolk.

Morgan raised his eyebrows. "Are you asking my intentions?"

She stuck out her chin. "Towards Zack, yes."

If he told her, she would throw him out. He shrugged. "I want to know my son."

"Any relationship you have with Zack has to be his choice."

He admired her determination to protect her family, even though he had no intention of being hampered by it. "And you trust his judgment."

She flushed. "No. That doesn't mean I trust you either."

"Yet I have been inside you," he murmured mostly for the pleasure of seeing her eyes flash.

"I was stupid then. I won't be stupid now. Not with my children's safety at stake."

He was annoyed. "I do not prey on children."

"I'm not talking about physical danger," she said. "But they're emotionally vulnerable. Zack is going through a difficult time right now. I don't want you confusing him even more."

"It may be I understand the boy better than you think."

"If I didn't consider that a possibility, we wouldn't be having this conversation," she said frankly. "But you don't really know him. You don't see him as an individual yet."

"Of course he is an individual. I only have one son."

"Listen to yourself. 'One son.' 'The boy.' He has a name. You could try using it occasionally."

He stared at her, oddly discomfited. Had he ever called the boy by name? He could not remember. Was not sure why he should care.

She cared. Elizabeth. Her passion lit her from the inside until she glowed with maternal warmth and anger. Vibrant. Desirable. Dangerous.

To distract her, to indulge himself, he moved in, nudging her back against the sink. "Zachary," he said deliberately.

He put his hands on the counter, caging her hips, watching the wild beat of her pulse under her jaw. "Elizabeth."

Lowering his face to her neck, he breathed her in, the sharp notes of her irritation, the sweetness of her arousal. He eased forward, teasing her with the brush of his body, letting her feel how she affected him.

"Satisfied?" he taunted against her throat.

She inhaled sharply, her breasts rising, and he raised his head and took her open mouth. He felt a flash of heat, of triumph, of delicious friction, before her fingers tightened on his arms and she bit his lower lip. Hard.

His head jerked back. Snarling, he met her gaze.

Her eyes were dark and dilated, her mouth resolute. He was confident enough of her, of his own skill and experience, to believe he could still have her. He almost lunged again for her mouth.

But she stopped him, slapping her palm against his chest. "My satisfaction isn't the issue. This is about Zack. He comes first."

Of course the boy came first. Morgan would not still be here on this island otherwise.

He leaned back slightly, his lip throbbing, his body tight. "So?"

"So." Her breath escaped in a short, explosive puff. "Any personal relationship between us, any physical relationship, complicates things."

Impatience licked him. "Without our physical relationship, the . . . Zachary," he said carefully, "would not exist."

"As far as you're concerned, he didn't exist. Not until a few days ago."

"And you hold that against me. Would use that against me."

She opened her mouth to deny it. "Pretty much."

Surprise held him momentarily speechless. Surprise and respect.

"It's not like you have this great track record of sticking around," she continued. "Until I'm sure you won't hurt

Zack, it's better if we take things slowly. Our relationship begins and ends with him."

Strong words. She was a strong woman.

But not, he thought, invulnerable. He surveyed her face. Her gaze was clear and fearless, her cheeks flushed with what might have been anger. But beneath the angle of her outthrust jaw, he caught again that tiny, betraying flutter of her pulse.

"Is it the boy you're protecting?" he murmured. "Or yourself?"

*   *   *

Liz's heart threatened to pound its way out of her chest.

"Is it the boy you're protecting? Or yourself?"

Both, she thought desperately.

"Zack, of course."

Well, it was half true, wasn't it? She nudged Morgan out of the way with her hip and opened the freezer door. She needed to get a grip on the situation and herself. "The kids are waiting for their dessert. Why don't you carry the ice cream out there while I make coffee?"

She thrust the carton at him.

His brows flickered upward. "You trust me alone with your children?"

Not really. But she trusted herself alone with him even less.

"I think you can deal with each other unsupervised for a few minutes," she said, her tone as dry as his.

She spooned coffee into a paper filter, trying to ignore the pounding in her blood and the trembling of her hands. She was not the kind of woman who quaked with lust. Not usually. Not since Copenhagen.

Maybe stress and deprivation were finally getting to her.

Or maybe Morgan was.

He set the ice cream on the counter and came up behind her, moving silently and too close. "I am not finished. I want you."

Her breath backed up in her throat.

"First lesson in parenting." She flipped the switch on the coffeemaker and turned, leading with her elbow. He stepped back, avoiding a jab to his ribs. "What you want doesn't come first anymore."

It was a good exit line. She grabbed four bowls and a handful of spoons and beat a retreat toward the dining room and safety.

Emily leaned her head on her wrist, plowing tunnels through her rice and peas.

Zack's place was empty. Of course. She should have known he'd escape from the table the minute her back was turned.

"Zack!" she called up the stairs. "Ice cream."

No answer.

"Sulking," Morgan observed.

"Regrouping," Liz corrected. "It's been quite a day."

For all of them. And it wasn't over yet.

"Em, would you go upstairs and tell Zack it's time for dessert?"

Emily's small face was tense, her gaze fixed on her plate. "He isn't there."

She pressed her lips together in annoyance. "Well, wherever he is, can you tell him—"

Emily looked up, her big eyes wide and clouded. "He went out."

A feeling tickled the back of Liz's neck like a spider crawling along her hair line. "Out where?"

Emily twisted, looking over her shoulder toward the front door.

"Beneath the wave," Morgan said.

"What?"

His face was grim. "I will go after him."

Liz quelled her unease. His urgency was infectious, but there was no point in overreacting. "That's not necessary. He's fifteen. It's still light out. How much trouble can he . . ." Her voice trailed off.

Morgan met her gaze. "Precisely."

Her heart hammered. "I'll call his cell phone."

"Do as you wish. I am going to find him."

"You can't. He left because of you."

Because he was hurting, angry, and confused, questioned by the police and confronted with his biological father. And she'd told him to get a job. She winced.

"You give him too much credit," Morgan said. "I doubt he is capable of rational thought. He is a young, rebellious male. He runs on instinct."

"Runs where?" She knelt by her daughter's chair. "Em, honey, did Zack say anything about where he was going? When he's coming back?"

Emily's lip trembled. She shook her head.

Liz strode to the living room and dug in her bag for her phone.

Morgan followed. "I need something that belongs to him. Something he sleeps with or wears next to his skin."

She lowered the phone from her ear. "Why?"

"You are wasting time." Morgan's gaze was cool and implacable. "Get it, please."

"I'm not going to . . . We don't need search dogs. Or psychics." With relief, she heard the connection to Zack's cell phone go through. But the call switched over instantly to voice mail. Her stomach hollowed.

Emily's sandals slapped as she ran upstairs. Upset, Liz thought.

She swallowed her worry and anger, struggled to keep her voice calm. "Zack, this is Mom."

She left a message, flipped her phone shut. She needed to check on Em. But even as she headed for the hall, her daughter reappeared in the entrance to the living room, hugging a pillow to her waist.

"Your brother's?" Morgan asked.

The little girl nodded.

His smile this time was no cool curve of lips but something warm and genuine. Liz's heart stuttered in her chest.

"Good girl." Morgan plucked the pillow from her small hands.

Emily gazed up at him the way she had in the police

station, like he was all the Disney princes and Anakin Sky-walker rolled into one.

Liz watched him strip the case from Zack's pillow, his movements swift and fluid, as if every second counted. "This is ridiculous. We're on an island. He can't go any-where."

Morgan ignored her, folding the pillowcase, shoving it in a pocket.

Liz set her jaw. "If anyone goes after him, it should be me."

"Where he has gone, you cannot follow."

"You know where he is?"

"I have some idea."

Which was more than she had. At least in Chapel Hill, she'd known Zack's few friends and his hangouts. Here, she was clueless. Doubts assailed her. She should never have moved them to Maine.

"Then I'll drive you," she said.

Zack was her son. Whatever mood had driven him from the house, whatever trouble he found, he was her respon-sibility.

Morgan stalked to the door. "You stay here."

"But . . ."

He glanced over his shoulder. "In case he comes back."

And before she could summon another argument, he was gone.

She kept staring even after the front door closed behind him. She wasn't Emily's age anymore. She wasn't looking for a prince to ride to her rescue, and she'd lost her belief in fairytale endings when Ben died. But inside her flickered the hope that this one time everything would turn out all right. With Morgan's help. For Zack's sake.

Even if it meant Morgan was more firmly entrenched in their lives than she'd ever imagined or wanted him to be.

*   *   *

Zachary glanced at his cell phone display, ignoring the blinking message icon. Almost nine, barely past sunset.

Man, he couldn't get over how dark it was here. He could
see in the dark since . . . His mind shied from the thought.
Well, he could see. Enough to avoid tripping over his feet
on the crumbling edge of the road. But the lack of street-
lights, headlights, made him feel even more alone.

No city glow stained the horizon. Only red clouds mark-
ing where the sun went down and silver clouds veiling the
moon. Nothing to do in this hick town but go to the beach—
*"Amazing the things one finds underwater," don't go there,
don't go there, don't*—or sit in his room jerking off.

His mouth hung open. He couldn't get air in his lungs.
His chest was hot and tight.

"She feeds you, clothes you, shelters you like a child."

But he didn't feel like a child. He felt . . . The pressure
in his chest built and pushed at his throat like a sob, like
a scream.

He walked faster along the broken road to escape it.

Occasional lights pierced the dusk and his solitude, the
pale flicker of a TV through a window, the yellow glow of
a lamp. Real families secure in their homes, with mothers
who didn't drag you off to Bumfuck, Maine, and tell you to
get a job, with fathers who didn't die or show up sneering
out of nowhere.

A screen door creaked and slammed. Something
thumped and was dragged rattling down a driveway.

He didn't want to see anybody. He couldn't talk to anybody, not with the weight sitting on his chest, cutting off
his air. He stopped in the shadow of the trees a few yards
away as somebody—a girl—lugged two garbage cans
down to the road.

It was her. The girl—his mind fumbled for her name—
Stephanie, from Wiley's Grocery Store. Stephanie Wiley.
Her dark red hair was almost black in the twilight, her
arms smooth and pale. He could smell her, the salt of her
skin, the freshness of her shampoo. Her gum. Inside him
something quivered and went still like a cat stalking a bird
on the lawn.

He didn't speak, but maybe he made a sound because her head jerked up.

She whirled toward the road, eyes widened against the dusk. "Who's . . . Oh." Her shoulders visibly relaxed. "Zack? It is you, isn't it? God, you scared me to death."

He unglued his tongue from the roof of his mouth and shuffled forward, no longer a stalker in the shadows, a sleek predator in the grass, but himself again, fifteen and awkward.

Her silver lip ring glinted as she smiled, flipping her hair back over her shoulders. "What are you doing here?"

"Oh, just, you know." He gestured largely. "Out. Walking."

"You could have made a little noise," she said. "Next time cough or say hi or something."

Next time. His heart swelled. Like she thought he would come by again, like she expected to see him.

Of course she's going to see you, dickhead. She couldn't avoid him if she tried. The entire island population was probably smaller than his old high school.

He cleared his throat. "Hi."

She cocked her hip, tilted her head. "So, where were you out walking to?"

"Nowhere." He was going nowhere. In more ways than one.

The porch light flicked on, and the front door opened, revealing a woman's backlit shape. "Steph, honey? Everything okay?"

"Fine, Ma," she yelled without turning around.

"What are you doing out there?"

"Just talking to a friend."

"Well, don't be long." The door closed.

"Parents." Stephanie rolled her eyes. "They worry, you know?"

Guilt needled him as he thought of his unanswered phone, his mother's strained face as she sat at the foot of his bed.

He swallowed the lump in his throat. "Yeah, I know."

Brilliant. Girls everywhere threw themselves at his feet because of his deep insights and sparkling conversation.

"It was even worse last summer," she confided. "Some lunatic was running around the island killing people."

"Yeah?" he asked, distracted. She was so interesting to look at, her mobile mouth with that silver lip ring, her small, firm breasts.

"Well, one person. A woman from Away was murdered on the beach. Then Regina Barone at the restaurant got attacked by some homeless guy. And after that, somebody broke into the clinic and beat the shit out of her and the doctor."

"Probably looking for drugs," Zack said. There. Practically a complete sentence.

"Probably. Anyway, my parents were really freaked." She stuck her hands into the hip pockets of her jeans, studying him in the dim light. "So . . . You want to sit for a while?"

His tongue felt too big for his mouth. "Sit?" he repeated stupidly.

"Out back." Her smile flashed like a fish underwater, bright and quick. "We have a swing."

"That would . . ." He cleared his throat. "That would be good. Great."

*   *   *

Morgan glided down the stairs and melted into the long twilight of northern summer.

Sex or the sea?

The boy would seek one or the other. He was young, male, finfolk. At dinner he had quivered with too much tension, too much energy, all of it unsatisfied.

He needed relief. That moment of entry into a body of water or a woman, the plunge and rock to completion, the ebbing peace that followed release.

Morgan's lips curled back from his teeth. It was not only

the boy who was frustrated tonight. But his own needs must wait.

Elizabeth's wry voice came back to him. *"First lesson in parenting. What you want doesn't come first anymore."*

He had to find the boy. Zachary.

At the fork in the road, Morgan raised his head, scenting the air. He could smell the fog rolling in from the water, heavy with brine, and the breeze rising through the trees, carrying the scent of spruce and decaying leaves.

Right into town? Or left to the beach?

He pulled the pillowcase from his pocket. The beach, he decided. The boy was young for sex and new to the island. He probably lacked an outlet beyond his own hand. So it would be the sea he aimed for.

More reason to find him and find him fast.

The finfolk charged with rebuilding Sanctuary sometimes had to be forcibly restrained to keep them on task and on land. Even an experienced elemental could slip permanently beneath the wave, could lose forever the will and finally the ability to take human form.

Zachary was not experienced. With an adolescent's raging hormones and lack of control, with no training or understanding of his nature or his powers, he was doubly at risk.

Morgan gripped the pillowcase, casting for scent or sign of the boy's presence. He had not found his only son to lose him again.

*   *   *

Zack was drowning. His armpits were drenched, he couldn't breathe, and there was a roaring in his head like the ocean, tumbling him over and over, rocking him, driving him on. He gasped. Shifted.

"Zack." Stephanie's cool fingers wrapped his wrist. She tugged his hand from her naked breast. His fingers curled reflexively. She felt so good, like satin, like velvet, like nothing he'd ever felt before. She wriggled under him on the bench of the swing, making the world sway and his boner very, very happy. "Zack, we gotta stop."

He couldn't stop. He was going to explode. She liked it when he kissed her, so he tried kissing her again, warm, soft kisses, deep, drowning kisses, trying to get closer, trying to . . .

"Zack, I mean it." She pushed at his chest, moved his hand again. With her elbow this time, sharp against the inside of his arm. The pain penetrated the rush in his head.

He swallowed hard and eased his weight off her. "I wasn't trying . . ."

"Sure, you were," she said easily. She sat up and wiggled her breasts into her bra. His brain blanked again. ". . . got to get in," she was saying. "My mom's expecting me. And I have work in the morning."

He watched her tug her shirt down over her flat, pale belly. He hadn't really thought she would do it with him in a swing in her parents' backyard. He hadn't thought at all. His body throbbed.

Dickhead.

He looked up, into her eyes. "Work," he repeated.

"You know, that thing you do to get money?" Her smile was warmer and softer than her voice. He really liked her. "I'm saving up for college."

"I'm getting a job," he said.

"Yeah?" She pushed her red-black hair behind her ears, interest in her eyes. "Doing what?"

"I don't know." Something that had seemed like the worst idea in the world when his mother proposed it was suddenly acceptable. Desirable, even, because of Stephanie. "I have to find something."

She stuck out her lower lip thoughtfully. The tiny silver ring winked in the moonlight. "My dad's looking for somebody to stock shelves. I could talk to him for you."

"You would do that?"

"Sure. Why not?" The swing swayed as she stood. "Maybe you could come by tomorrow."

"To the store," he said so there would be no misunder-standing.

"What, you thought I was inviting you back to the swing?"

He was silent.

"No reason you can't do both." She smiled at him over her shoulder as she turned and walked away.

Despite the erection straining at his zipper, he lurched to his feet. "Stephanie."

She waggled her fingers. "See ya. Tomorrow."

He watched her skip up the back stairs and into her house, his face hot and stiff as if he'd been crying, his body hot and stiff from what they'd done and all he hadn't been allowed to do.

He couldn't go home like this. He'd explode. Suffocate. His mother would be waiting with questions, always with questions, and he couldn't answer them tonight any more than he ever could.

"Where did you go, Zack?"

"Out."

"What were you doing?"

Stephanie.

Her breasts were so soft and surprisingly firm, the nip-ples a miracle under his hand.

He breathed through his mouth. Okay, that wasn't helping. Think of something else. Do something else. He couldn't stay here and jerk off in her swing. Suppose her parents came out? Or she did? He needed to move. Walk it off.

He pulled down the hem of his T-shirt and stumbled along the side of the house toward the street. A cool breeze washed his face. The sky pulsed with a billion stars. He ran a hand through his sweaty hair, filling his lungs with sweet, clear, twilight air, willing his body to settle.

"So." The man's voice came out of the shadow of the trees, lazy and amused. "It was the sex after all."

8

THE NIGHT WAS COOL WITH MIST AND MOON-
light, ripe with sex and frustration. Morgan surveyed the
boy, his big hands restless at his sides, his oversized T-shirt
hanging like a tent from his broad, bony shoulders, and
felt a twinge of something warmer and deeper than humor.
Sympathy, perhaps.

It had been a long time, centuries of time, but he
remembered—didn't he?—his first fumblings at sex. Fos-
tered in a Viking household, he and his twin Morwenna
had come quickly to adulthood. Even before Morgan was
fetched away to Sanctuary, he had his first female, a human
with curly pale hair and delightfully fast hands. He could
not remember her name or, truth be told, her face. But
he remembered the hot, sweaty anticipation, the primal,
almost painful relief.

His son had found distraction, apparently, but no
release.

"A swim would help," Morgan observed.

Hectic color stormed the boy's face. "Water's too cold."

"The colder the better, I'm thinking."

The boy jerked his shoulder, neither yes or no, and started to walk along the road.

Morgan fell into step beside him.

Zachary glared. "What are you doing?"

"I told your mother I would bring you back."

"I don't have to go anywhere with you."

"No," Morgan agreed. He felt the boy's start of surprise and pressed his advantage home. "But I'm not facing your mother without you, so you must decide how much of my company you will bear."

"I don't want to talk to her. Or you either."

Morgan was half tempted to drag the boy to the water, dump him in, and be done with it.

But it was not enough to prove the boy was finfolk. He wanted him as an ally, a willing tool. Dylan was right. The situation here and on Sanctuary would be easier if there was some understanding between them. It would take time to win the boy's trust.

"Your conversation is not so highly prized as you imagine," Morgan said dryly.

"You don't know my mother."

Morgan lifted a brow.

"She'll *ask* things," Zachary said desperately. His voice cracked on the word.

"She does not need answers," Morgan said. "Only reassurance. And perhaps . . . an apology."

"You're telling me to apologize."

"You worried her." *And me*, he thought. A new, disturbing notion. "The more you show yourself sensitive to her concerns, the less concerned she will be."

"You mean, the more I tell her, the less she'll ask," Zachary said shrewdly.

Morgan smiled a shark's smile in the dark. "Precisely."

* * *

Liz read to Emily and tucked her in, both of them comforted by the familiar bedtime ritual. She missed the years when Zack was small and could be protected with a nightlight and a kiss, when the only monsters were imaginary and could be banished to the closet.

She padded downstairs to switch on the porch light, her bare feet silent on the wooden treads.

The porch was empty. The yard was dark. The incessant whir of crickets filled the night.

The words of the storybook wrapped her heart like barbed wire, leaving a dozen tiny, bleeding punctures. *"And Max the king of all wild things was lonely and wanted to be where someone loved him best of all."*

Closing her eyes, Liz leaned her forehead against the cool glass by the side of the door. "Zack, come back," she whispered like a prayer. "Come home."

Where was he? For that matter, where was Morgan? She hated being stuck in the house with no way to reach them and no way to fix this.

Zack still hadn't answered her calls.

She took a deep breath and forced herself away from the door. Turning on another lamp, she settled into a deep chair and booted up her laptop. Work was a good antidote to worry. So she would work. Fifty-three-year-old Henry Tibbetts had come into the clinic after an unexpected fall on his boat. Listening to the lobsterman's halting explanation, Liz suspected he might have had a seizure. She took a careful medical history and ordered him to the hospital on the mainland for an EEG. In the meantime . . . The clinic stocked phenobarbital, but surely there were newer drugs with fewer side effects? Frowning, she pulled up the research online.

She was making notes when she heard a scrape on the porch, a rattle at the door. Her head rose. Her heart constricted with hope.

"Zack?" She uncurled her legs, sliding the laptop to the floor.

The front door opened.

Zack. Thank God. Relief crashed over her in a wave.

Her son loomed in the opening to the living room, shoulders hunched, watching her from under his thick, fair lashes. She jumped to her feet, barely registering Morgan coming in behind him.

Her son didn't want her touching him anymore. She didn't care. She grabbed him hard and hugged him tight. So tall, she thought, with a man's big bones and a boy's lean chest. When did he get so tall? His T-shirt smelled of young male sweat and grass.

He patted her awkwardly on the back with one arm. "Sorry, Mom."

Foolish tears, angry, grateful tears, filled her eyes. "Where were you?"

Zack's arm dropped.

She stepped back and saw him exchange a look with Morgan over her head. Unease brushed her spine like a cold hand in the dark.

He cleared his throat. "I went to Stephanie's. Stephanie Wiley? Her family owns the grocery store. She thinks her dad can maybe give me a job." Another quick glance at Morgan. "Stocking shelves and shit."

The fist in her chest loosened. "Zack, that's wonderful."

"Yeah." He shuffled his feet. "I should turn in. Got to be rested for my big day tomorrow."

"What time do you need to be there? Do you have clean—"

"'Night, Mom. Good night, um . . ."

Morgan's gaze met Zack's. Their eyes were the same, exactly the same, gleaming gold with thick, pale lashes. "Good night."

Zack practically bounded up the stairs, moving with more energy than he'd exhibited in months.

Liz faced Morgan. "Who are you and what did you do to my son?"

The gleam spread to a smile. "Perhaps he is simply growing up."

"You think?" Liz asked doubtfully.

"And perhaps it is the girl's influence."

"Stephanie," Liz said, committing the name to memory.

"He must have met her at the grocery store. I didn't know he had any friends on World's End."

"You are surprised."

"Thrilled, actually. And grateful." She reached out and squeezed his forearm. "Thank you. This whole thing turned out better than I expected."

His muscles were rigid under her touch. His gaze dropped to her fingers, pale against the black cashmere; lifted to her face. Her heart stuttered.

"Much better," he murmured and dipped his head.

Her bare toes curled on the hard floor. His voice was so cool, his body so warm. His heat infected her, spreading from her hand on his arm to the pit of her belly and the soles of her feet. She felt his swift inhale against her lips and then his mouth covered hers.

Hot. His kiss was hot and urgent. He didn't seduce, he devoured, licking at the seam of her lips, thrusting his tongue inside, blanketing her brain with heat.

This was wrong. Her children were upstairs. She should stop him. She would stop him.

In a minute.

For now she gave herself up to gratitude, relief, and lust, gave herself over to him. He bit, licked, sucked at her mouth, devastating her with liquid fire until she was soft and open, until her body was wet and clamoring for his. His hands found and claimed her breasts. His fingers plucked the tight little points.

"I want to taste you. Here." His breath seared her lips. His touch glided over the curve of her belly, along the crease of her thigh, and pressed between her legs. His palm circled slowly. "Here."

Her body strained toward his. She squeezed her thighs together, struggling to speak. To breathe. "I . . ."

He watched her face as his fingers rubbed her through her slacks.

"I'm not that grateful," she choked out.

"You would be."

Oh, God.

Laughter, shocked, excited, broke from her. She stepped back firmly, away from his touch, out of temptation. "The children," she articulated carefully, "are upstairs."

He shot a glance toward the empty steps, the darkened hall. "We are down here."

She ignored the thrill that ran through her veins and along her bones. He'd never married, she reminded herself. He didn't have kids, except for Zack. He couldn't understand.

"I can't do this," she said. "I need to set an example."

I need to be in control.

He stood very still, watching her, his eyes dark and considering between those thick blond lashes. Tension rolled off him in waves like heat from an oven. She could feel herself melting.

"You are in earnest," he said finally, flatly.

She inhaled. "Yes."

"Why? You are ready for me."

"Not ready for this."

"You are. I feel it. I smell it. Your body weeps for mine. Let me satisfy you."

Temptation almost overwhelmed her. "You can't. I need more than a quick grope on your way out the door. I need trust and tenderness and companionship and commitment. Can you offer me all those things? Or any of those things?"

"I am offering you sex."

"That's not enough."

His gaze met hers. "It was once."

His words thumped low in her midsection. An exquisite shudder went through her as she remembered the earth moving and the stars wheeling and his body plunging into hers again and again.

Remembered how she'd waited for his call the next day and all the days after, the sick realization she was pregnant as the result of a one-night stand.

She raised her chin. "It was never enough."

His eyes blazed. His mouth curled mockingly. "You

have changed your tune. You sang a different song when
you were open and under me."

She sucked in her breath. But before she could respond,
he tugged on the door. The night swirled in, and he was
gone.

*   *   *

The moon breasting the clouds left a wake of broken silver.
The fog flowed, a cool current from the sea.

Morgan welcomed the chill in the air, for he had a burn
in his blood that would not be satisfied this night.

His own fault, he acknowledged.

He had miscalculated Elizabeth's resistance. But then,
he had not expected resistance. He had never had a female
reject him before. Never known a woman who demanded
more than her pleasure as her due.

*"I need trust and tenderness and companionship and
commitment. Can you offer me all those things? Or any of
those things?"*

Of course he could not. Would not.

He was not bloody human.

But he should have worked harder to gain her trust, he
realized now.

A hunter must think like his prey. He had managed well
enough with the boy, observing from a distance, anticipating his moves. But with Elizabeth, Morgan had blundered
badly. He had allowed his hunger to compromise his skill.
Betrayed by appetite, he had struck too soon.

Something to think about when his blood was cooler.

He left the road, plunging down a slope thick with huckle-
berries, beach roses, and tall weeds.

The scent of the sea, cod and kelp, birth and decay, rose
like the mist to fill his lungs and head. The heavy surface
shone, opaque in the cloudy light. The tide sighed and murmured over the rocks, leaving behind bowls of rich water
brimming with life.

He rolled his shoulders, the tension leaching from his
muscles. Head erect, he strode over the deserted strand,

shedding the things that constrained him in human form: shoes, sweater, pants, worry, conscience. The finfolk were powerful shifters, and he was their lord. He could transform even his outer garments. But tonight he wanted nothing between him and his element.

He splashed through pockets and pools of water, his world revealing itself in stages, blue-green algae clinging like shadows to the rocks, small, complex fortresses of periwinkles and barnacles, rubbery mats of sea wrack and Irish moss.

The water seized his ankles like cold manacles in the dark. His balls tightened. He grinned fiercely and waded forward, the warden's medallion at his throat shining like a second moon.

The ocean surged to receive him, rustling around his knees, lapping at his thighs. He shook back his hair and dived, holding his breath against the shock of cold, the painful ecstasy, into the clear salt dark, into the pulse and surge and curl of the water, letting the joy take him, letting the water take him, one with the joy and the water.

Home.

Free.

His boundaries blurred and dissolved. His bones melted, stretched, fused. The pulse of the waves became his pulse, the heart of the ocean, his beating heart. He felt the Change rip through him like another pain, another ecstasy, tearing, convulsive, consuming as climax.

He retained just enough of his human mind to shape the Change as the hand of a potter shapes the clay. He was speed, size, strength, he was death in the water. He was the wolf of the ocean, *Orcinus*, seal killer, whale killer, killer whale. Scent disappeared. Sound enveloped him, vibrating through his bones, echoing in his head.

He plunged and breached, his breath a cloud, exhalation and exultation. He rocketed through the rushing dark, outracing human thought and the oily taint of humans in the water, propelled by cold and energy.

Home.

Free.

The lash of heat flicked like a whip across his belly. He reared, rolled, fearless and confused. He was predator, not prey. Yet even in orca form he recognized ENEMY.

Human? No.

He reached out with questing thoughts and rapid clicks, received them back as echoes in the dark. He felt the heat rising like a plume, like a stain, like blood from the broken breast of earth. A sea vent, he realized, on the ocean floor, seeping heat and malice.

"I feel your frustration, finfolk lord, even in the depths of Hell. Why do you not take what you need?"

Gau. He recognized the source of heat, the voice in his head. The demon lord Gau, Hell's emissary to Sanctuary, an old acquaintance and sometimes adversary who served the prince of Hell as Morgan served the prince of the sea. They knew each other well, fellow elementals equal in age and power, pride and position. They understood each other.

Perhaps too well, Morgan acknowledged. For in the demon lord, Morgan recognized his own lust for survival, his own personal ambition.

He bent his thoughts downward to the vent. *"Gau. I thought we buried you."*

The demon's amusement curled upward like smoke. *"I am immortal. Remarkably hard to snuff. Didn't I see you go down with the wall on Sanctuary?"*

The previous winter, the children of fire had attacked the merfolk's island. Morgan had stood with Conn on the walls of Sanctuary when an eruption of the earth's crust had turned the sea itself against them, sending a great wave down like a hammer on the castle.

"I am finfolk," he returned blandly. *"Remarkably hard to drown."*

"Ah, yes, I remember. You saved your lord that day and got small thanks for it."

Surprising the resentment that stirred. Or not so surprising, Morgan reflected, trying to shield his thoughts. Gau was very good at his work.

"*Better thanks, I am sure, than you received from your lord for your defeat.*"

A hiss of fire, another flash of heat.

"*Your lord is weak,*" Gau spat. "*He allies himself with weakness to the detriment of all your kind.*"

"*We make no alliances. The children of the sea are neutral in Hell's war on Heaven and humankind.*"

"*Not so neutral when your prince is fucking one.*"

Morgan had thought the same. But despite her human heritage, he respected the prince's consort Lucy, *targair inghean*, promised daughter of the merfolk. He gave a mental shrug. "*Neutral enough until you moved against us.*"

"*We seek only to restore the balance of power to what it was. To what it should be.*"

"*Enough games,*" Morgan snapped. "*What do you want?*"

"*Only your welfare and ours. Your people are dying.*" Gau's voice grated like sandpaper in his skull. "*Beset by humankind and neglected by the selkie pretender. Ally with us and you will survive. We can have primacy again.*"

Temptation struck, sharp and shining as a hook.

He dived deep, fighting the pull of Gau's voice. "*Water and fire make poor allies.*"

"*Are we not both elementals? Our interests are the same. Our quarrel is with Conn, not with you.*"

"*I am the prince's warden.*"

"*He does not deserve your loyalty. Why do you think he put you to work hauling stone? Because you are expendable to him. He would not care if you and all your people vanish beneath the wave.*"

In his chest, the warden's medallion pulsed like a heart. He needed to surface, Morgan realized dimly. He needed air. "*I pledged him my fealty.*"

"*A promise to his father, long past and easily forgotten. You are lord of the finfolk. You are more fit to lead than he.*"

"*You promise me rule over the children of the sea.*"

"*Ally with us, and together we can take back the world from the human vermin.*"

Vermin. The word stuck in Morgan's throat, a small indigestible lump that made the rest impossible to swallow.

Elizabeth was not vermin.

Zachary was not vermin.

He tried to turn his thoughts away from them, but Gau was too quick for him.

"*The boy is finfolk,*" the demon said.

Not a hook, a harpoon this time, straight to his gut. Somehow Gau knew what Morgan had only suspected.

Or, Morgan acknowledged, the demon merely said what he knew Morgan wanted to hear.

"*The future could be his,*" Gau continued. "*And yours. Only say the word, only pledge us your support, and you can have everything you desire.*"

He could not breathe. "*And if I decline?*"

Gau's response scorched the water. "*Then we will take them from you. The boy and the woman both.*"

9

≈

MORGAN STOOD ON THE MOON-WASHED LAND-
ing outside Dylan Hunter's apartment. The restaurant downstairs was shuttered tight. He pounded on the door, rewarded
when a light sprang on inside.

A lock clicked.

"Morgan. Jesus." Dylan scrubbed his face with his hand,
blocking the entrance to the apartment. "It's after eleven.
What do you want?"

"I thought you warded this fucking island."

Dylan's eyes narrowed. "I did."

"Who is it?" A woman's voice rose from behind him.
"Is everything okay?"

Dylan turned his head. "Fine, sweetheart. Go back to
bed."

An infant's thin wail wavered and fell.

"Shit." Dylan grimaced. "You better come in. Keep your
voice down."

Morgan followed him inside.

The rooms were small, shabby, and warm. Morgan

thought the entire apartment would probably fit inside the great hall at Caer Subai. Instead of English wood and Spanish iron, French silks and Italian marble, the place was littered with the debris of human existence, shoes under a table, bright throw pillows on the couch, bits of sea glass dangling in the windows. A child's artwork covered the refrigerator. Photographs hung on the walls.

The woman in the photographs stood in a darkened doorway, wrapped in a long red robe, a fussing infant on her shoulder.

"You remember my wife, Regina," Dylan said with obvious pride.

Straight, cropped hair; thin, angular face; dark, expressive eyes. Not a beauty, Morgan thought. But fertile and formidable, if what he had been told of last summer's events was true.

He inclined his head.

Regina cocked hers. "Kind of late for a social call."

"I am here on business."

She looked at her husband. "Selkie business?"

Dylan shrugged.

"Well, you can fill me in later." She soothed the infant, a pink scrap with her mother's cap of dark hair and her father's bold black eyes. "I'll feed Grace in our room."

Morgan noticed the shadows under her eyes, a faint bruising that reminded him of Elizabeth's fatigue. "I am sorry to have intruded," he said stiffly.

"'Sokay." Her quick smile transformed her face. She was not as lovely as Elizabeth, but he could see now what had attracted Dylan. "Grace usually wakes up about now anyway. If we're lucky, she'll go down until I have to get up at five."

Dylan rested a hand on the small of his wife's back, ran a finger down his daughter's cheek. "I'll make you some tea. You want that herbal stuff?"

"That would be good." She leaned into him a moment, a yielding, graceful gesture that made Morgan blink. And wonder. There was more between the selkie and his mate

than sex and progeny. Was this the trust and tenderness
Elizabeth sought?

*"Can you offer me all those things? Or any of those
things?"*

No. Why would he want to? He was not half-human, as
Dylan was.

Yet Dylan now bore little resemblance to the moody
adolescent Morgan remembered. He seemed stronger, more
self assured, more . . . *Satisfied*, Morgan thought with a
twist of envy.

Regina adjusted the infant's weight on her shoulder and
disappeared into the bedroom.

"So." Dylan grabbed a tea kettle, filling it at the scoured
white sink. "What drags you to my door at midnight?"

Morgan prowled restively in the tight space between
kitchen and living room. "I saw the demon lord Gau. Heard
him, rather."

Dylan banged the kettle on the stove. "When? Where?"

"Not an hour ago, two miles east."

Dylan clicked on the gas. Blue flames licked at the kettle's sides. "Two miles east," he repeated. "You're sure it
was Gau? We defeated him last winter."

"I recognized his voice." A whisper like fire, a taint like
oil in the water.

"There are other demons."

Morgan raised his brows. "So near?"

"Margred bound one in the waters last summer, near
where you think you saw Gau. And we've had attacks since
then. Not on the island, not since I set the wards. But you
know as well as I do it's impossible to shield every inch of
the sea bottom."

Morgan knew. The northern deeps around *Yn Eslynn*
were literally a hotbed of demons seething beneath the
crust, testing the limits of earth and the merfolk's powers
and patience.

His lips drew back in a silent snarl. The island was not
his territory. A week ago, the demons were welcome to it.
But they would not touch what was his.

"What I can do, I will do," he said. "For as long as I am here."

"I appreciate that," Dylan said. "Before they left, Conn and Lucy strengthened the protections on the island. But there are places the finfolk can go the selkie can't."

Morgan had not considered there was more to Conn's visit than his consort's whim. He did not like knowing he was not fully in the prince's confidence. Or that he might have misjudged him. "He did not tell me."

The kettle whistled. Dylan removed it from the fire. "Conn probably figured you didn't give a damn. He wouldn't know you had a personal stake on the island."

"Neither did I."

Dylan took a mug from a cupboard, shot him a glance. "You're sure, then, that this kid is finfolk."

"His name is Zachary," Morgan said. "No, I do not know. Gau said he was."

"You can't believe everything a demon says."

"I do not need your instruction," Morgan said coldly. "I was battling demons in the deep before your grandfather was born."

Long enough to fear that Gau, for once, might have spoken truth.

An unfamiliar fear crawled up his back. The island was warded. But once Zachary entered the water, once he was beyond the wards' protection, the boy was vulnerable. What would happen then?

Gau's threat burned in Morgan's brain. *We will take them from you. The boy and the woman both.*

* * *

He mounted her, pushing her thighs wide as she strained toward him, wet and open and aching under him, their joining sharp as orgasm, shifting as a dream.

In one shocking, glorious thrust, he shoved himself full length inside her, thick and hard. Filling her. Stretching her. She had never been so full. Only once. Only . . .

She moaned in pleasure and in need as he ground against

her, seated deep inside her. She ran her palms down the line of his back, dug her short nails into his buttocks, pulling him closer, urging him on, reveling in his hot, smooth, bare skin, in his strength and weight pressing her into the mattress. It had been so long. Too long. He slammed into her again and she arched, shuddering with sensation, delighting in the power of his body, the scent of his sweat, the healthy slap of wet flesh on flesh.

She panted. "More."

He reared up, his odd, pale eyes with their deep, dark centers gleaming golden in the dark.

Morgan.

She woke to the rasp of her own breathing and the emptiness of her bed.

Oh, dear God.

Liz lay on the damp sheets, willing her heartbeat to return to normal.

She was married. Had been married. After three years, she was resigned to rolling over at night reaching for Ben. Wanting Ben. She missed her husband beside her in their bed, the intimacy of touch and breath that was deeper than sleep, more satisfying than sex.

This was different. Dangerous. Disloyal.

This was Morgan, Morgan's face she had imagined over hers in the night, Morgan's weight on her, Morgan's flesh in her, Morgan filling her. Fucking her.

She drew a sharp breath.

"I am offering you sex," he had said to her.

"That's not enough."

Maybe not.

But the prospect, the promise in his voice and in his eyes, left her empty and aching for him.

The foggy remnants of her dream lingered the next morning, clogging her brain, pounding like a hangover in her head. She rummaged in the back of her drawer for underwear. She needed to do laundry. Her hand closed on a folded square. She pulled it out. Stared at it blankly.

And was transported back sixteen years in time.

Morgan, standing in the light of early dawn, the scratches of her nails on his shoulders. His face calm, composed, polite, as he turned to offer her something. His hand? A handkerchief.

She managed to sit up and take it, pleased to notice her hand was steady. Evidence of her awesome self-control, she thought, and winced.

Then he hadn't simply invaded her dreams, Liz reminded herself. He'd trampled them.

She finished dressing, dabbing concealer on the bags under her eyes. Her familiar reflection stared back from the mirror, pale, resolute, in control.

It bothered her she could not control her dreams. She felt betrayed, as if her mind and body were in collusion against her.

Stumbling downstairs, she fumbled through her morning routine, fueled by coffee and the need to maintain a pretense of normality. She packed snacks and a peanut butter sandwich for Emily, propped a note in the middle of the kitchen island where Zack would be sure to see it when he woke.

Walking into the front hall, she felt Morgan's presence from the night before like a ghost brushing her skin.

Steadying herself with a hand on the banister, Liz called up the stairs. "Emily! Time to go!"

It was a relief to get to work, to slip on the authority and armor of her white doctor's coat, to concentrate on her patients' needs and problems instead of her own.

Margred Hunter, in Exam Room 2, could be a problem. Liz glanced down at her notes; up at her patient. Sitting upright on the paper-covered table, Margred certainly appeared healthy. Glowing dark eyes, abundant hair and breasts, slight, mysterious smile. Like a poster model for pregnancy, Liz thought, or some pagan fertility goddess. Her physical exam confirmed her blood pressure was normal and she had only mild edema. Her baby was head down and settling nicely into her pelvis.

But the woman was less than two weeks from her due date. She could go into labor at any time.

"About your birth plan," Liz began.

Margred looked surprised. "We went over that at my appointment last week. When Caleb was here. He wants me to have our baby at the hospital."

"Which is great," Liz said promptly. "They have a wonderful birthing center there and the best neonatal unit outside of Portland. The thing is, you're already thirty percent effaced. Of course in an emergency, we can call LifeFlight or the Coast Guard. But given your progress, I wonder if you had considered staying on the mainland until after the baby is born."

"No," Margred said simply. "Caleb cannot be away from the island. And I will not be away from Caleb."

"As long as you understand the risks. We're a good ninety minutes by ferry from the mainland."

"Less than an hour if Caleb's father takes us in his lobster boat."

Liz blinked.

"That's how Regina got to the hospital," Margred explained.

"Right. All right." Liz blew out her breath. "I'm still learning how to live on an island. Just promise me you'll call if you have any questions or concerns."

"Or contractions."

"Those, too." Smiling, Liz put a hand under Margred's elbow to help her down from the exam table. "You can make an appointment with Nancy for next week. Assuming you make it that long."

"I had better. My baby shower is Tuesday night." Margred cocked her head. "You should come."

"Oh." Warm pleasure caught Liz unaware. But the situation was awkward. Margred's husband had picked up Liz's son for questioning yesterday. Automatically, she retreated behind her familiar doctor-patient barriers. "Thank you, but it's hard for me to get away in the evenings. I have a little girl."

"I saw her, I think. In the waiting room?"

Most people didn't see a resemblance. Liz felt the tension in her shoulders relax. "That's right. Emily."

Margred shrugged. "So bring her. Lobster bake at the point, seven o'clock. There will be plenty of children. Regina's son Nick is about your daughter's age."

"I . . ." Liz bit her lip. Why not? Obviously any awkwardness was mostly in her own mind. And wasn't this why she moved to the island? To form connections, to be part of a community with her children. "Thank you."

"Thank you." Margred's mouth curved with sly humor. "Now if I go into early labor, I won't have to leave the party."

Liz was laughing as she escorted her out front.

While Margred scheduled her appointment, Liz scanned the waiting area. Her daughter was camped in a cluster of chairs pulled seat to seat into a makeshift fort.

And crouched on his heels at the entrance, his white blond hair even with the top of the chairs, was Morgan. He looked up, eyes gleaming, golden, intent, like the eyes of a predator or the eyes in her dream.

Hot color swarmed her face.

"Elizabeth." He rose to his feet with smooth, animal grace. He nodded as Margred finished at the front desk and came up behind them. "Margred."

"Morgan. I did not expect to find you here."

"Nor I you."

"Then what . . ." She looked from Morgan to Liz. Speculation glinted in her eyes. "Ah."

Liz cleared her throat. There was an odd resemblance in the two faces that were otherwise so different, male and female, dark and fair. Something in the expression or the eyes maybe, something fierce and proud and primal. "You two know each other?"

"Not well," said Morgan.

"Years ago," Margred said at the same time.

Which? Liz wondered. *Not well* or *years ago?*

Margred shrugged and smiled. "I remember so little."

"I am pained to be so forgettable," Morgan murmured.

"No doubt you have improved with time."

He threw back his head and laughed. Liz felt an absurd flutter that might almost have been jealousy. Totally unprofessional, she thought. Inappropriate.

Terrifying.

"Mom." Emily tugged on her white doctor's coat. "Are you done yet?"

Liz knelt, grateful for the distraction. She hated making Emily sit through her clinic hours, but there hadn't been time this morning to make other arrangements. "Not yet, honey. I still have a couple of patients to see."

"Then can we go to the beach?"

"We're going to the community center, remember? To enroll you in summer camp."

Emily's bottom lip poked out. "I don't want to go to summer camp. I want to go to the beach."

"I can take her."

She looked up. Margred was gone. There was only Morgan, staring down at her with those knowing yellow eyes. Her heart jumped. Her brain blanked. "What?"

"I will take your daughter to the beach," he repeated, his tone patient and amused.

Emily jigged from foot to foot.

"No," Liz said. "Thank you, but we can't impose."

"It is not an imposition. I came to see you in any case, you and your daughter."

"Why?"

He hesitated. "Companionship," he said finally.

"I need trust and tenderness and companionship and commitment," she had said to him last night. *"Can you offer me all those things? Or any of those things?"*

Her breath escaped. "Emily isn't your child."

"No, but I will keep her safe." He met her gaze. For once his eyes weren't distant and amused but warm and direct. "Let me do this, Elizabeth. For you and the child."

"Please, Mom," Emily begged.

"I get off in two hours," Liz said.

"I will have her back to you before then," he promised.

She looked from her daughter's eager face to Morgan's inscrutable one, feeling herself teeter on the edge of a decision, on the brink of a precipice. "What's your cell phone number?"

"I do not have a cell phone. Not . . . with me."

There was simply no way she could let her daughter go off without any way to reach them. "Then . . ."

"You could give him yours," Emily said. "Pleeease."

"Trust must go both ways," Morgan said quietly.

He was right, damn it. Of course he was right. But she hadn't counted on anyone but herself in a long, long time.

Slowly, she unhooked her cell phone from her belt. "The clinic's number is already programmed in. Just hit the contacts key."

He glanced curiously at the phone before slipping it into his pocket.

"Yay!" Emily dragged her backpack from under the chairs. "Thanks, Mommy."

Liz swallowed the sudden lump in her throat. "You should thank Mr. Bressay."

His gaze locked with hers. "You can thank me." Her chest tightened as a corner of his mouth curled in a smile. "Later."

*   *   *

"Where's your car?" Emily asked.

"I do not have one."

"Why not?"

Morgan glanced down at the bobbing dark curls on a level with his waist. "I do not need one."

He was finfolk. He had no use for human technology and little patience with human questions.

The little girl beside him chattered on, unaware of either predisposition. "Can't you drive?"

"I could," he answered shortly.

"Then why don't you?"

"I like to walk."

"Me, too." She sounded out of breath.

It occurred to him her questions might be driven by more than curiosity. Her legs were very short.

He reduced the length of his stride. "Shall I carry you?"

She stuck out her chin. "I'm okay."

Dauntless, he thought, amused and admiring. *Like her mother.* "Give me your backpack, then."

She wriggled out of the straps. "Where are we going?"

He kept his tone casual as he hitched the small pink bag over his shoulder. "Not far." He hoped. Zachary did not have a car either. "Why don't you take me where you went yesterday with your brother?"

He could not enter the water with the girl watching. But he could mark the place, assess the danger, return later to set wards.

Her gaze slid from his. "It's kind of a secret."

"You do not have to tell me," Morgan said. "You can show me."

She did not answer. But where the road dipped down to the beach, she turned off the paved way and onto a narrow track through the tall grass. Beach roses and blackberry bushes pressed in on both sides. Thorny vines like trip wires crossed the uneven ground. Her short legs were soon scratched with thin pink lines.

"Careful." Morgan cleared a trailing cane from her path.

She flashed him a smile before flitting ahead.

He smelled the sea before he saw it, shining like mother of pearl in the sun. The path broke up in a welter of rocks. The rocks tumbled down to a crescent of gray sand littered with pebbles and shells.

Secluded, with soft footing and a deep draft. A smart choice, a safe choice, for a finfolk youth learning to Change. A perilous place for the human child left on shore.

Morgan frowned. "Do you come here alone?"

Emily shook her head. "I'm not allowed."

"And where do you wait when your brother goes in the water?"

Those big eyes widened before she hung her head.

At a loss, Morgan regarded her soft, dark curls. The child had not yet developed her mother's defenses or the human facility with lying, but she was clearly keeping silent. To protect her brother?

He could understand that. He could even applaud her loyalty. He had his own secrets, his own loyalties. But he had promised Elizabeth to keep her daughter safe.

"You must not go into the water."

"I don't." She scrunched her small face. "It's too cold for swimming anyway. Not like the beach at home."

"Home?"

"North Carolina. Where we lived before."

"It is the same."

"No, it's not." She skipped down the rocks.

He felt an unfamiliar qualm at the possibility she might slip and break her little neck. He took her arm to prevent it. Under his palm, her skin was as smooth as the inside of a shell, her bones delicate and fragile as a bird's.

"The sea," he explained. "It is always changing and always the same. You are always at home with the sea."

She tipped up her face. "But I don't know anybody here."

He stared at her, baffled. "You know your mother. And your brother Zachary."

"They're family. I don't have any friends." Her childish mouth trembled.

Morgan felt a flicker of panic. He had little experience with children. None at all with crying ones. "You know me," he offered desperately.

The alarming moisture retreated as she assessed him with her mother's clinical, critical eye. "You're old."

"Very old," he agreed. "Hundreds of years old."

She gave a watery chuckle.

The sound woke a memory in the cavern of his heart

that had been still and cold and silent for centuries—the echo of another child's laughter. His sister, his twin, Morwenna. He had not let himself think of her in years.

"You're not that old," Emily said. "You could be my friend, I guess. If you want."

The tentative hope in her eyes struck like a barb in his heart. He was one of the First Creation, elemental, immortal, solitary. He did not make friends.

"Mr. Bressay?"

He stared down at her.

"I'm hungry."

He was, too. In his heart. In his soul, if he had one.

"I can take you back." Now that he had marked the place, he had no need of the child's company. None at all.

"I have a sandwich. Peanut butter. In my backpack."

Wordlessly, he slid the pink bag from his shoulder and handed it to her.

Taking it from him, she settled herself on the rocks and patted the flat place beside her.

He froze.

She did not appear to notice. Her small, grubby hands pawed through the pack, pulled out a squishy plastic bag. Peeling it open, she extracted the mangled sandwich. She regarded it a moment and then carefully tore the bread in two. Smiling, she offered him half.

The hook in his heart dug deep. An unfamiliar emotion welled in his chest. He did not need her food. But he was touched by her determination to share what she had with him.

The way Elizabeth had last night.

Folding his long legs, he eased down on the rocks beside Elizabeth's daughter. Solemnly, he accepted the sandwich. "Morgan," he said. "If we are to be friends, you must call me Morgan."

10

~≈~

"I DON'T CARE ABOUT THE HAIR." GEORGE WILEY glanced at Zack's new dye job and away. "As long as it's clean and out of your face. And I don't care about your clothes as long as you don't smell and I'm not staring at your underwear all day. I don't care about your lifestyle either."

Zack swallowed. His *lifestyle*? Shit.

"I'm not gay, Mr. Wiley," he wanted to say. *"Actually, I'm very interested in having sex with your daughter."*

But that wouldn't get him the job or Stephanie, so he kept his mouth shut.

Wiley shifted his weight, making his desk chair creak. The small office was at the back of the store, crammed between the meat counter and the stockroom. The cold air smelled of bananas and spoiled milk. "Islanders, once they get used to you, tend to live and let live," he said.

Zack nodded to show he was listening, but inside he was wondering how long it would take for the Nazi twins, Todd and Doug, to get used to him. And how he could avoid them if he was working at the grocery store.

Wiley cleared his throat. "This time of year, though, we get a lot of summer people. They think they want local color, but they don't want to see anything that makes them uncomfortable."

Again, his gaze flickered to Zack's aggressively black hair. Zack's stomach sank as he waited for Wiley to tell him he didn't get the job after all.

His hands clenched between his knees. Screw it. It's not like he *wanted* to sweep floors and carry boxes for minimum wage.

Only . . . He wanted an excuse to hang around her. Stephanie. And a job would prove to his mom he wasn't a kid anymore. It was something to do, something to hold on to.

"So I'll tell you what I told my daughter," Wiley continued. "If customers are distracted by your makeup, you're wearing too much. This is a store, not a circus. I'm not hiring you as a clown."

Zack's heart thudded. "You're hiring me?"

Wiley ran a hand over his receding hairline. "Looks like it. I can use you thirty hours a week. Friday and Saturday are our biggest days, Wednesday and Sunday you're off. Monday and Thursday we stock shelves, do the weekend store displays. Out by eleven."

"Eleven at night," Zack repeated to be sure he understood.

Wiley's eyes—blue, like his daughter's—narrowed. "That a problem for you?"

It wasn't like he had school the next morning, Zack reasoned.

His chest expanded with the power of making a decision, taking an action, without checking first with his mother. He met Wiley's gaze. "No, sir."

Wiley gave a short nod. "I'll see you tonight, then. Six o'clock."

*   *   *

"Six," Liz repeated. "But what about dinner?"

She bit her tongue the instant the words left her mouth.

She was the one to insist Zack get a job. But she hadn't expected him to find one so soon, she thought, torn between guilt and pride. And she'd never intended him to work nights.

Despite their sometimes competing schedules, throughout her husband's illness and after his death, Liz had made the family dinner a priority, a constant, a way of demonstrating to her children and herself that life went on.

And life did go on. Life changed. Zack was changing right before her eyes. He was barely wearing makeup tonight, she realized, just a touch of liner to offset his long gold eyes.

He shrugged, apparently uncomfortable with her inspection. "I'll grab a sandwich before I go."

"I'll make you something."

"You don't have to."

She needed to do something, to connect with him somehow, to make up to him in some way for whatever failures had brought them to this place. "I want to."

"Whatever. Thanks," he added in a voice that meant *"Leave me alone."*

She fixed tuna melts, and the three of them ate dinner together. Early, so Zack could leave for work on time, although Liz had no appetite and he kept looking at the clock.

At least he ate, she told herself as she carried their plates to the sink. But he hadn't spoken a word to her.

The doorbell rang.

"I'll get it." Emily, always sensitive to tension, jumped up from the table.

Zack followed her into the hall.

Liz shut off the water with her elbow and reached for a dishtowel. "Make sure you see who it is before you open the—"

"Morgan!" Emily said.

Liz's heart bounded as high and glad as Emily's voice. Stupid heart. It was only the memory of her dream, the rush of sex, the contact high she got from being in the same room with him, that caused that erratic jump in her pulse. Or maybe it was the relief of having another adult in the house.

"And he brought a kitten!" Emily shouted.

Liz's jaw dropped. She closed her mouth. Swallowed.

Adult, my ass, she thought, and went to deal with the situation.

Morgan stood in the entryway, tall, dark, and formidable with winter pale hair and eyes. Against his chest in one large hand he supported a small striped kitten. Emily danced around them as Zack watched from the stairs.

"What are you doing?" Liz asked, keeping her voice low.

Morgan raised his brows at her tone. "Your daughter already told you." He unhooked tiny claws from his sweater and handed the kitten to Emily. "I brought you a cat."

"She's so cute," Emily crooned, cuddling the little head under her chin. "What's her name?"

"His name," Morgan corrected, "is up to you."

Her eyes widened with delight. "I can name him?"

"You can keep him."

"Now, just a minute," Liz said.

"Can I?" Emily whirled, clutching the kitten to her breast. "Can I, Mommy?"

Liz's heart sank at the mingled hope and appeal in her daughter's face. She had enough to deal with already. They all did. Morgan had no right to dump this on her. "We need to talk about this, Em," she said gently. "You're just starting camp. A pet is a lot to take on right now."

"That means no," Zack said.

Emily's face fell.

Liz drew a careful breath. "It means we need to talk. You caught me by surprise."

"That's 'Hell, no,'" Zack translated.

"We have to be responsible," Liz insisted. "We have to consider the consequences."

"Why?" Morgan asked.

She turned on him. "Excuse me?"

He took a step toward her, holding her gaze. "You are taking something simple and making it complicated. Your daughter wants a cat. I found her a cat."

"You found it."

He nodded. "Behind the restaurant."

A stray. It probably had germs. Fleas. Parasites.

And none of that mattered compared to the look on her daughter's face. Emily sat on the floor with the kitten in her lap, happiness shining in her eyes.

"We don't have anything to feed it," Liz said weakly.

"Regina has been feeding it scraps from the kitchen." Morgan moved closer, lowering his voice so only she could hear. "Let go, Elizabeth. Give in. There is no harm in losing a little control."

Her face burned. "This isn't about us. This is about what's best for Emily."

"Your daughter needs friends. She needs this."

Oh, God, he was right. How could she have missed it? How could he understand what her children needed better than she did herself?

Her sense of failure tightened her throat. She forced herself to smile. "Advice from an expert?"

"Easy enough to give her what she wants." His smile gleamed. "You are more difficult."

Her breath shuddered out. No one else looked at her the way he did. Wanted her the way he seemed to. How could he say such things to her now, in front of her children? Emily, thank God, was too young to understand, but Zack . . .

"I can bring home the food and litter and stuff," Zack said from above them on the stairs. "When I get off work."

"It's too much for you to carry."

"I can do it."

"I'll pick you up," she said. "When do you get off, eleven? It'll be dark anyway."

"And Em will be in bed," Zack said. "Stop treating me like a kid, Mom."

He was a kid. Her kid. She didn't want to coddle him,

but life had taught her how unexpectedly things could go suddenly, horribly wrong.

"I'm still responsible for you."

Zack shook his head. "I'm out of here." He thumped down the stairs, stepped over Emily in the hall.

"Zack . . ."

"See you." He brushed by Morgan and slammed out the door.

Liz closed her eyes.

"If you want him to be a man," Morgan said, "you must let him take a man's part."

It was a relief to have someone her own age to fight. She opened her eyes to glare. "He's only fifteen."

"Old enough to pull at a tight rein. Did you never take the bit in your mouth when you were his age?"

"Not really. I was a good girl. A good student." Her voice was only faintly bitter. "I spent my time cramming to get into a good school."

"Ah, yes. The Plan." His lips curved, cool and amused. "I remember."

She blinked. "You do?"

His gaze met hers, and her heart jolted. His eyes were not cool at all. "There was a time you wanted more than your parents wanted for you."

She swallowed. "And I got more than I bargained for."

"An adventure," he said softly.

Memory thumped in the pit of her stomach.

"More than an adventure," she reminded him. Her rash decision that night had life-changing consequences. Morgan had given her a baby.

And now, it seemed, he'd given her a cat.

She looked at Emily, playing with the kitten on the floor. The little pucker between her brows was gone, her expression open and more relaxed than at any time since their move to World's End. Liz would accept anything and anyone who put that smile on her daughter's face.

And the kitten was responsible, she thought. No, Morgan was responsible.

He arched an eyebrow. "Regrets?"

"No," she answered honestly. "Thank you. For the cat."

Emily's head shot up. "We're keeping him?" She sought confirmation in her mother's face. "We're keeping him!"

Scrambling from the floor, she launched herself at Morgan, hugging as high as she could reach. "Thank you! Thank you, Morgan."

He stiffened like a startled dog.

Liz bit her lip, a pang at her heart. He wasn't used to children, she reminded herself. Emily wasn't his. Despite his kindness this afternoon and his gesture with the kitten, he could not give her open-hearted daughter the affection she sought.

"It's Mr. Bressay, honey," she reminded gently.

He raised his large hand and slowly, carefully stroked her daughter's curls. "Morgan." His voice was harsh. He cleared his throat. "I told her to call me Morgan."

Emily tipped back her head and beamed. "Because we're friends."

"Yes." His deep voice made the word sound like a vow. "We are."

He crouched beside her. "Now that the cat has a home, you must give it a name."

They both watched the kitten. Deprived of Emily's attention, it stalked across the floor and pounced on Morgan's boot.

Emily giggled. "Tigger."

His brows rose in question.

"From *Winnie the Pooh*," Liz supplied. "He bounces."

Morgan looked blank.

Poor man. He really was out of his element.

Yet there was nothing false about his interaction with Emily, none of the fake heartiness of her male colleagues who had tried to hit on her with her children around. He treated Emily with the same grave courtesy he might have shown an adult.

And Emily, Liz saw, soaked up his masculine attention

like a flower turning its face to the sun. "I'll take good care of him," she promised. "He can sleep on my bed."

"In a box," Liz said.

"In a box on my bed," Emily said without missing a beat.

"I saw big boxes in your garage," Morgan remarked. "Big as houses, if you were the size of your kitten."

Emily's eyes rounded. "We could make a Tigger house."

"I imagine we could," he agreed.

Smooth, Liz thought. He was very good at getting what he wanted.

"*I want you,*" he had said last night, his tone low and thrilling, dark desire in his eyes.

She gnawed her lower lip again. She appreciated his intervention with Emily. He was perceptive, he was kind. But he was not safe.

"The moving carton is a great idea," she said. "Emily, honey, why don't you look in the linen closet and see if we have any towels to make a bed for Tigger? The green ones."

"Can I take Tigger?"

"Tigger will be fine down here with me. Now scoot. The faster you get the towels, the sooner we can get started on his house."

Her daughter bolted up the stairs.

She faced Morgan, trying to ignore her stuttering heart. "What are you doing?"

That beautiful mouth curved. "I believe I am turning a carton into some kind of cat accommodations."

"You didn't come over tonight to build a kitty condo."

"My plans will wait."

"But you had plans." For God's sake, why was she pushing this?

"I have . . . hopes."

The look in his eyes made her stomach jump. It was uncomfortable and intoxicating to flirt like this, to want like this, with her daughter only a flight of stairs away.

"I can't . . ." She inhaled and tried again. "This isn't appropriate."

"I have slightly more finesse than the cat, Elizabeth." There was an edge to his voice now, sharp and dangerous. "I will not pounce in front of your children."

The focus in his eyes made her blood tingle. "And what happens later?"

"What is later? A year, a month, a week from now?" He shrugged. "I am here now with you. It is enough for me."

She'd told him she needed trust, tenderness, companionship, commitment. Could the first three be enough? Could passion be enough?

Her heart pounded. She felt dizzy, as if she stood on a cliff above a raging sea. *Step back from the edge?* she wondered. *Or take the plunge?*

Swallowing hard, she took one step closer to the fall. "I meant later tonight."

His hot gaze locked with hers. "That is up to you."

* * *

He could eat her up in a few hasty bites.

But he had promised her finesse, and he was experienced enough to know greed could be his undoing. So he controlled his hunger with a hunter's patience, making himself useful, biding his time. He hauled a moving carton upstairs. While Elizabeth unearthed bowls and her daughter shredded newspaper, he cut down the sides of the box so the kitten could not climb out and the girl could not fall in.

He made Emily giggle, lying on her floor to inspect her room from a cat's eye perspective. Retrieving an elastic hair band from under her dresser, he presented it to her with a bow. She rewarded him with a smile and a smacking kiss on the cheek before bouncing into bed.

Morgan's empty hands curled into fists at his sides. The little girl's kiss left him gasping, struggling like a fish out of water.

With the fatalism of his kind, he accepted that he would

eventually lose his battle for survival, that he would one day surrender to the lure of the sea, lost finally and forever beneath the wave, without will or ability to take human form.

But he never imagined he could become stranded on land, snared by something as foolish as a child's affection, as transitory as a woman's desire.

In its box, the kitten mewed and fretted, trapped by Emily's love and Elizabeth's care.

The children of the sea were solitary by nature and by choice. Perhaps with Morwenna . . . But his twin had turned her back on him, and Morgan had never forgiven her defection. Even swimming with the whaleyn, the great, mild giants of the sea, he had resisted the seductive security of the pod. He could survive longer as a shark: focused, ruthless, predatory.

Nothing lasted forever but the sea, not love or faith or hope or strength. The child's affection, like her memories, would fade. His attachment to her and to her mother could only be temporary.

And yet . . .

He watched Elizabeth tuck her into bed, smoothing her hair and the covers with a tender hand, the murmur of their voices like the rising and falling of the sea, and felt pieces of his heart slipping away, eroded by longing.

Elizabeth leaned over her daughter's pillow, the bend of her body graceful in the spill of light from the hall.

"Good night, Mommy." Emily's gaze sought Morgan, waiting in the doorway. "'Night, Morgan."

He had to clear his throat before he could speak. "Good night."

"Sleep tight." Elizabeth eased the door shut on the kitten's piercing cries. She smiled ruefully at Morgan. "Assuming they can sleep at all."

Before he could respond, she slipped by him, disappearing through a shadowed doorway at the other end of the house. Her room? He wanted to follow, to ravage, to possess. But he did not think she would invite him into her bed, take him into her body, with her wakeful child down the hall. He heard water running and the slide of a drawer before she reappeared, her cheeks faintly flushed.

Avoiding his gaze, she preceded him down the stairs. The kitten's mews pursued them, stopping abruptly as they reached the front hall.

Elizabeth cocked her head. "She has that cat in bed with her."

"Almost certainly," Morgan agreed, amused.

Indecision warred in her face. "I could go up."

"You could." Resting his hand on the small of her back, he steered her gently into the living room. "But you won't."

She turned to face him. He liked looking at her, those clear, dark eyes, that long, mobile mouth, the slightly squared jaw. "Why won't I?"

He brushed a strand of hair back from her face, pleased at the sudden intake of her breath. "Because you know they will both be happier this way."

"Em has camp in the morning."

He tucked her hair behind her ear, letting his hand linger, letting her grow accustomed to his touch. "You said yourself she would not sleep with the kitten crying across the room."

He could feel her weakening, but she still argued. The woman would argue with the angels. "She could still have allergies. Asthma."

"Worrier."

"Worrying goes with the job description, I'm afraid."

He cocked an eyebrow. "Doctor?"

"Mother."

"You should not worry over what you cannot control." He stroked his thumb down the side of her throat, pressed against her rapidly beating pulse. "Let go, Elizabeth."

Her breath sighed across his lips. "I suppose you're right. I just don't want this sleeping together thing to become a habit."

He kept his face straight with an effort. Did she still

think they spoke of her daughter and the cat? "One night," he murmured. "One night won't change anything."

He covered her mouth with his, keeping his eyes open to gauge her response. Her lashes drifted shut. Her lips warmed and yielded. The surrender in her kiss, the faint resistance in her muscles, combined to drive him wild. But when he deepened the kiss, she turned her face away.

"Maybe you're right." She retreated toward the kitchen.

He let her go. Elizabeth might let him take her, but only after the required preliminaries. Trust. Tenderness.

Conversation.

"You were good with her. Emily," she said. "Good with both of them, really."

He understood the change of subject was another step back, another way of regaining distance and control.

He leaned his hips against the counter, admiring the stretch of her back as she opened a cabinet. "It is because I am a stranger. I see them differently."

"I thought it was because you were . . ."

"Zachary's father?"

She bit her lip. Shot him a glance over her shoulder. "Male."

"I am gratified you noticed."

"Wine?" she offered.

Another preliminary.

"Whatever you want," he said.

She stood on tiptoe to reach for glasses. "White or red?"

"Either." He ran his tongue over his teeth. "Or we could have sex."

She went still for one tiny, betraying moment before she turned. "Wine first."

The spark of reaction caught him by surprise. Wine *first*. His patience was to be rewarded, then. His body stirred and thickened in anticipation.

"The counselor said the children need a male role model," Elizabeth continued. Her small, neat doctor's hands dealt competently with bottle and corkscrew. "Before we moved here, I tried reestablishing contact with my parents in Philadelphia, but things didn't work out."

He pulled his mind back to the conversation. She was estranged from her parents, he remembered. "Because of Zachary."

She poured the wine—red—into two glasses and handed him a glass. "Because of Zachary. And Ben." Grabbing the bottle and the second glass, she nodded toward the back door. "Would you get that?"

He complied. The cool night air flowed through the door, easing his tension. He felt more himself outside, in the open, in the dark.

Not completely open, he noted. The screened back porch was latticed for privacy, with rolling blinds to keep out the rain and a double skylight to let in the moon. Bright cushions covered two chairs and a hammock, bleached by the silver light. The breeze carried the scent of pine and stirred the wind chimes dangling in one corner.

Elizabeth set the bottle on the floor and sat sideways in the hammock like a mermaid caught in a net. The sag in the webbing forced her to lay back, legs parted, toes barely touching the floor. Deprived of support, she looked softer, looser, off balance. His predatory instincts sharpened, edged by an odd tenderness.

He sipped his wine, watching her over the rim. "Your parents disapproved of your husband?"

She hesitated. "Yes."

"But he is dead."

"Emily is his daughter."

He did not understand. "She has your eyes."

"She has her father's name. His skin color." She took a gulp of wine. "To my father, Zack looks like a freak and Emily looks like the gardener's daughter."

Comprehension gave way swiftly to rage. "Your father is an ass."

"Yes, he is." There was no bitterness in her voice, only a weary acceptance. "But he is their grandfather."

"Your husband must have family."

"In Puerto Rico. I take the children to San Juan to visit once a year, but it's not enough." She stared into her wineglass. "Zack seemed to be doing all right for a while, but the last year or two he's been so angry. Withdrawn. He can't focus. His grades have dropped. His sleep patterns have changed. I have to nag him to shower." She looked up, and the distress in her eyes made him want to kill something for her. "I'm worried he's doing drugs."

"Not drugs," Morgan said.

"What else could it be?"

The Change, he thought. The timing was right. Like puberty itself, the Change would affect every aspect of the boy's development and feel completely beyond his control. On Sanctuary, adolescents were guided through the Change by an experienced warden. Ignorant and alone, Zachary would be helpless to understand or mitigate the compulsion that seized his body.

Poor little bastard. No wonder he hid in his room and avoided the touch of water.

"His therapist didn't think it was drugs either." Elizabeth struggled to sit up, cradling her glass in her hands. "But therapy wasn't helping. I thought the move up here— new friends, new environment, a fresh start—might do him some good. Emily, too. She's more resilient than Zack, more open, more eager to please. But she hasn't been truly happy in, oh, way too long. They both need something so much." She pressed the fingers of one hand to her temples. "And whatever it is, I can't give it to them."

She was wrong, Morgan thought. Even without understanding her son's true nature, Elizabeth had given him the tools to survive.

She was strong enough not to need his comfort. Not to need him. But it annoyed him she gave herself so little credit.

"You underestimate yourself," he said. "And your children. You have been giving to them since they were born.

They can be who they are, they can be angry or scared or miserable in your presence, because they know you will be there for them. Will always be there for them."

As no one else had been, he realized. Certainly not him.

"Even when they leave you, they will take your example with them," he said. "Your strength. Your compassion. Your determination to do what is right. They could not ask for a better teacher, Elizabeth. Or a better mother."

"Oh." Sudden moisture swam in her eyes. "Thank you."

Something sharp lodged in his chest. He had not intended to make her cry. "Do not thank me."

She blotted her eyes with her fingertips. "Sorry. I'm not usually this emotional."

"Neither am I." The admission made him uneasy. He set down his wineglass, ill-prepared to deal with her tears or his own reaction to them. "Elizabeth . . ."

She shook her head. "I didn't mean to dump my problems on you."

"Do not apologize." He sat beside her in the hammock and felt her weight roll warm against his thigh. His blood surged at the contact. "You should talk to me. I am Zachary's father," he said, and the words this time had new meaning.

"That doesn't solve anything. In fact, it makes things more complicated."

"More than you know."

Her chin lifted. "I'm used to dealing with things by myself."

Good. Her strength would make it easier when he had to leave her.

But not yet, he thought.

"Not tonight," he said.

The prospect pleased him more than he would have thought possible a week, a day, an hour ago.

Taking her wineglass from her, he set it beside the hammock. He brushed his mouth across her temple. Her cheek. The corner of her eye. The salt of her tears was nectar to him. Her body was soft and warm and trembling, undeniably human, irresistibly female.

She pulled back, eyes wide in the darkness. "I'm not having sex with you because you feel sorry for me."

He froze, affronted. Disappointed. She did not want his comfort, it seemed.

He could, of course, seduce her into compliance. Even without magic, he had the skill to overcome her scruples. Yet he was oddly reluctant to lay siege when her walls were already down. He had seen her angry and composed, passionate and determined. Now she was vulnerable and alone. She deserved better than to have her power of choice stripped from her.

"Your choice," he said coolly. "Your loss."

And mine. The realization set his teeth on edge.

For the humiliating truth was he wanted her still, beyond breath, beyond lust, beyond reason.

She struggled to sit upright in the rocking hammock. "I didn't say we weren't having sex." With her eyes on his, she reached for the buttons of her blouse. "Only that it wouldn't be out of pity."

11

❦

IF HE LIVED ANOTHER THOUSAND YEARS, MORgan would never understand humans. Until Elizabeth, until this moment, he had not cared enough to try.

Her fingers trembled on the buttons, and his heart stopped. He covered her hand with his. "Let me."

Let me touch you. Let me help you. Let me please you.

Her breasts rose with her breath. Her hand fell away.

Lovely, practical Elizabeth, prepared to do everything herself. In this one area, at least, he could lavish her with care. Not from pity—she was right about that—but as a kind of tribute to her beauty and her strength. She deserved no less.

The thought slid into his mind that she might in fact deserve much more, but the surge in his blood swept thought away. He was drowning in her, her eyes, her throat, her breasts.

He undid one button. Two. A third, his knuckles grazing the smooth skin above her waistband. She sucked in her stomach, her hands closing over his. To stop him? Or aid him?

"Let me," he said again.

She lay half under him, unresisting, as he pulled her blouse free.

Her breasts gleamed in the shadows, full and pleasing, cupped by underwear that bound her narrow ribcage. He lowered his head, inhaling her scent, soap and Elizabeth. Lovely. He licked her, running his tongue over the top slope of her breasts. Her breath hitched. Nuzzling one cup aside, he found her pebbled nipple with his mouth and suckled her hard, arousing them both, pleased when she moaned.

He felt her fingers in his hair, scratching delicately against his scalp, and shivered under her touch like a dog. But this wasn't about him, not only about him, not yet. He obeyed her silent tug on his hair, raising his head, covering her mouth with his. He kissed her above, deep, penetrating kisses, thrusting his tongue into her mouth while his hand played her below. He craved her taste, seasoned by wine and desire. He stroked down to her knees and up again, down and up, until her thighs loosened and she made a sound, pleading or approval, in the back of her throat. He cupped her, feeling her moist heat through the fabric, and caught her gasp in his mouth.

He dragged her pants open, worked his hand inside. She was hot, slick, wet.

Ready for him.

Fondling her with one hand, he raised his head. Even in the dusk, he could see her cheeks were flushed, her lips glazed and parted. She lay back against the webbing, watching him, her eyes dark and aware.

Not the gaze of a woman mindless with passion.

He frowned. Not that he wanted her mindless, exactly.

"It's all right." She raised her hand to the back of his head, toying with his hair. "Em's asleep. No one can see us back here."

He had not considered the possibility of an audience. But she had.

Morgan's eyes narrowed. Despite the bloom on her skin, the lush wetness between her thighs, she was still thinking like a mother, like a doctor. Still conscious, still careful, still in control.

Bugger that.

She thought too much. Worried too much. He wanted to plunge her into passion, drag her into the moment, away from the everyday concerns that swarmed like gnats around her head.

He pushed to his feet, making the hammock bounce like a boat in the waves. "Good. Then we won't be interrupted."

He yanked his sweater over his head, baring himself to the waist. His medallion swung against his chest. Elizabeth rolled to one elbow, reaching for him. Capturing her hands, he pressed them to the hammock. "Hold on."

He stripped her pants and underwear away.

Beautiful. He took her with his eyes, letting his gaze roam where his hands had already gone. Beautiful and feminine and his.

"What are you . . . Oh." Her voice trailed off as he crouched between her thighs. She tried to press her knees together, but his shoulders blocked the way. "You don't have to . . ."

"Yes. I do. I want to eat you alive." When her hips hitched, he shoved a pillow under her, cushioning her. She could not focus on pleasure with ropes chafing her skin. He wanted her to think only of this. Only of him.

He did not ask himself why. Reasons did not matter when she was spread wet and open in front of him. Leaning forward, he set his mouth on her most succulent flesh.

He lavished her with licks and nips, bites and kisses. She strained toward him and away, her fingers twisting in the webbing. Her response flooded them both, inflamed him like whiskey, warmed him like wine. Her smooth, firm legs tensed and stretched. Her toes flexed and curled against his knee, against his shoulder. She was helpless to stand or to stop him, at the mercy of his hands, his tongue, his teeth. He held her captive, his hard hands on her buttocks while he feasted. He was drunk on her, her scent, her cries, her soft, wet, luscious center.

Slowly, he thrust a finger inside her, then two, glory-
ing in the slick, convulsive clench of her body. His blood
pounded in his head, in his loins. His rod demanded release.
Now, now, now. He fumbled with his clothing, desperate to
take her.

Pressing her thighs wide, he braced his feet against the
floor. He tipped the hammock, angling her just the way he
wanted her. *There.* She arched. So hot. So wet. Taking himself in hand, he set himself to her, male to female, naked
flesh to naked flesh. *Now.*

"Wait," she choked out.

His lips pulled back from his teeth. She could not be
serious.

She jackknifed in the hammock, her head nearly clip-
ping his chin.

He grabbed for her before she tumbled them both.
"Easy."

She groped on the porch around his feet, nearly upend-
ing the hammock in her eagerness. As she fumbled with
her discarded pants, her smooth hair brushed his groin. He
sucked in his breath.

"There." She righted herself, face flushed, eyes sparkling. Between two fingers, she gripped a small square foil
packet. "Now."

His mouth compressed in distaste. "A sheath."

"Condom." She cleared her throat. "I got it while we
were upstairs."

When she disappeared into her room, he realized. She
wanted this, had planned for it. He could not get any harder,
but the thought sent another flood of warmth through his
veins. But . . .

"It is not necessary," he said.

"Yes, it is."

"I will not make you sick."

The immortal children of the sea were not subject to the
diseases of humankind.

"You could get me pregnant."

Again. The unspoken word reverberated between them.

Under the circumstances, he did not think he could explain how unlikely that outcome was. Or how desirable. The finfolk population was declining. The begetting of children was an issue of practical and political survival.

Yet Elizabeth did not desire another baby, that was clear.

And at some point, her desires had begun to matter to him.

Her firm jaw set at his continued silence. "If we do this, we use protection."

Morgan gritted his teeth, frustration pounding in his blood.

If?

His kind were legendary for their sexual allure. With the slightest exertion of magic, he could overwhelm her resistance, make her so wild for him she would let him do whatever he wanted to her without brake or barrier. But he would not violate her will in such a way. He respected her too much. He . . . liked her, he realized, with a vague feeling of discomfort. He wanted her not only willing but *with* him, in body and mind. Not any woman, but Elizabeth.

If that meant he must sheath himself, so be it.

"I suppose that is your usual practice," he said stiffly.

She folded her arms across her naked breasts. "My usual practice?"

Had he said something to offend her?

"With your other partners," he clarified.

Human partners. "*I can have sex with whomever I want, whenever I want,*" she had said.

Her eyes narrowed. "I don't have other partners."

"Do you not?" he asked softly.

And why in the name of God and all the angels should he be concerned about whom she slept with or when? He was not bound by the silly strictures of human behavior. The children of the sea were free to follow the lusts and whims of the moment, their passions as powerful and changeable as the ocean which gave them being.

"That condom is almost four years old. I had to check the damn expiration date before I took it out of the box."

Morgan felt his face go blank with shock. Four years. Her husband had been dead three. Did that mean . . . Surely that did not mean . . .

"There must have been others," he said.

She did not answer.

Ah.

No others since her husband, then. And given the timing of her pregnancy and marriage, likely few before.

Only him.

The thought was humbling and strangely arousing. She was not simply hungry for sex, Morgan realized. For whatever reason, she wanted *him*. She had chosen *him*.

Which meant there was more involved here than a moment's comfort or the easing of lust. The act took on weight, substance, significance.

Morgan felt a flicker of panic. For the first time, he doubted his ability to give her what she needed. He only knew he felt compelled to try.

She raised her chin another notch. "If you've changed your mind . . ."

"Do I look," he demanded, "as though I have changed my mind?"

Her gaze fell to his ruddy cock, jutting proudly from between his thighs. "No," she admitted.

"Perhaps," he suggested, only half joking, "I am simply intimidated by your trust in me."

She smiled wryly. "You don't appear particularly intimidated either."

Indeed, under her gaze, he was swelling, hardening further.

"Not on the outside," he acknowledged. "But how lowering if you concluded, after so long a wait, that your patience was not adequately rewarded."

With relief, he watched the light spring back into her eyes. "Maybe—after so long a wait—I won't be very picky. Either way, it's my choice."

He really did like her, he thought. Even now, she took responsibility for her actions and reactions on her own shoulders. It made them equal in a way they had not been sixteen years ago.

"Shall we put it to the test, then?" he asked.

Wordlessly, she held up the condom.

He had never acquiesced to a partner's demands or desires before. But Elizabeth was not like any other partner. For the first time, sex was not about taking what he wanted, but about giving what she needed. He could do this for her. He could give her one less thing to worry about tonight.

He took the foil packet from her hand.

Of course, being Elizabeth, she was not passive. As soon as he opened the packet, her hands were there. Her head bent gravely to her task, her smooth hair sliding forward. Her fingers stroked and encircled his aching shaft, pushing the sheath firmly to its base. When she was done, she cupped his stones gently in her hand, scraped her nails lightly over him. Exquisite sensation shot from his balls to his brain.

He clenched his fists in near agony. "I promised to make your wait worthwhile. I'll have no chance at all if you do that."

She shook back her hair and smiled up at him, her eyes gleaming in the dark. "Maybe I'm tired of waiting."

* * *

She was tired of waiting, tired of thinking. She wanted to feel something besides responsible and alone.

Maybe Morgan wouldn't give her what she needed in the long run. But he was exactly what she wanted tonight.

She was no longer a naïve twenty-one-year-old dreaming of adventure, no longer a hopeful bride dreaming of forever. She was done with dreams.

Tonight, she would take what she could get: tenderness, trust, companionship, sex.

Her heart hammered. And Morgan could give them to her.

With her fingertips, she explored him, learning his textures. Sleek and then rough, cool and then hot, silky smooth and unyielding as stone. She rubbed her cheek against his stomach. She loved the way he smelled, musky and male.

Expelling a harsh breath, he caught her wrists and pulled her hands away from his body.

Startled, she looked up. She couldn't see well. Only his body, smooth and strong and pale against the night, the gleam of his eyes, the glint of the medal on his chest.

It was Copenhagen all over again.

She pushed the thought away. No, it wasn't. She knew what she was doing this time. She knew him.

"I want you." His low voice resonated through her.

She quivered like a violin string in the dark. Deliberately, she smiled. "Then take me."

He swooped. The sky swung and her world tilted as the hammock dipped and climbed like a skiff in a storm. His hands, his mouth, streaked everywhere, fast and hot and even a little rough. Pummeled by sensation, saturated with pleasure, she could do nothing but hold on and respond.

She heard herself cry out as the whirlpool dragged her under. Her body arched, her fingers tangled in the webbing. A quickening pulse beat in her blood.

Take me now.

She felt him at the entrance to her body, heat to her heat, hard to her soft. Her eyes slid closed.

"With me," he demanded. "Elizabeth."

His command recalled her from the depths. She opened her drowned eyes and saw him above her, the moonlight on his shoulders, his face a dark blur, her fantasy lover made flesh, pushing inside her, plunging inside her. Real. Here. Now.

The shock contracted her stomach, flung her to another peak. Her short nails gripped his sides as he worked her, as she met him, thrust for thrust, stroke for stroke. His feet braced on the deck, his hard hands bruising her hips, he pounded into her, strong and relentless as the sea. She was drenched, battered, swept away.

Until the long crest rolled through her like a gathering wave and took them both.

12

〜

ZACK HACKED THROUGH THE SEAMS OF THE CAR-
ton, exposing the soup cans inside. Almost through his first
shift. Picking up the price gun, he shot numbers in a row:
two-sixty-nine, two-sixty-nine, two-sixty-nine.

Wiley's Grocery didn't have scanners in the checkout
lines.

"No need for them," George Wiley had explained earlier that evening as they were shifting cartons from the
back room. "I know my store. This isn't America, son."

He meant the mainland.

I'm not your son, Zack thought.

A vision flashed into his brain of Morgan, tall and
broad-shouldered, standing too close to his mother in the
hall. His mom had looked strange, not like a mother at all,
her cheeks too pink, her eyes too bright.

Zack's chest tightened as if he'd been running. He
stabbed the gun down another row of cans. *Two-sixty-nine,
two-sixty-nine, two-sixty-nine*, and done.

Straightening, he slid the old cans to the front of the
shelf and face out. Rotating stock, Wiley called it.

The work was physical. Mindless. Zack didn't have to think, just follow instructions. He liked that, liked working alone. At the beginning of his shift, he'd had to help Mr. Wiley haul boxes from the afternoon's delivery to the appropriate aisles. But now Wiley was arranging displays at the front of the store. He was okay, even if he was overweight and going bald and Stephanie's dad besides.

Zack's dad, his real dad, Ben, started losing his hair even before the chemo. You could see it in pictures, this dark, W-shaped hairline above a high forehead and warm brown eyes. The details of his father's face were fading away, blurred by time, overlaid by images of his illness. Zack wasn't sure anymore what he remembered and what he'd reconstructed from photographs.

A picture of his dad sat on his dresser, taken on a fishing trip to Holden Beach when Zack was ten years old. His dad had one arm around Zack's shoulders, and they were both squinting at the camera and grinning. Zack's hair was hidden by his ball cap, and his skin had tanned a golden brown. They looked related, like father and son.

But when Zack looked in the mirror this morning, it wasn't Ben's face he saw.

It was Morgan's.

Hands shaking, he grabbed cans, slung them to the back.

"Last aisle," Wiley said behind him.

Zack's hand clenched around a can of chunky chicken soup, *two-sixty-nine*. He faced it out carefully before he turned. "Yes, sir."

"You did good tonight. We'll finish early."

The praise made Zack uncomfortable. He hung his head, staring at his feet. Big feet, like his . . . like Morgan's. "Yes, sir," he said tonelessly.

Wiley chuckled. "Southern boy, aren't you?"

"Excuse me?"

"Calling me sir. Makes me feel damn old."

Zack didn't know how to respond. He *was* old, as old as Zack's mom, anyway. Too old for . . .

Another image of his mother standing with Morgan at the foot of the stairs seared his brain.

Too old for . . .

"Any questions before we call it a night?" Wiley asked.

"No, sir. Um, Mr. Wiley."

Maybe his mother didn't feel old either. The tightness returned to Zack's chest. Maybe . . .

"I need to buy cat food," he blurted. "Oh, and some litter. To take home."

"You have a cat?"

"We do now," Zack said grimly. Morgan's cat. But they could take care of it without Morgan's help.

Wiley rubbed his chin. "You can't buy anything now. I already closed out the register. But you pick out what you need. You can settle up when you come in tomorrow."

"Sure. Thanks. What time?"

"Be here at twelve. I post the schedule on Monday."

"Twelve o'clock," Zack said, committing it to memory. His heart knocked against his ribs. "Is Stephanie working tomorrow?"

Wiley shot him a sharp glance. "Everybody works weekends in the summer."

Zack swallowed. "I just, um, wondered. Since she wasn't here tonight."

Oh, God, could he please shut his mouth?

"She stayed home," Wiley said. "Some guy coming over, I think. You need a ride?"

Zack's gut churned. She had *some guy* coming over. Not him.

Disappointment nipped at him.

Wiley was watching him with astute blue eyes like his daughter's, waiting for an answer.

"No," Zack said. "I don't need a ride."

Not where he was going.

*   *   *

Liz was breathing. Barely.

She lay cocooned by the hammock, pinned by Morgan's

weight, dazed, sated, satisfied. Her legs were numb below the knee, her mind empty and at peace.

If she could have summoned the energy to smile, she would. For the first time in years, she hadn't thought like a doctor or a mother. She hadn't thought at all. She had let herself desire and be desired, let herself feel like a woman again. She was more than relieved. She felt smug. Triumphant.

Gradually her heart rate slowed. Her skin cooled. A chorus of discomforts and doubts crept back, pervasive, persistent as the tree frogs in the yard, and began to compete for her attention. A crick in her neck. A cramp in her thigh. A knot digging into her back. She was wet from sex and nearly naked, hot where Morgan covered her and cold everyplace else.

She ran her hand down his back, savoring the feel of smooth skin and solid muscle. She didn't want to get up. Didn't want to let him go. The realization trickled down her spine like ice dripping.

She was a grown woman, she reminded herself. She could have sex—heart-stopping, mind-blowing, jungle-thumping sex in a hammock if she felt like it—without things falling apart. Without falling in love.

She could have Morgan.

She pressed her lips together, staring over his head into the dark. As long as she didn't think too hard, say too much, feel too deeply.

Life had already dealt her the bitterest blow it could and she'd survived. Surely she could survive . . . she could *enjoy* an affair without romanticizing reality? Without expecting promises or guarantees, without neglecting her children or responsibilities.

Her children.

Her heart jolted with panic. Her mind clicked back into gear. "What time is it?"

Morgan's lips moved against her neck. "What does it matter?"

It mattered. Her world hadn't changed, even if for one magical moment the earth had rocked on its axis.

She pushed at his shoulder, dragged her arm from under him to peer at her wrist. The dial of her watch glowed in the dark—10:05.

Her head dropped back in relief. She had time to clean up, to compose herself, before Zack came home.

If she could move. Morgan's solid weight still pressed her into the webbing.

She poked his upper arm. "You're heavy."

He trapped her arms and rolled with her, somehow avoiding overturning the hammock. A quick lurch, and she sprawled against his naked chest, straddled his naked thighs. Her breath caught.

"You are delicious." His warm mouth captured one nipple. His big hands kneaded her butt.

She trembled in discomfort and delight, trapped between his hot body and cold reality. "I'm cold."

Conflicted.

He nuzzled her other breast. "I can warm you."

Yes.

No.

"That's not . . ." His erection rose against her stomach, hot and hard. *Oh.* She sagged. "The point," she finished weakly.

He ran his fingertip along her jawline, blew his hot breath in her ear.

For one moment, she let herself be tempted, let him drag her into the warm sea of desire. Her body yielded, softened, and flowed over his.

Mistake.

She may have temporarily lost control. That didn't mean she'd lost her mind. Her perspective. Her heart.

Her breath hissed.

What was she doing?

It was one thing for her to risk her own happiness on a relationship that would not last, on a man who would not stay. She would not compromise her children's sense of stability.

"I have to get up." She pushed on his shoulders. Their legs tangled. She blundered from the hammock, knocking over the glass of wine. "Shit. Oh, shit."

"Elizabeth, what is the matter?"

"Nothing." All she could see was an image of Zack walking through the house and out the back door to find them. To find her, naked. "It's not broken, see?" She set the wineglass by the back door, the cool air tickling her bare ass, and tugged on a sleeve of her blouse until Morgan rolled to release it. "I need to get dressed."

Slowly, he sat upright, watching as she scrambled for her clothes.

Hopping on one leg, she shoved her other foot inside the damp fabric. "Damn, I have to change my pants."

"Then you will change."

"Right." She pulled herself together, summoned control and a smile. "No use crying over spilled wine."

He eyed her oddly. "Indeed."

"Thank you." She buttoned her waistband, bundled his clothes, and thrust them at him. "That was wonderful. You should go."

"Why?"

A flutter of panic. Because her voice wanted to shake, she sharpened it. "Zack will be home soon. I don't want him to find you here. To find us together."

"The one has nothing to do with the other."

Maybe not. But she couldn't separate out the pieces of herself, the mother and the lover. And she couldn't put them together.

"You can say that because you're a guy. Men can compartmentalize."

"Zachary is male," he pointed out.

"Zack is . . ." She bit her lip. "He's not ready for this."

She wasn't ready for this.

"I am here. He must accept that."

"Not now. Not like this. You said it yourself."

"Said what?"

What was his problem? Sixteen years ago, he couldn't roll off her fast enough. Now, when she wanted, needed him to go, he was stalling.

She stuck out her chin and looked him in the eye. "One night doesn't change anything."

* * *

Zack found the beach, his private cove, even in the dark. There were some advantages to being a freak after all.

He shifted his grip on the grocery bags. Ten pounds of cat litter, seven pounds of cat food, a plastic litter box, and two metal bowls, everything the kitten would need or his mom could want. But he couldn't face her yet, her anxious eyes, her too bright smile, her questions. *How was work? What did you do? What do you mean, think, feel, want?*

His throat closed. He couldn't breathe. He dumped the bags at the foot of the trail where he'd be sure to stumble over them on his return.

He wanted to be left alone. Alone in his bed, listening to his music, with the Victoria's Secret catalog stashed under his mattress. He grimaced. Not that he could beat off with his mother and Morgan downstairs. If Stephanie . . .

But Stephanie was seeing somebody. Some guy. Not him.

And now he would be stuck seeing her every day at work, knowing he owed her his job, knowing she liked him but not . . . enough.

He sat on a clump of weeds to pull off his boots. Maybe he'd just get his feet wet this time.

His heart beat faster with shame and excitement. His clothes chafed. Maybe not. Probably not.

He stood.

The night swam with stars and scents, throbbing, close. He couldn't pick out the constellations, but he recognized the smells, pine and brine, kelp and loam. The sky was black and soft as velvet, the sea gleaming with reflected light. Zack couldn't see where one left off and the other began. The waves ran over the rocks with a sound like chains. They called to him, dragged at him hard. Pulling his shirt over his head, he dropped it on the sand.

His skin pebbled in the night air. His nipples poked out. So did his dick. The water chuckled and rustled closer as he shivered with cold and energy and desire.

There was no one to stop him, no one to see. Anyway, he wasn't hurting anyone. He could do it once, once and get it over with, and then he wouldn't come back for a long time. A week. He had a job now. He might not get another chance to come back anyway.

He undid his pants, stripped off his underwear and socks.

The waves' chant filled his head. The cool air caressed his body. Inside him, needs twisted and stirred like eels in an aquarium, like the monster in *Alien*, fighting to burst out.

He took a deep breath. It would be all right. He knew what he was doing now. He knew where he was going. Everything would be all right once he got into the water.

Barefoot, naked, he padded over the narrow strip of hard, damp sand. His body tightened in anticipation. His mind drifted to the slow, warm summer nights of childhood, fishing from the pier with his dad, the floodlights on the foam, the smells of brine and bait, beer and blood, the sound of the surf and men's voices.

He raised his head, absorbing the stars and the murmur of the tide. He was a man now. This was his place.

He waded into the water.

Cold.

It seized his balls, locked his knees, jolted his blood. This was the worst part. Baring his chattering teeth, he slogged forward, the waves surging from calf to thigh, from thigh to waist, grabbing at his balls, pumping through his veins. He shuddered with tension and cold. His belly and legs trembled. Deep, deeper, almost . . .

There.

The Change ripped through him, convulsive as orgasm.

His heart pounded, his lungs exploded, pain and ecstasy coursing along his bones. So good. So hard. He let himself go, let everything go, as the spasms went on and on, milking his body. He arched helplessly under the waves, under the water, flailed and felt the flat slap, the cool slide, of fins and tail.

He gasped, and salt flooded his mouth, pushed into his chest and choked him. He floundered, suffocating in the oxygen-rich water. Oh, shit, oh, Christ, oh . . . Gills ripped from his throat, shuddered and swelled. Terror melted into triumph and relief. All right, then. All right.

The water was in him, he was in the water, rushing, pulsing, free. Everything else forgotten.

He spiraled into the depths, and the cold clear darkness claimed him.

*　　*　　*

Morgan stalked along the broken asphalt in the dark.

He never stayed with a woman after sex. Over the centuries, he had left hundreds of lovers for spurious reasons or no reason at all.

But he had never before left at the woman's insistence. Elizabeth's insistence.

A muscle twitched in his jaw. He'd given her what she wanted, had he not? All he knew how to give. Yet still somehow it had not been enough, or he would not be walking back alone to his room at the inn, pushed out of her house to accommodate the whims of an adolescent boy.

"One night doesn't change anything."

But it had. She was inside him now like a virus, like a fever, an ache in his belly, a pang at his heart.

An irritable wind swirled around him. Shadows scudded across his path. Morgan glanced at the clouds threatening the moon and realized he had allowed his foul mood to leach into the atmosphere.

His lack of control disturbed him. Weather magic was the first learned and most easily mastered of elemental powers. But judging by the turbulent sky, those clouds would start spitting soon. He needed to cool his blood, to clear his mind, to calm the turmoil inside him and above.

He turned left, following the track to the beach.

And nearly stumbled over some grocery bags dumped at the foot of the trail. Human litter. He almost passed it by, but a familiar scent teased at his nostrils, tickled his attention.

Zachary?

Morgan's head snapped up. The boy's scent mingled with the weeds, lingered on the plastic.

Zachary had been here. Was here still?

Morgan's gaze raked the beach, found boots, shirt, pants. No boy.

His lips drew back in a silent snarl. Zachary had gone into the water alone and unwarded. Dangerous enough for an inexperienced shifter with no guidance or instruction. But for Zachary . . .

Cold fingers traced Morgan's spine. There were demons in these waters. Gau knew the boy was finfolk, had threatened him already. *"We will take them from you. The boy and the woman both."*

Morgan's throat closed. Swearing, he yanked at his boots, tore off his jacket. He ran for the water, breaking the surface in a low, fast dive.

If Gau touched the boy, there would be Hell to pay.

* * *

The orb rested on the sea floor, glowing with blue green phosphorescence. It was the light—not warm, not cold, eerily beautiful—that had attracted Zack the first time, almost a week ago. He'd felt it flickering like a fallen star and followed it to this crevice at the base of another island, hidden in the roots of the earth.

The glow spilled from a fissure in the rock. He felt a catch of excitement. Like when he and Ryan used to go into the woods behind the middle school looking for snakes. Once they'd found a copperhead coiled under a log and poked it with a stick to watch it strike.

The danger was part of the thrill.

The light pulsed like a heartbeat, piercing the darkness, reaching, seeking, drawing him on. Everything else faded and fell away from that blue radiance, the flowing kelp, the twisting worms, the armored crabs and mollusks. The sea bottom around was barren. The odd light played over stones and bones and the shells of small creatures that had died.

Zack felt a brush of caution, a moment of misgiving, an instant's unease.

He shook it away. He was invulnerable in the water.

He was close enough now to see the orb itself, half-buried in the sand. The opaque surface ran with color like a garden globe, blue, green, silver, pink. The light throbbed around him, moved into him, its beat reflected and magnified by the surrounding rock

like the surge of the sea

like the flow of his breath

like the rhythm of his blood

like a mother's heartbeat to the child swimming in her womb.

Closer. The whisper reached into his head.

Closer. The command twined around his heart.

Touch me. He shivered with excitement.

Release me. Entranced, he drifted nearer, trapped by the primal beat.

The water shivered. Faint vibrations dragged along his skin, tugged at his attention.

Not the orb.

His sharpened senses identified turbulence. Something coming, hard and fast. Boat?

Predator.

Panic pumped his heart. *The globe.* The thought slid into his primitive brain, sharp as a heated knife. He couldn't let his precious orb be seen, touched, taken by another.

A small, rational part of his mind protested another shark would hardly covet a submerged garden ornament, but its voice was drowned by the rush of fear, the possessive swell, the compulsion beating in his brain.

Hide. He must hide it.

He backed clumsily, confined by the narrow crevice in the rock. Sand stirred and settled over the orb's surface, veiling the glow. *Yes, yes.* He writhed around, swept the sea bottom with his tail. A great dark cloud of debris boiled and billowed, choking him, cutting off the light.

Yessss.

He shot from the cloud into the clean salt dark, his blood pounding as he raced through the open sea, adrenaline and triumph coursing through his veins. Free, clear, fast, fearless, at the top of the fucking food chain.

WHAM.

The impact exploded out of nowhere, catching him broadside, slamming his ribs, knocking him yards off course. He floundered, struggling to orient himself in the dark sea.

Aggression flooded his brain. He turned to attack.

BAM.

Another punch from below. The force hurtled him to the surface. He lashed wildly, twisting to defend himself.

In the shadowed depths beneath him, a monster slid into sight. Broad white snout, massive pale sides, a flat, dark gash of a mouth . . .

Another shark.

Holy shit.

The thing was huge, twice his size. Panic stabbed his chest. His heart hammered. His ribs throbbed.

Flight or fight? His shark self screamed for blood. But he was battered, bruised, afraid. In open sea, the monster shark would certainly outswim him. Maybe, if he could make it to the island, he could lose himself in the rocks?

Zack dived.

The other shark glided to intercept him. Zack switched course, but his pursuer changed direction, too, anticipating his moves. He braced for another blow.

But instead of striking with its snout, this time the monster merely brushed him, bumping his side. Zack bunched his body, whipped his tail to get away.

The shark circled after him, its movements graceful, almost lazy in the clear black water. Zack plunged and zipped, back and forth, making another run for the rocks. The shark cut him off with a second warning bump. Abandoning his plan, Zack fled.

Water streamed. Fish scattered. The monster pursued, moving occasionally to bump or block him.

He was being driven. Herded, Zack realized, with the portion of his brain that still functioned in his terror. Forced in the direction of World's End.

His body was stretched, his strength depleted. His sides hurt. He couldn't concentrate. His mind darted behind, ahead. If he could reach the cove, the shallow water might save him.

In a last burst of hope and energy, he drove himself at the shore. Waves churned. His belly scraped bottom. With luck, the monster behind him would beach itself on the rocks.

Frantically, he flailed and felt his limbs pop and change, felt his skin shrink and wrinkle, felt his tortured lungs expand. His mouth gaped as the surf foamed around him, as the cold air struck his shivering back, his starving lungs. He was naked. Vulnerable. Human. If the shark caught him now . . .

He clawed his way up the beach on numb knees and frozen hands, desperate to get up, get out, get away from the rush of the water.

He collapsed for a moment, his cheek pressed to the sand, the webbing melting from between his fingers, his face wet with salt and tears and terror. Must breathe. Must move. Summoning his last strength, he crawled to his discarded clothes. Stared, dumbfounded, at the pile on the sand.

That wasn't his shirt. Those weren't his shoes.

"You must not go into the water," Morgan said behind him, "until you have learned to defend yourself."

13

HIS SON SPRAWLED, BEACHED, BLINKING, NAKED on the sand. No longer shark, but human.

The fear and temper that had driven Morgan to herd the boy ashore threatened to explode in all too human ways now they were on land. He clenched his fists, willing them to subside.

The boy was back and safe for now.

He strode out of the surf. "Get up."

Zachary spat. "Get away from me."

Not an auspicious beginning to the discussion they must have.

Perhaps he had been rough on the boy, but the threat, and his own pumping terror, had taken him by surprise.

"Are you all right?" Morgan asked.

Zachary curled to a sitting position, covering himself. "Leave me alone."

Morgan's eyes narrowed. The boy appeared unharmed. Bruised, embarrassed, angry, but unharmed. But there had been a definite taint of demon in the water where he found him. The children of the sea were immortal, but they could still be killed. Possessed. Zachary, half-human and inexperienced, was particularly vulnerable even before he was targeted by the demon lord.

"You have no idea of the dangers out there."

"I was fine until you came along."

"Which only proves how little you know."

Zachary tossed back his wet hair. His gaze speared Morgan's, his eyes accusing and curiously adult. "Whose fault is that?"

Morgan was silent. In truth, he could have spoken to the boy before this. He had an obligation to his prince and his people. Zachary belonged on Sanctuary, where his power could be assessed and trained. Morgan should have made an opportunity and forced the issue. He had not, because of Elizabeth.

Because he wanted to bed her.

A flare of remembered fire licked his belly.

His plan had been simple and ruthless: claim Zachary, fuck Elizabeth, and go. Now that he had achieved both goals, he had no excuse to dally on World's End.

The fire sank down to chill and ash.

"*One night doesn't change anything,*" Elizabeth had said.

But she was wrong.

They both were wrong.

"Put your clothes on," Morgan said. "Your mother will be worried about you."

"She doesn't know anything."

"She knows when to expect you home."

Sullenly, the boy rolled to his feet and reached for his clothes. He hitched up his pants, fumbled with the buckle. Without looking at Morgan, he asked, "Are you going to tell her?"

He heard and understood the desperate anxiety in the boy's voice. The days when the children of the sea were acknowledged, feared, and revered were gone. There was no guarantee Elizabeth would believe their son.

Or accept him.

"That is your responsibility," he said as gently as he could.

"I can't." Panic made his voice higher, like a child's. "She wouldn't believe me."

Morgan stifled a flash of compassion. "Then you must show her."

"Forget it. She already thinks I'm a freak."

"You are not a freak. You are finfolk."

Zachary sneered. "What is that, like, a mermaid?"

"Merfolk."

"Whatever. It's not me. I turn into a shark."

Morgan reached for patience, remembering what it had been like for him so many centuries ago. The boy had a lot to learn, in more ways than one. "Not only a shark. You could take another form."

"No, I can't. It's always a shark."

Morgan sighed. Was this what Griff had gone through with the new changelings on Sanctuary? It had been almost a century since the young roamed Caer Subai, free and feral as dogs. But Morgan was fast developing new respect for the gruff castle warden who had taken them in charge.

"The finfolk are shape-shifters," he explained patiently. "With enough skill, enough practice, we can control the Change and determine what we become. But your fears control you. You turn into a shark because you fear the shark."

The boy's chin jerked up. "I guess then you're afraid of them, too."

Morgan bared his teeth in a smile. "No."

Zachary's gaze dropped. He scooped his shirt from the sand. "Anyway, I'm not telling her."

"She is your mother. She cares for you. She has the right to know."

The realization made him deeply uneasy.

"Then you tell her."

Morgan opened his mouth. Closed it.

"Yeah, that's what I thought," Zachary said with bitter satisfaction. "You never told her either."

"The children of the sea keep apart from humankind," Morgan said stiffly.

But their neutrality had not preserved them in Hell's war to regain primacy on earth.

Conn argued their people's survival depended on a closer alliance with mortal kind. The old divisions were blurring, no more so than on World's End with its muddle of human emotions and selkie bloodlines. Margred and Caleb, Dylan and Regina, Conn and the *targair inghean* . . .

"Not that far apart," Zachary sneered. "Or you wouldn't have me."

The look, the tone were a younger version of Morgan's own.

Another tie, another link, Morgan thought. *My son.* The recognition left him shaken and oddly moved.

"The point is, we did have you," he said coolly, reaching for his customary distance. "And now we must all deal with the consequences."

Zachary jammed his feet into boots. "We were dealing just fine before you showed up. We don't need you." He stomped for emphasis. "I don't need you to take care of me."

Morgan heard the bravado behind the boy's boast. *Little boy*, he thought, *you have no idea what you need.*

* * *

"Zack!" Elizabeth opened the front door wider, as much caution as pleasure in her voice. She had changed her pants, Morgan observed, and caught her rich hair back in some sort of clip. Her cheeks were faintly pink. "How was your first day of work?"

"Fine." He thrust the grocery bags at her. "For the cat."

"Oh, that was so nice of you." Her determined cheerfulness was almost painful to hear. "Thank you! How much was it? Do you need—"

"No."

Her gaze darted from him to Morgan. Responding, he

guessed, to the tension in the atmosphere. "Something to eat?"

"No. Thanks." Zack brushed by her on his way up the stairs. "I don't really feel like talking right now."

Insolent whelp.

But the boy was right about one thing. Elizabeth was not likely to accept the truth about her son without proof. Which meant any words tonight would be wasted.

He met her gaze, dark with confusion and the lingering shadows of desire, and was abruptly reminded he had been inside her only an hour ago. He wanted to be inside her again.

"What are you doing here?" she asked.

"I ran into Zachary." Quite literally. "After work."

And hauled the boy's ass home before he could take it into his head to flee.

Zachary shot him a cold look over his shoulder. It would have been more effective if Morgan hadn't recognized the sneer from his own mirror. "I'm going to bed," he announced.

Morgan let him go. Nothing could be settled tonight anyway.

"Good night," Elizabeth called after him. She turned back to Morgan, her teeth denting her lower lip. "Do you want to come in?"

"Yes."

Her flush deepened. "To talk."

Ah.

"Not right now."

"Then . . ." Her fingers tightened on the door.

"I do need to talk with you," he said. "About Zachary."

Apprehension darkened her eyes. "What happened?"

He could not tell her. But after tonight, he had a new understanding, a fresh sympathy for her fears. He hastened to reassure her. "About his future."

"*Tell* me."

Apparently he was not as reassuring as he thought. A

lack of practice, perhaps. "I believe I have tested your . . . flexibility enough for one evening."

Her eyes met his, a wry smile in their depths. "When you foisted that cat on me."

Deliberately, he held her gaze. "When I foisted myself on you."

Her throat moved as she swallowed. But she was not distracted, his Elizabeth. "You were going to tell me about Zack."

"Tomorrow," he said.

She searched his face. "He's really all right?"

"He is fine." Gau's threat beat in his brain. *I will take them from you. The woman and the child both.* His jaw set. "I swear it."

Elizabeth exhaled, her shoulders relaxing. "The clinic closes at two. Say, sometime after that?"

He would have another day with her, he thought. The relief he felt was new and troubling. "Tomorrow afternoon," he agreed. "We will go to the beach."

Her brows drew together. "The beach? But . . ."

"To talk about Zack," he added.

"All right," she said slowly. "If that's what you want."

It was not what he wanted at all. But he owed her the truth.

He could not rob her of their son without offering her even an explanation in return.

*   *   *

The next afternoon, Zack loaded groceries into the back of an SUV while its owner watched him closely. Like he was going to steal her beer or break her eggs or something.

"Thank you for shopping at Wiley's," he said before he closed the hatch.

Which was stupid, they were on a fricking island, where else was she going to shop? But Wiley said to say it, and Wiley was paying him, so he did.

He pushed her empty cart out of the way while the SUV

backed up. The overcast parking lot was still half-full of cars from the two o'clock ferry. He jammed carts together, feeling the impact in his shoulders. He was stiff and sore from the night before, from hauling boxes and from the other thing.

The shark thing.

His throat closed. The parking lot blurred like the world underwater. Blinking fiercely, he grabbed at another cart. What was he going to do? He couldn't escape what he was anymore. Couldn't hide. Not with Morgan here, watching him. Knowing.

Sweat broke out on his face. What if Mom found out? Or Em. He felt sick to his stomach just thinking about it, guilty and excited and miserable. He'd always known he was different from the rest of his family, but at least when his dad . . . when Ben was alive, he'd felt like he belonged.

Where did he belong now?

He should never have left them alone last night, his mother and Morgan. The words ran together in his head, *hismotherandmorgan*, making him uneasy in a different way.

Had he told her yet? Maybe not. Probably not. She hadn't said anything this morning. Just drank her coffee and packed Emily's lunch and asked him the usual mom sort of questions. But it was getting harder and harder for both of them to pretend that everything was normal. That *he* was normal.

Morgan's deep voice rolled in his head. *"You are not a freak. You are finfolk."*

Whatever.

At least while he was at work he could forget for a little while. He rolled the carts toward the store entrance, letting their rattle jar his arms and fill his head.

He wasn't going to think about it. Any of it.

He dumped the carts at the front of the store. While he was outside loading groceries, Wiley had taken his place bagging for the older cashier, Dot. Which meant . . .

Gritting his teeth, Zack walked to the station at the end of Stephanie's checkout line.

She tossed her red-black hair without looking at him. "Where were you?"

"I had to take some woman's groceries out to her car. Paper or plastic?" he asked the customer.

"Oh, plastic."

Stephanie's hands never missed a beat, pushing, weighing, ringing up the items sliding past her register. Her nails today were painted dark purple. "I meant last night."

His mind slid away from the memory of the orb and the cold, terrifying rush through the water.

"I was here." He piled cold cuts into a plastic bag, topped off with napkins. "Working."

"After work."

"Like you care," he said bitterly.

"I do. I thought we were friends."

He dropped a can of baked beans on top of some Kaiser rolls. "Right. That's why you were home waiting for some guy last night."

"Waiting for . . . Your total is seventy-three dollars and twenty-nine cents," she said to the man standing in line. "Thank you for shopping at Wiley's."

She waited until the shopper collected his bags before she hissed at Zack, "I was waiting for you, dummy."

His mouth gaped.

She turned to the next customer in line. "Did you find everything you need today?"

Zack's mind whirled as he bagged the items that came at him down the line, crackers, dish soap, chunky chicken soup, *two-sixty-nine*.

Stephanie's voice broke into his concentration. "So, if you weren't with me, who were you with last night?"

She couldn't be jealous. Jesus, he was a freak, whatever Morgan said.

"My father," he mumbled.

She shot him a sharp look over her shoulder. "I thought your father was dead."

"My biological father."

"Oh." Her fingers paused their dance over the register. "Wow. Wait . . . Is he the really hot guy staying at the inn? Looks kind of like you, but older? Blond."

Zack felt his face get red. "I don't know." Was he hot? Did she think he was hot? "He's got light hair."

"That's the one. Your total is thirty-two dollars and eighty-five cents," she said to the woman in line.

Cans were piling up in front of Zack. He stuffed them into a bag.

"I'm sorry, this register is closed now. Dot can take you over there. Dad." Stephanie raised her voice, calling over to the other register. "I'm taking my break now."

"Stephanie, it's Friday."

"I get breaks on Friday." She flashed him a grin. "Please."

He huffed. "Fifteen minutes. Not one second more."

"Thanks, Daddy. Come on," she said to Zack.

He finished loading the woman's cart. "Where?"

"Break. Hurry up."

He followed her back to the storeroom, drawn by her quick, firm steps and smoothly moving hips, helpless as a fish on her line.

She dropped into a metal folding chair, waved him to another. "So, what did he want?"

"What?"

"Your father. What's he doing here?"

He looked into her sharp, interested face. Some of the tension churning inside him eased. "I don't know."

"Maybe he's dying and he wants to leave you all his money."

He shot her a disbelieving look.

She shrugged. "Okay, my fantasy, not yours. He probably has another family tucked away somewhere."

"I don't think so." Zack swallowed. "According to my mom, he never got married."

"He could still have kids. You could have, like, half

brothers and sisters running around someplace and never know it."

Zack's chest felt tight. He was having enough trouble figuring out where he belonged without the thought of others like him out there somewhere.

"I have a half sister already," he said. "I don't need anybody else."

"Still, it's kind of cool. Him looking you up after all these years. Although it's weird, him waiting so long."

"He didn't know about me," Zack heard himself saying. "When my mom got pregnant. She didn't know how to get in touch with him."

At least, that had been the story she'd always told him. Who knew anymore what was true or not?

"So it was kind of not his fault," Stephanie said.

Zack jerked one shoulder, unwilling to admit it.

"I wonder if he's carrying a torch for your mom."

He recoiled. "What are you talking about?"

"You know, because he never married. And then your dad dies and your other dad, he finds her again and—"

"Stop," Zack said.

"Sorry. Awkward."

"Yeah."

"I hate to think about my parents doing it."

"He's not my . . ." Zack's voice cracked, humiliating him. It hadn't done that in months. He cleared his throat. "My father is dead."

Under the black liner, her blue eyes were serious and sympathetic. "It doesn't take anything away from your dad if you get to know the new guy."

Morgan's voice rolled through his memory. *"You have no idea of the dangers out there."*

"I was fine until you came along."

"Which only proves how little you know."

Zack stood, his chair scraping on the concrete floor. "I don't want to know him. I don't want anything to do with him."

"Why not? You might have more in common with him than you think. You probably take after him, at least a little bit."

Zack's pulse pounded in his head. "That's what I'm afraid of."

"It's not like he's an axe murderer or something."

His hands clenched into fists at his sides. Inside his boots, his toes curled. Not an axe murderer. A shark. Merfolk. Finfolk.

Whatever the hell he was.

She studied his face. Her own expression softened. "Anyway, he made the first move. I guess what happens next is up to you."

Her words steadied him, made him feel as if he had a choice, a measure of control.

It was up to him.

He met her gaze, profoundly grateful. "Thanks."

"No problem." She strolled closer, tilted her head up. She was so pretty, so forceful, it was almost a shock to realize he was actually taller than she was. Standing on tiptoe, she touched her lips to his. Her lips were sweet and slightly sticky. Cherry Chapstick. Her silver lip ring brushed the corner of his mouth.

His head swam. He put his hands on her waist, tried to kiss her again.

She shook her head and took a step back.

He was wanting, aching, confused. "Stephanie . . ."

"Break's over. My dad will be looking for us."

"But—"

She tossed her red-black hair. "I made the first move. What happens next is up to you."

*   *   *

The forecast called for fog and rain. *Summer in Maine*, Liz accepted with a shrug. There would be no walk on the beach today.

They could meet in her office.

All those interruptions, her practical side protested.

Or at the inn.

All those beds, temptation whispered.

But when she called the inn to suggest a change of location with Morgan, he dismissed her concerns.

"The weather will clear," he had predicted.

He was right.

By the time they emerged from the trail, blooming with Queen Anne's lace and goldenrod, overgrown with blackberries and beach roses, the clouds had pushed offshore. Liz could see the storm over the mainland, the dramatic gray slant of rain over the water. But here was sunshine and the piercing cry of gulls.

The cove was wild and deserted. No picnic tables or access signs disturbed the natural landscape, only a peeling wooden rowboat and an orange fiberglass canoe drawn up above the water line.

Liz sat on rocks warmed by the sun, listening to the sigh of the wind and the murmur of waves, soothing as a child's bedtime story. Heat soaked the shoulders of her sensible blouse. She looked up at Morgan, the shape of his head black against the bright sky, and everything inside her flowed and moved to the rhythm of the wind and the waves. All the muscles she'd used last night went lax, all the nerves woke and reminded her they'd like to be used again.

He dropped a couple of towels from the inn on the sunlit rock.

She blinked. "You're not going to swim. It's too cold."

"I may." His eyes were opaque, his mouth a hard, flat line. "If it becomes necessary."

Necessary?

She couldn't imagine any circumstances that would drive her into that water. Someone drowning, maybe.

He nodded toward the two craft beached above the straggling brown line of seaweed. "I thought we would take a boat."

She felt a spurt of surprised pleasure. She hadn't expected him to plan a romantic interlude on the water. "You rented a boat?"

"No." He padded across the hard, damp sand and ran an assessing hand over the rowboat's upturned prow.

She expelled her breath. "We can't simply row off in someone else's property."

"I am an excellent oarsman," he assured her. He tugged off his boots, set them on the sand.

"Yes, but . . ."

His feet, she thought. Something about his feet . . .

His muscles bunched. She watched, distracted, as he flipped the heavy boat and hefted it into the air as if it weighed no more than a canoe. Goodness, he was strong.

"I'm sure you are," she said. "It's still stealing."

He turned. His smile revealed an edge of teeth. "My people do not see it that way."

She had noticed islanders had a more relaxed attitude toward crime and property than people who lived on the mainland: doors left unlocked, cars left running with their keys in the ignition. One of the advantages, she supposed, of knowing all your neighbors.

But Morgan was no more an islander than she was.

Barefoot, he waded into the shallows. The surface of the water heaved and sighed, expanding in ripples around his legs. Wet denim clung to his calves.

"Come." He swung the boat down with barely a splash. Its bottom scraped sand. "I have something to show you."

Her heart fluttered. It felt dangerous, delicious, to be doing something as illicit as joyriding in a borrowed boat. He made her feel like a girl again, irresponsible, carefree, sneaking onto the locked grounds of Kastellet in search of adventure.

"I thought we were here to talk about Zachary."

"We will," he promised. "In the boat."

She climbed slowly to her feet. "This really isn't necessary."

"Yes, it is." His eyes glinted. "Otherwise, I cannot be sure you will not run away."

She laughed. Putting her hand in his, she let him lead her to the water's edge, leaving solid ground and her scruples behind.

* * *

The sea was the color of mossy slate, flashing with sparks like fool's gold. Pale green bladders of seaweed floated just beyond the reach of the oars.

Liz trailed her fingertips in the cool, dark water, enjoying the surge against her hand, the tingle up her arm.

Tiny, sensory details impressed themselves on her consciousness. The rush of water and the rattle of the oarlocks. The shape of Morgan's hands and the turn of his head. The faint gold glitter of beard by the edge of his jaw where he'd missed a spot shaving.

He rowed with a fluid, easy strength that sent warmth curling through her midsection. It occurred to her, idly, that she'd never seen him sweat. Not that it mattered. It was remarkably pleasant to be with him like this, to be gliding without effort or destination over the sunlit water while he did all the work. A passenger instead of the captain, enjoying the ride.

She flushed almost guiltily. Not that that arrangement would suit her in her everyday, real life.

She pulled her hand from the water. "So, about Zack. I take it he was rude to you last night."

Morgan stroked the oars. "We exchanged . . . words," he acknowledged in that precise way he had, as if English were his second language.

"I know he can be difficult." She bit her lip. "He was very close to Ben."

"So you have said."

"It's hard for him to accept another man in his place."

Morgan's eyes glinted. "To accept me."

"I . . . Yes."

"I am not a substitute for your dead husband, Elizabeth."

She flushed. Ben was never so blunt. "I never said you were."

"Only that you wanted me to be."

That gleam must be mockery. It could not be pain. But in her rush to get rid of Morgan last night, she had been rude, too. She owed him. If not an apology, then an explanation.

"I miss the closeness I shared with Ben," she admitted carefully. "When you're married to someone for fourteen years, when you raise two children together, you develop a certain familiarity. Intimacy. Trust. But I chose to be with you last night. I wanted . . ." She sucked in her breath. "I want you. I'm just saying it's an adjustment."

"For all of you." His tone was dry.

"The past few years, there's only been the three of us. Under the circumstances, is it any wonder we're a little—"

The oars checked. "Possessive?"

She firmed her mouth. "Protective."

He dipped the paddles back into the water. "Zachary is almost a man. It is natural for him to want to protect you."

"And I'm his mother. I need to protect him."

He turned his head, his gaze colliding with hers. "You cannot. He is different, Elizabeth. More different than you can imagine."

The intensity in his voice alarmed her. "You mean, he's growing up."

"Growing up. Changing."

What was he getting at?

She searched his face, his eyes, for a clue, unease constricting her throat and roiling her stomach. She knew that feeling. Every mother in the world knew that feeling. "Are you talking about puberty?"

"I am talking about the Change in Zachary." He expelled a harsh breath, letting the oars trail in the water. "This would be easier if you still believed."

"Believed what?"

"You have a story you tell in your churches." He didn't move, but she felt the coiled tension in him, the energy bunching under his skin. "About the Creation."

Her anxiety spiked. "Is this a religious thing? Is Zack involved in some kind of cult?"

He shot her a look, flat and sharp as a scalpel.

She held up both hands. "Sorry." Though why she should apologize she had no idea. He was the one who had changed the subject. "Go on."

"In the time before time, the elements were formed from the void. And as each element took shape, its people were called into being—the children of earth, the children of the sea, the children of air, and the children of fire."

His voice was deep and lulling as the waves that lapped the boat. Liz folded her hands together, forcing herself to focus on his words.

"Then the Creator made humankind, breathing His immortal soul into mortal clay. Not a popular decision," Morgan said, "with any but the angels. The children of fire—you would call them demons—rebelled, declaring war on the children of the air and humankind."

"I'm sure Emily would enjoy this story," Liz said. "But what does it have to do with Zack?"

"More than I imagined. More than you could dream. Forced to share their territories with this upstart creation, the children of earth and sea retreated, the fair folk to the mountains and wild places of earth and the merfolk to the depths of the sea. Generally, the elementals avoid contact with humankind."

"Okay," Liz said cautiously. Where was he going with this?

"But some encounters are inevitable," Morgan said. "Some are sought. And such meetings always have consequences."

For no reason at all, her heart began to pound. "What kind of consequences?"

"Art. War. Rumors. Legends." His eyes, deep black with rims of gold, locked with hers. "Children."

Her mouth was dry, her mind blank. She stared at him, wetting her lips. "I don't see . . ."

"I am finfolk, Elizabeth," Morgan said deliberately. "Merfolk. Our son Zachary is one of those children."

14

〰

LIZ LAUGHED, A SHORT, SHOCKED, DISBELIEVING
sound. "You're kidding."

You're crazy.

But Morgan appeared perfectly sane, his odd golden-
colored eyes unwavering, his hard face composed. He
didn't look delusional.

He also didn't look like he was joking.

A different fear seized her throat.

*"I am finfolk. Our son Zachary is one of those chil-
dren."*

"You mean Finnish," she said.

"I am a shape-shifter, Elizabeth."

No. Her body stiffened in rejection. Her mind reeled
in shock. This was Morgan, a man she'd admitted into
her home. Allowed alone with her children. Had sex with.
Twice. And he was . . .

Joking, she told herself firmly.

Or insane.

"This isn't funny." She wet her dry lips, glanced over
her shoulder. The shore seemed suddenly very far away.

His words on the beach came back to her. *"Otherwise I cannot be sure you will not run away."*

Dear God.

She twisted on her seat, forcing herself to hold his gaze, to speak calmly. One of them had to be rational. "You look human to me."

He *was* human.

How could he be anything else?

"I am finfolk. A man on land," he explained. "In the sea, we take the form of creatures of the sea."

Her stomach lurched. She was trapped on a boat with a madman. Should she try to humor him?

But this was *Morgan*, her heart insisted, who had shown such insight with Zack, such patience with Emily. There must be some way to reach him, to reason with him.

"Morgan, I'm a doctor. I've spent years studying and treating the human body. What you're suggesting simply isn't possible."

"Your medicine is based on human science. I am not human. I am an elemental."

She ignored his outrageous statement, seizing gratefully on the one word she trusted. "Exactly. Based on *science*. Reliable knowledge acquired through empirical evidence and critical thinking. Not speculation based on some cock-eyed interpretation of the Bible or, or fairy tales. You can't believe . . . You can't expect me to believe . . ."

"I expect nothing. I had hoped . . ." Morgan shook his head. "No matter."

The oarlocks creaked. The paddles flashed as he raised them, dripping, from the water. Shrugging out of his jacket, he laid it on the seat beside him.

Liz's face felt stiff. Her lips were numb. "What are you doing?"

"Providing you with the empirical evidence you require." He tugged his shirt over his head. His shoulders were broad, his torso as pale and smoothly sculpted as marble in a museum. His silver medal gleamed on his chest. "We cannot discuss Zachary's future until you believe."

Her heart stuttered. "Let's not do anything"—*crazy*—"hasty now. I'm a doctor," she repeated, holding on to her professional identity like a talisman against madness. "I know people you can talk to. People who can help you."

"Other doctors."

"Yes," she admitted.

"No." The boat bobbed in the mild chop. "We are deep enough here."

Liz clutched the sides, apprehension coiling in her belly. "Deep enough for what?"

He met her eyes. "For me to show you what I am. What our son is."

Even though she knew nothing was going to happen, a primitive chill chased across the back of her neck and down her spine. "You really don't have to."

"Yes. I do."

She bit her lip, tempted to say she believed him just to keep him in the boat. "Just don't drown trying to prove anything."

Sudden laughter lit his eyes. "I can promise you that."

He stood, one foot on either side of the rocking boat, balancing with an athlete's ease and a dancer's grace. His toes spread. Gripped.

Liz caught her breath. Surely that wasn't . . .

In one smooth move, he dove over the side. The boat lurched and wallowed. Water sprayed. She closed her eyes against the splash.

When she opened them again, Morgan had disappeared.

Still gripping the sides, she peered into the cloudy water, relieved when she saw him gliding below, the pale, smooth curve of his shoulders and back flowing into his long, dark legs. His body appeared almost cut in two, black and white, light and shadow, his pale hair almost green in the half light. Watching him swim, it was easy to understand the old legends of half-human creatures under the sea.

Even though his story was nonsense.

She waited for him to surface.

Time slowed.

Waves rolled the boat.

Morgan remained underwater. She watched his shadow slide under the boat and hung anxiously over the other side.

Shouldn't he come up for air?

A great gray body erupted from the water, all smooth speed and flashing curves.

She cried out and recoiled. *Shark*.

Horror gripped her. Morgan was in the water. He would be attacked, eaten, killed.

"Morgan? Morgan!" she called desperately, praying for a glimpse of him, searching for signs of life. Or blood.

A plume of spray shot skyward. The creature arced and leaped. She glimpsed the long jaw, the curved fin, and her heart resumed beating.

Not a shark. Her pulse drummed with fear and excitement. *A dolphin*.

It reared from the water, almost dancing on its great fluke, its massive body gleaming against the sky. Its round eye was deep black with a glint of gold.

Recognition squeezed her throat, quivered in the pit of her stomach.

Her mind slammed shut. No.

The dolphin plunged, a shining pewter arc disappearing in a burst of speed and foam. She stared, transfixed, as it shimmered, darkened, spread. The sea rippled and flashed.

She blinked.

A shadow, as wide as the boat was long, glided like a kite through the depths below. Her brain fumbled. A ray. Magic, alien, other, moving with primitive purpose and grace, breaking the planes of space like a bird.

It circled the boat, once, twice, drifting close. One wing tip slid above the surface, furled in a lazy salute. She inhaled in shock and fear and amazement.

Sunlight struck the water, striped its back in patterns of

light and shadow, black and white. She stretched out her hand.

"In the sea, we take the form of creatures of the sea."

Her breath shuddered out. *Impossible.* Her fingers curled into a fist.

She watched the shadow grow bigger than the dolphin, bigger than the boat, pushing through the water. Blood rushed in Liz's head. The shadow shot past, developing length, strength, bulk. The boat rocked. A black dorsal fin rose like the sail of a pirate ship cutting through the water, rose and fell, rose and . . .

Orca.

White gleamed against black, a patch of cheek, a flash of tail. She should have been terrified. She *was* terrified, her mouth dry, her pulse racing. And yet . . .

Joy, power, freedom surged just beyond her reach, too huge to understand or encompass. What her mind refused, her heart welcomed in awe and wonder.

"Morgan," she whispered. Not a question, not a warning this time.

The whale broke the bounds of the water, its motion like flying, like dance. White and black, dark and bright, magic as the night sky over Copenhagen sixteen summers ago.

"I want an adventure," she'd said to him then.

She had never dreamed of anything like this. Moisture beaded her eyelashes. She tasted brine on her lips, like tears or spray. Saltwater, the source of life.

The whale fell back into the sea in a flourish of foam.

"Oh." She cried out in loss. In longing.

As if he heard her call, the sleek black shape surged and circled. She watched him speed toward the boat, deep and fast. She trembled, clutching the sides as the whale slid beneath the bow.

The water boiled. Burst.

And Morgan emerged from the sea on the other side.

She met his eyes, golden eyes, animal eyes, with wide black centers and no expression. Her heart threatened to beat its way out of her chest, everything she'd believed, everything she thought she understood, suddenly upended.

His large hands gripped the sheer line. Between his fingers, something shimmered, sheer and shining as insect wings. She blinked as it faded away. His powerful shoulders flexed. In a rush of water, a blur of movement, he surged into the boat.

Her mouth opened and closed silently. *Like a fish*, she thought, and shivered. Bad analogy.

Morgan folded himself on the bench opposite hers, his big, square knees jutting into her space. Rivulets of water ran down his smooth skin. "You are all right."

A question? An observation? Or a command?

"Fine. How . . ." She stared, riveted at his feet, ankles, arches, toes. His *toes*. Between his joints, a faint webbing stretched, iridescent as scales. *Oh, God.* She forced her gaze to his face. Cleared her throat. "How are you?"

"I am well. Usually, I do not change forms so quickly. The danger of losing concentration is too great. But today I felt anchored. You anchored me."

She swallowed. "Is that good?"

"Yes."

"Then I'm glad."

He studied her face. "You are a remarkable woman."

"And you are . . ." *Impossible. Unthinkable. Unreal.* "Remarkable, too."

She itched to touch him, ached for the reassurance of his solid flesh. His human flesh. She clasped her hands together tightly in her lap. "I thought you'd have a tail," she blurted.

"I beg your pardon."

"You said finfolk. Merfolk. And in Copenhagen, at the statue, you said . . ." She could no longer remember exactly what he'd said at the statue of the Little Mermaid all those years ago. "Anyway, I thought . . ." She gestured toward his legs, encased in wet black denim. Avoided looking at his feet.

"Ah. No. One chooses to be one or the other, a man on

land or a creature of the sea," he explained patiently. "To be both at the same time denotes a lack of control. I chose the forms most likely to be acceptable to you."

"Flipper," she said, only a trace of bitterness in her tone.

His eyes narrowed. "The *muc marra* and *whaleyn* were land mammals once. The closest to human of the creatures of the sea."

She turned his words over in her mind like a child with a shape puzzle, struggling to make things fit. "What?"

"Eons ago, they gave up the land for the ocean. I thought it might help you to know that. To see their choice as right and natural."

Her focus sharpened. Her maternal instincts woke. She straightened on the narrow seat. "Zack isn't a dolphin. He's a fifteen-year-old boy."

"Already past his first Change."

"You can't know that."

Everything in her rejected what he was saying. They were talking about her baby, her firstborn.

But the pieces fit.

"I saw it. I saw him last night. Elizabeth." Compassion deepened his voice. "Where do you think he got the lobsters?"

Oh, God.

Her face felt stiff. "I thought he was having trouble adjusting to the change."

"He was."

She was too upset to appreciate his irony.

In the distance, an early lobster boat headed home, the chug of its motor traveling over the water. Liz's mind spun, picking and discarding memories, testing pieces of the puzzle.

"The grief counselor said he was okay. 'As well as can be expected.'" She bit her lip, the small pain a distraction from the ache at her heart. "But about six months after Ben died, Zack changed. His hair color, his hygiene, his clothes."

Those damn boots, she thought. He never went barefoot anymore. Even in the house, even in the summer, he wore socks.

Morgan nodded. "The Change comes on at adolescence. He would try to control it. Failing that, to hide."

Liz swallowed painfully. "He started spending all his time in his room. I thought—he's a teenager. But then his grades dropped. He didn't want to see his friends."

"He could not confide in them."

"He could have come to me." The hurt burst out of her. "I'm his mother. I've always told him he could come to me about anything."

"He would not have the words to tell you what was happening. To explain. How could he? He did not know himself."

Her heart broke for him. Her poor boy. Emotion clogged her throat. "I never suspected . . ." Wasn't that what parents always claimed while their children suffered teasing, addiction, abuse? *"I didn't know." "I never dreamed." "He never said anything."* Useless now to look back and wish and wonder. "I thought he was doing drugs."

"You must not blame yourself."

She shook her head. He didn't understand. "I knew something was wrong. I should have found a way to fix it."

"He does not need to be fixed. He is not your patient."

"No, he's my son." She pressed her fingers to the headache pounding in her temples. "I could have handled drugs," she muttered.

How did she handle this?

"There is nothing you can do," Morgan said.

She raised her head and stared at him.

"Zachary needs to be with his own kind now," he continued calmly while her world crashed around her ears. "On Sanctuary."

Her blood chilled. The drumming in her head made it difficult to think. "Excuse me?"

"It is dangerous for him here. He needs the guidance of

his own kind. When I return to Sanctuary, Zachary goes with me."

* * *

She stared at him, her warm brown eyes huge and accusing.

A completely foreign emotion gripped Morgan's chest. Guilt.

He resisted the urge to look away. He had faced down demons in the deep, stood unfaltering on the wall of Caer Subai when Hell's own flood had crashed down on his head. He would not flinch before one mortal woman.

But that look harpooned his heart.

Even when he had left her at dawn sixteen years ago, even when their son was arrested, even when Morgan had Changed before her eyes, Elizabeth had retained her essential courage, her indomitable determination.

Now she looked shaken. Vulnerable. Betrayed.

He gritted his teeth. Of course he must take Zachary with him. The boy could not be left to bumble on his own.

Especially not with Gau hunting these waters.

She inhaled audibly. Her chin jutted out. "Over my dead body."

He felt a rush of relief. He would rather fight her than feel this grinding guilt.

"Let us hope it does not come to that."

She narrowed her eyes. "Threats?"

Over the water, a gannet folded rigid white wings and plunged into the sea after unwary prey.

He was handling this badly, Morgan realized. His emotions were a nameless, toxic brew, a witch's cauldron seething and bubbling inside him, corroding his customary detachment.

He had never before concerned himself overmuch with the truth, only with survival. Compared to the preservation of his people, the fate of one human female could hardly be allowed to matter. Her good opinion should matter even less.

And yet . . . Elizabeth mattered.

He had to make her understand without terrifying her. Zachary was a target. They both were. Removing the boy to Sanctuary would protect him and divert any danger to Elizabeth.

Or leave her alone and defenseless.

Doubt slid into Morgan, cold and sharp as a blade. The island was warded, he reminded himself. Elizabeth would be safe as long as she remained on the island.

But his uneasiness lingered like the stain of blood in the water.

"I do not threaten. But until Zachary receives the proper training, he is a danger to himself and others."

Water lapped against the boat, filling the silence.

"You said you could choose," Elizabeth said at last. "What if he chooses to be human?"

"He is not human."

"He's not an animal either."

"An elemental. Immortal. One of the First Creation."

"Immortal?"

He hesitated. "The children of the sea can be killed. Or lost beneath the wave. But as long as we live in the sea or on Sanctuary, we do not age and die as humans do."

"You don't age." She considered him, her head tilted to one side. "Exactly how old are you?"

He had stretched her credibility enough for one day. But he would not lie to her or hide the truth any longer. If she rejected him, it was no more than he deserved.

But his palms were sweating.

"I was born on the isle of Bressay," he said carefully, "in the year of your Lord seven hundred and fifty-eight."

She looked down at her hands, clasped tightly in her lap, then up at him. The reflection of sunlight on the water danced across her face. He drank in the sight of her, the deep brown, intelligent eyes, the lines of laughter and loss, the firm, slightly squared chin. He wanted to cup her face in his hands, to comfort her, claim her. But his kind did not touch, only to fight or to mate. And he was no longer certain she would welcome his embrace.

"Zack is only fifteen," she said. "He's not even ready to choose a college yet. How can he make a decision about something like this?"

"There is no decision. He has no choice." His voice was harsh. No choice for any of them. "He is what he is."

Her hands rose and fell in a gesture of frustration. "Then why are we even having this discussion?"

"Because of you," Morgan said with brutal honesty. "Because of my feelings for you. As soon as I knew the boy was finfolk, I would have taken him and gone. For no other woman—for no other force on earth—would I have stayed."

His declaration shook them both.

Wild color stormed her cheeks. Her eyes were dark and confused. "I don't know what to say."

Morgan's jaw clenched. He was no mortal man to beg for her love, no *sidhe* lover to seduce her with promises. "What do your instincts tell you?"

Her gaze met his. "My instincts apparently are not very reliable."

"Fight?" he offered softly. "Or flight?"

She shook her head. "I don't want to fight you. And I'm not going to run away from my responsibilities as Zack's mother. I'm not like you. I believe we always have a choice. My heart hopes Zack will choose to stay, will let himself be human, will let himself be a boy a little longer. He'll leave eventually, whatever I say. To college, to an apartment, to a girl or a job in another state. I have to be prepared to let him go. But not now. Not yet."

The look in her eyes tore at his heart.

"Then why," he quoted back at her, "are we having this discussion?"

"Because of you. Because you were honest with me. You are Zack's father. I need to think about what that means before I decide what's best for Zack."

She could not fail to see that what was best for Zachary was to return with Morgan to Sanctuary.

He had won.

Elizabeth would let him win, would sacrifice her own happiness for the sake of their son.

Morgan would have everything he wanted, everything he came for.

He had not realized victory could leave such a hollow in his chest, such a bitter taste in his mouth.

15

∼≋∼

"WATCH ME, MOMMY," EMILY YELLED FROM THE top of the slide at the island community center.

Camp had been dismissed for the day, but children still lingered, running, shrieking, playing, as if everything were normal. As if the rules of the playground still held true even when the laws of the universe shifted and Liz's world turned upside down.

"Mommy."

"I'm watching," she called, standing near the other mothers.

Here, at least, she could be like other mothers. Watchful. As if her simple presence could protect her child in this strange new world, a world where the old tales were true and lovers walked out of the sea and changeling children were stolen by the fairies.

She wrapped her arms across her stomach, holding herself together.

Emily hit the ground running, chasing after a skinny dark-haired boy a year or two older.

Liz caught her breath. *Emily.* What on earth was she going to tell Em about her brother?

Nothing, she decided. Not yet. There was no need if Zack stayed. And if he left, telling Em was several notches down on her list of things to obsess about.

"Never gets any easier, does it?" a woman next to her remarked.

Liz blinked, trying to place her. Chopped black hair, thin, attractive face, big, Italian eyes. "Sorry, what?"

"Parenthood." The woman nodded toward the playground. "You think when they're babies that's the scariest time, and then they're toddlers and getting into everything, and next thing you know they're trying to kill themselves on the monkey bars. Must be even worse having a teenager."

"I . . . It has its challenges."

Like finding out your son's avoiding bath time because he turns into a . . . dolphin? Whale? She hadn't asked, didn't want to imagine.

"God, I'm sorry. You don't have a clue who I am." The woman smiled, quick and wide. "Regina Hunter. That's my son Nick on the playground. And you saw my daughter Grace when my husband brought her in for her well-baby checkup last week."

"Oh. Yes." Liz struggled to pull herself together, straining her facial muscles to smile back. "Nice to meet you. How is Grace?"

Liz flipped through her mental file of patients. Grace Hunter, three months old, father Dylan.

She felt an almost audible click in her skull as another piece slid into place. "You're married to Dylan Hunter."

"That's right."

Liz resisted the urge to grip her arm. "Your husband works with Morgan. Morgan Bressay."

Regina eyed her cautiously. "Sometimes."

"Environmental protection." Her heart pounded. "Underwater exploration."

Caution morphed into suspicion. "So?"

She was scaring her, Liz realized. She scared herself.

She was taking a risk she wasn't prepared for with a woman she didn't know. The children's voices faded in and out like the sound from a television a room away.

"I just wondered . . ." Her nerve and her voice failed her. "Have you known Morgan long?"

"Never saw him before this trip. You?"

She licked dry lips. "He's Zack's father. Zack is my son."

"The teenager."

Liz nodded. She couldn't do it. No matter how desperate she was for information about Morgan and insight about their son, she couldn't unload her deepest fears and secrets on this friendly, normal, uncomprehending stranger.

"Puberty's rough. All those changes," Regina said.

Liz caught her breath.

"I can just imagine," the other woman continued deliberately, "what you must be going through."

Her heart beat in her throat. "Can you? It's harder for Zack, I think, because he . . ."

"Takes after his father."

Liz swallowed hard. "Exactly."

Their eyes met. Held.

Regina smiled crookedly. "Dylan takes after his mother in almost exactly the same way."

"His mother," Liz repeated, afraid to guess. To hope.

"His mother was the sea witch Atargatis."

Liz stared blankly.

"Selkie, merfolk, whatever you call them. The children of the sea."

A wave of gratitude and disbelief swept over Liz, making her dizzy. There were others. She wasn't alone.

Regina's arm slipped under hers, warm and supportive. "Here, you look like you need to sit down."

She led her to a bench beside some play equipment, fortunately deserted.

"I'm fine." Liz raised her head, a bubble of panic rising in her blood. "Em."

"Right over there with Nick," Regina reassured her. "That's my son, Nick."

A dark-haired boy launched himself from the top of the fort, arms and legs wrapped around a pole. He looked so normal, so much like Zack at his age, Liz's chest ached.

"Is he . . ." She stopped. She was a doctor, trained to ask the right questions, to find the right answers, to respond quickly and decisively in a crisis. But Morgan's revelation had left her floundering.

"Dylan is Nick's stepdad," Regina said.

Liz nodded, feeling like a bobble head doll.

Regina sat beside her on the bench. "How long have you known?"

"I didn't. I guessed. Honestly, I'm not trying to pry into your personal life, I just—"

"About Morgan," Regina interrupted. "When did you find out?"

"This afternoon. He took me out on a boat."

Regina nodded, her eyes sympathetic.

"I thought he was crazy." Liz drew a deep breath. "Or I was."

"Not crazy. In shock maybe."

"Not seeing things?" She'd meant to sound ironic, but there was a wobble in her voice that shamed her.

"If you are, then half the island is hallucinating along with you."

"Half the island?" Her voice rose.

One of the other mothers glanced over curiously.

"Okay, slight exaggeration. Listen, we can't talk here." Regina stood. "Come to my house. The kids can play video games while we talk."

"Talk," Liz said.

She hadn't had a close girlfriend since Allyson ditched her for Gunthar sixteen years and a lifetime ago. She'd been too busy, too immersed in her studies, her work, her children. Her grief.

Connections, she reminded herself. She'd moved to the island in search of a community where she and her children would belong.

She'd never needed a friend more than now. Never

imagined she'd bond with another woman over their lovers from the sea.

Regina shrugged. "Talk, open a bottle of wine. Frankly, you look like you could use a drink."

*   *   *

"So, the sea witch Atargatis had three children with her human husband." Regina counted them off on her fingers. "Caleb—he's our police chief. He's human. Dylan, my husband, who's selkie. And Lucy."

They sat at her kitchen table, sturdy oak with a blue bowl of ripening peaches and tomatoes in the center. Liz was comforted by the child's artwork on the refrigerator, the framed handprints on the wall. Bits of sea glass wrapped in fishing line and silver wire caught the light in the wide apartment windows. She looked around the eclectic, comfortable, normal home and felt like Alice after she'd tumbled down the rabbit hole.

She set down her half-full glass of wine, a good red Italian Montepulciano. "I'm sorry. Did you say selkie?"

"Seal in the water, sheds his pelt on land to take human form," Regina explained.

Dear God, was all Liz could think. She made it sound so ordinary.

"They're all children of the sea," Regina continued. "Selkie and finfolk both. But the selkie only take one form in the ocean. The finfolk can change into anything. Have some more wine."

"I rule!" piped Emily's excited treble from the open door of Nick's room.

"Shit. No way," Nick said.

Regina winced.

"It's all right," Liz said. "She has an older brother."

"That explains why she's winning." Regina refilled Liz's glass. "Anyway, the third kid, Lucy, Caleb and Dylan's sister, was supposed to be human. Nice girl. Island schoolteacher. Taught Nick. Anyway, turns out she's selkie, too, a big deal magic worker. She ends up as consort to Conn ap Llyr, who's kind of like their king. Are you following this?"

"Caleb, Dylan, Lucy. One human, two . . ." *Not.* She gulped her wine. "Did you know your husband was . . ."

"Selkie," Regina supplied.

"When you married him?"

"When I married him, sure. Not when I got pregnant."

"You, too?" Liz blurted.

"Is that what happened with you and Morgan?"

Liz nodded.

"Must be something in the water," Regina muttered.

"Excuse me?"

"Joke," she explained. "So now he's found you again."

Liz stared broodingly into her wineglass. She was very, very grateful to Regina for finding her and bringing her home. "He said it was destiny. That fate brought us together twice."

Regina snorted. "Whatever. I heard he was here to haul Conn's ass back to Sanctuary."

Liz blinked. "Conn?"

"The sea lord."

"Right." A headache threatened behind her eyeballs, compounded by stress and Montepulciano. "Why are you telling me all this?"

"Who else am I going to talk to? Who else would understand? We are a small and extremely exclusive club."

Liz smiled wryly. The wine helped. Talking helped even more. "Women who have sex with merfolk."

"Oh, there are lots of those around. No, we belong to the much more exclusive club of women who got knocked up by their merfolk lovers."

Her smile died. "But if they have sex with so many women . . ."

"Low birth rate," Regina explained. "Sort of the downside of immortality. Their population is declining. That's why children are so important to them."

"*My son,*" Morgan had insisted. "*My seed.*"

Pain sliced her heart, pounded in her head. She willed

her hands to steady on her wineglass. "How many are there?"

"A few thousand, maybe. But no kids. Not for years. And three of their youngest were lost less than a year ago."

"I meant how many on the island."

"Well, we get visitors. Not just summer people, you understand. We're right between the Arctic current and the Gulf Stream, which is convenient for merfolk making the north crossing. But living here? Dylan. Lucy, until last fall. Oh, and Margred."

Liz thought of that awkward moment of recognition in her waiting room between Morgan and beautiful, exotic, pregnant Margred Hunter, their two faces so different and yet somehow alike. "She's one of them."

"Yes and no. Margred chose to live as a human with Caleb," Regina continued. "She'll grow old and die just like the rest of us. But she has her own magic. And I don't just mean the way every man on the island falls over himself when she walks into a room either."

"She chose to live as human." Liz grabbed the phrase like a life raft.

"That's right."

"What about your husband?"

"Well, sure." Regina considered her a moment and then said, "Look, I don't know what Morgan told you about your son, but he's a lot like Dylan. Which means he has a chance for a normal life. A human life. With you."

Liz wanted to hug her in gratitude. But she couldn't afford to lose her head. "If that's what he wants."

"What does he know what he wants? He's fifteen."

Liz flushed. "You're talking about Zack."

"Who else would I . . . Morgan?"

Liz dropped her gaze to her wineglass. "You said they were alike."

"Dylan and *Zack*," Regina clarified. "They're both half-human. Morgan is a coldblooded son of a bitch."

Liz shivered.

"*Because of you*," Morgan had said, his eyes alight with

intensity, his body throwing off heat. "*Because of my feel-ings for you. As soon as I knew the boy was finfolk, I would have taken him and gone. For no other woman—for no other force on earth—would I have stayed.*"

He hadn't seemed so cold then. Or last night on her porch.

But he wanted to take their son away.

Liz straightened her spine. All her life, she'd had to fight for what she wanted. Med school. Her baby. Ben's life. Sometimes she lost, but she didn't give up.

Just because her world had changed in the past few hours didn't mean that she should.

"I need to talk to him," she said, not sure if she meant Morgan or Zack.

"You want to leave Emily here?" Regina offered.

Liz looked at her, surprised and grateful. She hadn't expected an ally. "I don't want to inconvenience you."

"You won't. Let her stay for dinner. It's family movie night at the community center. Popcorn and a double feature. Dylan can take the kids and bring Emily home afterwards."

"That would be great. Thank you. What time?"

"Ten, ten-thirty?"

More than enough time to have things out with Zack. Her head pounded.

"I'll have to ask her," Liz said. Her seven-year-old had spent all day at a new camp. She might object to spending all evening away from her mother and a new kitten.

Which meant any serious discussions with Zack might have to wait, Liz thought, and tried to feel disappointed instead of relieved.

Summoned from her video game, however, Emily showed no sign of separation anxiety.

"Cool. Thanks, Mom." Her smile flashed. "Thanks, Mrs. Hunter."

"Hurry up!" Nick shouted. "You're going down."

"Bring it!" she yelled.

She turned back at the door to his room, her big dark eyes seeking reassurance. "You won't forget to feed Tigger."

Liz's throat ached. They were growing up, growing away from her, both her children. "I promise."

She watched her daughter bounce off before turning back to Regina. "You're sure this isn't a problem for you?"

"Not at all. Nick's thrilled. He needs more people his own age to play with."

"Don't we all." She walked with Regina to the landing outside the apartment. "I don't know how to thank you."

"Then don't. You good to drive?"

Her obvious concern touched Liz. "I'll walk. It's not far."

A walk would give her time to clear her head and plan her strategy. She thanked Regina again and went home, preparing to fight for what she wanted.

A future where she wasn't alone.

*   *   *

Stephanie set her hands on her hips. "Zack, when I said the next move was up to you, I was expecting a little more than, 'Hey, can I come over tonight.'"

Zack's face heated. "Okay. What do you want to do?"

She tilted her head, considering. "There's a movie at the community center tonight."

No movie could be as interesting as her backyard swing, but he wanted to make her happy. "You want to go?"

"I am going. Seven o'clock." And then, apparently taking pity on him, she smiled and added, "Maybe I'll see you there."

That smile—and the hope that she would sit with him, be with him, in the back, in the dark—was enough to lighten his mood on the walk home. When he thought about Stephanie, her smile, her eyes, her small, firm breasts, he didn't have to think about anything else. He didn't want to talk to anyone else.

Maybe now he wouldn't have to.

They barely had time for dinner before the movie started. Mom would be careful what she said in front of Emily, and Morgan wouldn't be around. Not two nights in a row. Mom was careful about stuff like that, too, with the guys she dated—or didn't date—since Dad died. She didn't want them getting ideas, or she didn't want him and Emily getting ideas about anybody taking their father's place. She'd made an exception for Morgan, but only because Morgan was Zack's . . .

Father.

He shook his head. Not thinking about that. Think about Stephanie instead, her sharp blue eyes, her red and black hair, the smooth silver ring at the corner of her mouth. "*The next step is up to you,*" she'd said.

Which took him back to Morgan and his mother. Shit.

He pushed open the front door, planning to escape to his room.

His mom was sitting where she always sat, in the corner of the couch by the reading lamp, cradling her open laptop. She worked all the time, making patient notes or doing research. When his dad was alive, they would sit together, not really talking. Every now and then, his mom would read something out loud about drug interactions or complications from herpes and his dad would reach over and pat his mother's foot.

Good times, he thought sarcastically. But the memory, so ordinary, so clear, clogged his throat.

"Hey, Mom."

She glanced up from her monitor, her face lighting in that way that made him feel loved and annoyed at the same time. "Hi, Zack."

He waited for the familiar litany of questions. *How was your day, your lunch, the walk, your life?*

When it didn't come, the tension leaked out of him like air from a balloon.

"Mom."

She looked up again, her eyes dark and questioning.

Morgan thought he should tell her.

But he wouldn't. He couldn't.

He cleared his throat and took the coward's way out. "Is it okay if we eat early tonight?"

"Hungry?"

"Yeah." He was always hungry, so that wasn't a lie at least. "Actually, I've got to be someplace at seven."

"Where?"

He hunched his shoulders. She was always after him to get out of his room, to go out. What did it matter where he went? "Some movie. At the community center."

Her face cleared. "Maybe you'll see Emily there."

"Em?"

"She's going with a friend from day camp. His parents are taking her. Do you want a ride?"

Stephanie was sixteen. All the guys she dated probably had their driver's licenses already. Hell, they probably had cars.

"I'll walk." He heard the sullen note in his voice and made an effort. "Thanks, though."

"No problem. I'd better get started on dinner, then." Her smile flickered as she uncurled from the couch. "So you won't be late."

She set her half-closed laptop on the coffee table. A minute later he could hear her in the kitchen, banging cupboards, opening drawers.

He hovered in the living room, caught between coming and going, between his past and his future, between what he had and everything he wanted. He could follow her and talk to her. He could go upstairs and hide.

He flopped on the couch, thumbed the remote for the TV, and picked up his mother's laptop, prepared to dull his mind into quiet.

His mom was still online. He ran his finger over the keypad to shut the application. Froze, with his finger raised and his heart thudding in his ears.

THE FINFOLK OF ORKNEY, he read. *These sorcerous*

shape-shifters of Scotland are frequently confused with the more benign legend of the selkie. While some scholars have argued that the tales have roots in the invasions of the Viking longboats, Hallen's Scottish Antiquary of 1886 refers to . . .

*   *   *

Tuna melts, Liz decided, grabbing the can opener out of the drawer. Simple and quick. And Zack liked them. Tigger mewed as the opener bit into the can, releasing the smell of tuna. Adolescent boys were like strays. As long as they were eating, they didn't run away. She'd set his plate in front of him and say . . .

And say . . .

"You Googled me," Zack accused behind her.

Her heart sank. Not the opening she was searching for.

"Like I was a disease or something," he continued.

She turned. "Zack."

He stood in the middle of their new kitchen, a skinny, black-haired version of Morgan with stormy face and glittering eyes. "*He* told you, didn't he? My . . . Morgan."

"Someone had to." His head snapped back as if she'd slapped him. She bled for him, her man-child, her first-born, struggling with a fate and a secret too big to bear. "It doesn't make any difference," she said gently.

"It does to me."

"You're still my son. I love you."

"I'm a freak."

She shook her head. "You're unique."

"Mom. That's what they say to kids they put in special classes."

Despite her heartache, she smiled. "Nothing wrong with special classes."

Except that Morgan wanted to take him away. For training, he'd said.

A pang struck her heart.

She dumped the tuna into a bowl. Tigger quivered at

her feet. "You're the same on the inside," she said firmly. "Anybody who cares about you will see that."

"I turn into a shark. Did he tell you that?"

Her throat closed. A shark. Well. The skin on her arms prickled.

"*I chose the forms most likely to be acceptable to you,*" Morgan had said. "*The closest to human of the creatures of the sea.*"

Bending, she set the nearly empty can on the floor for Tigger. The kitten's vibrating little body pressed against her ankles. "He said you were a shape-shifter. An elemental. A child of the sea."

"A shark. It's fucking scary."

"I imagine it is." She straightened and faced him. "Especially for you."

His chin thrust out. Trembled. The glitter in his eyes was tears.

She melted. Stepping over the kitten, she crossed the kitchen, reached up, and put her arms around him. His shoulders were broad and bony. His head loomed above hers.

His arms, his chest, his whole body stiffened. And then he made a sound deep in his chest and sagged against her. His forehead leaned against her shoulder. His body shook.

She closed her eyes.

"It's okay," she said, the way she had when he was a little boy, with a little boy's hurts and fears. She stroked his black-dyed hair. No matter what he was, what he could become, how old he got, he was still her Zack. "Everything's going to be all right. It doesn't make any difference."

She hoped.

"Why did you sleep with him?" Zack asked when the meal was done and they were clearing the dishes away.

Her heart bumped guiltily. "What?"

"Morgan. Did you know what he was before you . . ." Zack ducked his head. "You know."

She exhaled in relief. He wasn't referring to last night.

But where was he going with this? "No, of course not. I didn't know until today."

"So it would have made a difference," Zack said. His eyes were bleak and curiously adult.

"Oh, sweetie."

But he didn't need a child's reassurances now, she realized. His tears earlier had steadied him, strengthened him somehow.

"The point is, whether your father was finfolk or not, I should have known better, I should have known *him* better, before I slept with him. We can't always know the consequences of our choices. But we can try to learn as much as we can so we can make informed decisions."

He twisted his mouth in a smile. "You mean, by looking stuff up on the Internet?"

"Sometimes," she admitted. "And sometimes we just need to talk."

He absorbed that for a beat, maybe two. "Is it okay if we talk later? Because the movie starts in like ten minutes."

She stared at him in disbelief. How could he even think of going to the movies with so much undisclosed, undiscussed, and undecided?

Because he was fifteen, she realized. Still a child, still a boy, no matter how "unique" he was.

She was glad, relieved to have any evidence he was still a normal teenager.

"That's fine." She dried her hands on a dish towel. "You have a good time. Be home by eleven."

"Mom. It's Friday."

She draped the towel over the bar on the oven door. "And you have work tomorrow."

"Not until noon. Noon to six."

He was growing up some, if he remembered his work schedule.

"Eleven," she repeated.

"Fine."

"I love you, Zack."

He met her gaze. His eyes were Morgan's eyes, pale gold

with deep black centers, but his smile was pure Zachary, sweet and careful. "Yeah. Me you too."

Her heart swelled.

Maybe love would be enough, she thought when he'd said good-bye and the house was empty.

She filled the kettle and set it on the stove to make a cup of tea. The gas flared, too high, too fast. She frowned and adjusted the dial.

Maybe love was all you had, and all you could hold were the moments snatched before the ones you loved were gone.

As Ben had gone.

And Morgan.

Blue flames jumped and licked at the kettle's sides. The spout burped water as if it were boiling already, which it wasn't. Odd. Fat drops sizzled against the steel. The little hairs lifted on the back of her neck.

She adjusted the heat again carefully. Old stoves could be temperamental. Nothing to worry about. She'd had this one inspected with the rest of the house before they moved in.

Tigger mewed, plaintive, insistent.

She opened a cupboard to get a mug and the tea canister. She smelled . . . Not gas. Something fecal, something fetid, something rotten.

A hiss, a whoosh behind her made her turn.

A sheet of blue and orange flame shot upward from the stove.

"Shit," she yelled and dropped the mug and lunged for the burner control.

The fire reached greedily for her, a flash of heat, a howl of glee. She ducked, twisting the dial. The gas snapped off. The fire wavered. Dropped. Died.

Heart hammering, she backed away. The broken mug rolled at her feet.

Tigger cried.

"It's okay," she said shakily.

The burner was black, the kettle quiet. She glanced

down and saw the kitten puffed with fright, backed against a table leg.

She blew out her breath. "It's okay, baby."

She stooped to comfort him, and the dish towel hanging on the oven door burst into flame.

16

❦

THE PREMONITION OF DANGER TRICKLED THROUGH Morgan like smoke.

He raised his head from his whiskey like a wolf testing the wind, his hunter's instincts alert. But he could detect no threat in the quiet bar at the inn.

"Can I get you another?" offered the waitress. She shifted her weight, her hip brushing his arm. "Or anything? Anything at all."

"No." He remembered human manners and added, "Thank you."

She was young, clear eyed, smooth skinned, and eager. But he did not want her. He did not want any woman but Elizabeth.

The realization made him almost as uneasy as that sly tickle on the back of his neck, in the pit of his stomach. For the first time ever in his existence, he was uncomfortable in his own body. Not because he needed sex or the sea, but because he wanted her. Elizabeth. He worried about her.

How did humans bear it? This edge of impatience, this

itch of anxiety, this awareness of another like the slide of
water over his skin.

She wanted time alone, she'd said. To think.

The lingering bite of whiskey could not dispel the bitterness in his mouth.

She needed to pick up her daughter, service her car,
resume her life.

And Morgan, moved by her pale face and huge dark
eyes, aware he had pushed the bounds of her acceptance
enough for one day, had acquiesced like a besotted fool.

A mistake, he thought now. Like any warrior, Elizabeth
would use the respite to count her losses and regroup. He
should have stayed with her.

He should be with her. Now.

The thought cleaved his skull, sharp as an axe or
instinct.

He stood.

"Can I add that to your tab?" the hovering bar girl
asked.

He nodded, thanked her, and left, driven by an urgency
he could not explain and did not question.

The parking lot stank of gravel and gasoline, the moist
loam of the neglected gardens, the pervasive tang of the
sea. And under it all, an acrid taint like ash.

His nostrils flared. Like demon.

His lips pulled back from his teeth. The premonition of
danger flooded back, stronger than before. *Elizabeth.*

Before he reached the end of the drive, he broke into
a run.

*   *   *

Red flames shot to the ceiling. The burning towel fell
to the floor. Liz's heart hammered against her ribs. She
dropped to her knees, fumbling in the under-the-sink cabinet. Dish detergent, garbage bags, cleaning bucket . . . fire
extinguisher.

Thank God. She grabbed it.

She'd never used one before, had no idea if it had

expired. Could expire. She stumbled to her feet, yanked the big round pin, and aimed the nozzle at the fire.

Nothing.

Sweat broke out on her face and under her arms. Her pulse raced. *Do not panic.* She was a doctor, trained to respond calmly in crisis. She squeezed, pressed, prayed. A burst of chemical foam shot out, smothering the stove. Flames and foam collided in an oily, stinking mess. She coughed. Sprayed. The fire subsided with a sullen hiss and a flicker of orange. She sprayed until the canister sputtered and died, until the stove and surrounding floor were coated with greasy, caustic foam. Her hands trembled. Her legs shook.

She shuddered and lowered the extinguisher.

The fire erupted in a geyser of flame.

Holy shit. Smoke boiled, swirling with all the colors of a bruise, yellow, black, purple.

Get out, she thought.

Get help.

Nothing she could save was worth her life. Zack and Em needed her. She couldn't afford to die.

Tigger yowled, a long, unearthly cry of feline despair. She couldn't leave the kitten behind either.

She threw down the canister and reached under the table, cutting her palm on the broken mug. Tigger backed away.

"Damn it, cat."

She scooped him up, ignoring the dig of kitten claws and teeth, and dashed for the back door. Smoke coiled and slithered around the ceilings, flowed down the walls. Her sweaty palms twisted the doorknob. It stuck. With the kitten dangling in the crook of her elbow, she yanked, tugged, rattled the door in the frame.

It didn't budge.

The cat's cries pierced her eardrums. Coughing, she abandoned the door and stumbled toward the dining room. Her eyes stung with smoke. A chair loomed in her path. Pain cracked across her shins. She shoved it aside, lurched forward on her knees, still cradling the protesting Tigger against her stomach.

A curtain of fire sprang up like a wall, blocking her escape. Heat blasted her, nearly singeing her hair. She cried out in terror. Which way? Forward or back? The door? *Stuck.* Or the fire?

The back door burst open. The fire howled and flung itself at the draft.

A cold, wet blast of air struck back.

Morgan.

Relief swept over her. He filled the doorway, black as a thundercloud, bringing the storm in with him. Rain drove into the room, slashing, silver. The air trembled with fog and fury as energies collided.

Trembling, she stared as power flashed around him.

"Gau!" he shouted. "I cast you out!"

The fire roared, curled, retreated. In the door to the dining room, the curtain of flame tore like a veil, disappeared in a shower of diamond drops.

A gust scattered the choking fumes.

The fire on the stove muttered, spat, and died.

Tigger cowered, mute, in her arms.

Morgan stood in the dissipating smoke like a soldier on a battlefield. Liz could feel the energy pumping through his blood and pouring off his skin. His gold-rimmed eyes blazed.

Striding across the kitchen floor, he hauled her to her feet and yanked her against his iron body. "Are you all right?"

"I . . ." Her lungs weren't working properly. Neither was her brain. "Fine," she managed before his mouth crushed hers.

His kiss was fierce and needy. Hot. His mouth claimed and conquered hers. She clung to him with one arm, her short nails digging into his muscled shoulder, battered by a storm of sensation, a tempest of relief and desire and need. She couldn't get her breath or her balance. He swept away her control.

She gave herself up to his kiss, grateful simply to touch, taste, be.

The kitten squirmed and clawed between them.

"Ouch."

With one hand, he plucked the kitten from between them and dropped it on the ground. He gripped her hips to pull her more firmly against him and then stopped, his mouth compressing in apparent displeasure.

Her heartbeat thundered. Her head hazed with lust. "What?"

He took her arm and turned it over, exposing the long, thin lines of red cat scratches against her pale skin, her bleeding palm. "You are hurt."

"It's nothing. Thank God you showed up." She pulled her arm back. "Why did you show up?"

"You needed me," he said, so simply her heart stuttered.

He didn't mean it the way it sounded, she told herself.

"I did," she said. "I've never been so glad to see anyone in my life, but . . ."

The kitten edged closer to the door, quivering. Morgan snapped a word Liz didn't recognize and Tigger ran back under the table.

Liz regarded the open door, her mind working now, turning, churning. "How did you get in?"

He raised his brows. "In the usual way."

"The door was locked. Not locked," she corrected herself. "Jammed."

"No. Gau used your fears to hold you captive."

"Excuse me?"

"It was an illusion," Morgan explained. "Like the fire at the other door. Demons are masters of such deception."

Fire. Demons. In her house.

She drew an unsteady breath. "I think," she said carefully, "I need to sit down."

Before her knees gave out.

He righted the overturned chair with one hand. She sat,

the cat scratches throbbing on her arm. The broken tea mug rolled at her feet. Piles of chemical foam dripped from the stove. Rain puddled on the floor. The kitchen curtains were limp, damp, and dirty, and wet paper napkins had been blown around the room. The storm had been no illusion. But there were remarkably few signs of fire: a blackened towel, a scorched kettle, a smudge of soot on the wall. A breeze blew through the open door, clean and smelling of salt.

She shivered. "You're saying this wasn't a regular fire."

"It was a fire," Morgan said. "Fire is the demons' element."

"I was making tea. It's an old house. Maybe a gas leak . . ." He met her eyes, and her voice died. Okay, she didn't believe the gas leak theory either.

She picked up Tigger, stroking his vibrating little body for comfort.

"The flames provided the medium," Morgan said. "But Gau should not have been able to manifest so completely."

She felt ignorant. Helpless. "Who is Gau?"

His eyes, black and gold and guarded, met hers. "An old acquaintance."

"A demon."

"Yes."

"An enemy?"

"He has made himself so."

Fear sharpened her voice. "You know, you could stop with the ominous, cryptic statements. We're talking about my life here. My children's safety. I need to know what's going on."

He inclined his head. "You are right. I am not used to confiding in another." His smile showed the edge of his teeth. "I hunt alone."

She looked at his teeth and his eyes and was suddenly reminded of something she would prefer to forget. *He was not human.*

Inside her something quivered and froze like a rabbit spying a hawk, a flutter of purely animal panic. For a moment the impossibility of what he was overcame even the improbability of what he was saying.

She bit down on her lip—*This was Morgan*, she told herself firmly—and the fear passed. "Well, you're not alone now. You've got Zack to think about." And me, she thought. And Em. "If we're in danger, I need to know."

Morgan hesitated. Debating what to tell her? Or deciding what to leave out? "I am the leader of the finfolk. If I ally with Hell, if my people side with the children of fire against the selkie and humankind, Gau has offered me rulership over the sea."

"So he's angry because you said no."

He went still, that quality beyond stillness that reminded her again he was something more or other than human. "You sound very certain of my answer."

"No one who knows you could think you are a traitor."

His gaze rested on her, dark and unreadable. "Not everyone shares your confidence in my loyalties."

"You gave my daughter a kitten. You told me about our son." *You made love to me as if I mattered to you.* "You saved my house and probably my life. That earns you a certain amount of trust."

"You give me too much credit. You were in danger because of me. I could hardly do otherwise."

He would see it that way, she thought. Whatever Morgan was, whatever he had done, he had his own spare, warrior's code.

She frowned. "I still don't understand why Gau attacked me. Does he want revenge?"

"He wants my support."

"Killing me won't accomplish that."

"Threatening you might. He sees you as a weakness to be exploited."

She held her breath. "And how do you see us?"

"I have no weaknesses."

She struggled to hide her disappointment. "Then we have no value as hostages."

"Elizabeth."

She looked up and met his gaze. The look in his eyes was as warm, as fierce, as intimate as a kiss. Her blood began to pound.

"Your *value* is something Gau cannot begin to comprehend. He will not touch you again." Morgan's words had the weight of a vow, quiet and intense. "I will not leave you unprotected."

For a moment, she let herself be reassured, as if he would save her, as if he could love her, as if he would be there for her through all the Bad Things that life threw at you, like adolescence and illness and demons and death.

Except he was leaving.

Absently, she stroked the kitten in her lap. She had always known he would leave.

The only question was, how many pieces of her heart would he take with him?

*   *   *

Zack stood just inside the doors of the community center gym. Testing the waters, haha.

The odor of sweat competed with the smell of fresh coffee and stale popcorn drifting from the lobby. Moviegoers eddied and swirled around him. He recognized some of them from the store, summer people dressed from the L.L. Bean catalogue or the outlet in Freeport, islanders in faded jeans and ball caps. Kids squirmed on laps or ran around the wooden floor. Family groups settled into the rows of folding chairs that straggled from foul line to foul line.

He spotted Emily, sitting near the front with a skinny, dark-haired kid her age. The friend from day camp, Zack guessed. At least one of them was making friends. The tall dude who was with them must be the kid's dad. He couldn't go sit with them. The generations appeared to mix more on the island than they did back home in Chapel Hill, but he was pretty sure such a move would brand him forever as untouchable. A loser.

The big cop who'd picked him up for questioning was

there with a really pregnant woman. Her face looked like something in a magazine, all lips and eyes. Her breasts and stomach stuck out about a mile. Zack didn't know where to look at her or if he should look at all. He felt his face getting red and glanced away.

There she was. Stephanie.

His heart beat faster.

She sat with a bunch of her friends on a pile of mats under an extra hoop at midcourt. She waggled her fingers when she saw him, but she didn't get up or wave him over.

Zack stood frozen. Uncertain.

"The next move is up to you," she'd said.

That big asshole, Doug, sprawled beside her, leaning close to whisper in her ear. She laughed and punched him in the arm.

Zack walked over. "Hey, Stephanie."

She glanced up, her smile lingering in her eyes. "Hi, Zack."

He nodded to Doug. Todd was there, too, and a couple of girls he hadn't seen before.

"Everybody, this is Zack. Zack, everybody."

"Hey."

"Hi." One of the girls dimpled. "Cute accent."

"He's from Alabama," Stephanie said.

"North Carolina."

"Redneck flatlander," Doug said.

"Yankee asshole," Zack replied without heat.

Introductions concluded, it was easy enough to fit into the space on Stephanie's other side while they waited for the movie to begin.

A woman who looked like somebody's Italian grandmother, with hard red nails and lips and black athletic shoes, got up in front of the screen to welcome everybody to the summer movie series on World's End.

"Who's that?" Zack murmured to Stephanie.

"The mayor. Antonia Barone."

The mayor announced the movies, *Transformers II* and

something else. He was distracted by Stephanie, by how close she was and how good she smelled, like strawberry Jolly Ranchers.

The back of his neck crawled. Warning.

He looked at Doug, but the older boy had his hand draped on a girl's thigh, Hailey or Bailey or something. He didn't seem like a threat at the moment.

Zack took a deep breath, willing his muscles to relax.

The tall man sitting with Emily suddenly stood. Zack felt his own pulse accelerate as the man scanned the crowd. His gaze collided with Zack's, and this time the sizzle of warning shot clear down his spine.

Holy shit.

"What's the matter?" Stephanie asked.

Zack shook his head. "Nothing."

He watched as the man crossed the gym to talk with the police chief. Emily and the other kid trailed behind him, their short legs trotting to keep up. Chief Hunter frowned and glanced at Zack, apparently asking a question. Zack's throat tightened. He hadn't done anything wrong. But his creeping feeling of unease grew.

The mayor was still talking. "Fifteen-minute intermission," Zack heard, and "selling cookies in the lobby to support community programs."

He turned to Stephanie, trying desperately to ignore whatever was going on at the front of the room. "You want a cookie?"

"Give it up, dude," Todd said. "She doesn't put out for cookies."

"I might consider it." Stephanie smiled up at Zack. "But not for anything less than chocolate chip."

Zack jerked to his feet. "I'll see what they've got."

A piping treble pierced the hum of the crowd. "I don't want to stay here."

Emily.

Zack froze.

"I want to go home." His little sister's wail rose to the rafters.

"I've got to go," Zack said.

"But you just got here," Stephanie objected.

"I know. I'm sorry." He gestured toward the front of the gym, where Emily stood dwarfed by two big men. Two strangers. "It's my sister."

"The little black girl?" Hailey asked.

Doug snorted. "You'd rather make out with your sister than Stephanie? Man, that's sick."

Zack flushed, frustrated, furious. But he couldn't ignore the edge of panic in Emily's voice.

"I'm sorry," he repeated, and went to his sister's rescue, a loser after all.

"You need to stay here," the tall man was saying as Zack approached. "Half the island is here. Along with your wife."

"Don't tell me how to do my job," the police chief said. "You can't walk into an unknown situation without backup."

"I have no choice."

"Where's Morgan?"

"I wish to God I knew."

"Zack!" Emily ran and clung to him.

He put a hand on his little sister's shoulder, speaking over her head to the tall guy. "Morgan's staying at the inn. Maybe you could find him there."

The man appraised him. "You're his son."

"Yes, sir. What's going on?"

"I was going to watch the movie with Nick," Emily said. "But now Nick's dad is leaving, and he wants me to stay here, and I don't know the lady who's watching us." Her lower lip trembled dangerously. "And I want to go home."

"I can take her home," Zack said.

The police chief rubbed his jaw. "It would be better if you both stayed put for now."

"Why?" A sick ball formed in his gut. "Is it our mom? Is she okay?"

"I'm sure she's fine," Chief Hunter said.

"I'm leaving," the other man announced. "I need to find the breach in the wards."

The cop nodded. "Maggie will watch the kids."

Em's grip tightened on Zack's leg. "Zack?" Her voice rose.

Zack looked from his sister to the two adults, both alert, calm, grim. In charge. Next to them, he felt young and awkward. He didn't have a clue what was going on. But he couldn't stand here and do nothing.

"I can watch them," he said. "Em and . . ." Her friend. He didn't know the kid's name.

Chief Hunter looked at him sharply. Zack wondered if he would object.

Like lifting lobsters disqualified Zack as a baby-sitter.

He thrust out his jaw. "Emily's my sister. I'm responsible for her."

"I can help," somebody said behind him.

Zack turned. "Stephanie."

She cocked a hip, hooking her fingers into her back pockets. "I've baby-sat for Nick plenty of times. They can watch the movie with us." She smiled, making her silver lip ring gleam. "If that's all right with you."

"That would be . . ." Emotion clogged Zack's throat.

"Fine," the police chief said.

"Great." Zack cleared his throat. "That would be great."

                    *   *   *

Liz thrust the wet, wadded-up napkins into the garbage and grabbed the cleaning bucket from under the sink. Her hands shook. It was getting harder and harder to pretend even to herself that everything was going to be all right.

Dumping the bucket under the faucet, she twisted the tap. As long as she was mopping up puddles, she might as well scrub her floor. Keep busy. Keep the fear at bay.

What if Zack had been home when the fire struck? Or Em?

Panic glazed her mind. She struggled to focus, drawing up a mental list of Things She Could Control, clean the floor, check on the cat, buy a new fire extinguisher.

Not that the old one had done her any good.

She drew a ragged breath, standing next to the sink, waiting for the bucket to fill, waiting for her life and her heartbeat to return to normal, and saw Morgan pull the scorched remnants of the dish towel out of the trash.

She shuddered. She never wanted to see that thing again. "What are you doing?"

"Gau must have had a way in," Morgan said, spreading the wet and blackened towel on her kitchen table. "I am trying to find it."

He was doing something. Maybe she could help.

"Try the stove," she suggested.

A long shadow fell across the doorway. Her heart raced as she braced to face this new threat.

But it was only Dylan Hunter, Regina's husband, standing on her back stoop. She sagged against the sink.

Morgan glanced up. "About time you showed up."

Liz's gaze searched beyond him, looking for Em.

Nothing.

A different anxiety squeezed her chest. "Where's Emily?"

"At the community center with your son Zack. And my son Nick and my brother and Margred." Dylan smiled reassuringly. "She is in good hands."

He stepped over her threshold, surveying the wet floor, the shrinking foam, the black V on the wall above the stove. "What happened here?"

"Gau," Morgan said.

Dylan's black eyes widened in shock. "That cannot be. We buried him under half the ocean, Lucy and Margred and I."

"Buried, not extinguished. I told you he was back."

"But the island is protected."

Protected how? Protected from what? Demons? Whatever they'd done, it hadn't been enough.

"Not sufficiently," Morgan said, echoing her thought.

Dylan scowled. "I know my job. He could not have breached the wards without an invitation."

Liz shut off the water in the sink, struggling to find a footing in the conversation. "I thought that was vampires."

Both men looked at her.

"Buffy?" she offered. "The Lost Boys?"

Morgan turned back to Dylan. "She did not invite this. She would not."

"What about the kid?"

"Zachary is my son," Morgan said, cold as ice.

"That's what worries me."

Their eyes clashed, black and gold. There were undercurrents here Liz did not understand, but she could feel the tension swirling in the air. *"Not everyone shares your confidence in my loyalties,"* Morgan had said.

She stiffened in his defense, in Zack's defense. "It couldn't be Zack. He isn't even here."

"He wouldn't have to be," Dylan said without taking his eyes off Morgan.

"Perhaps a former occupant," Morgan suggested. "A dabbler in the black arts."

"Witches in Maine?" Dylan sounded skeptical.

Morgan shrugged. "We are not so far from Massachusetts."

"I can ask Caleb to check with the real estate office," Dylan said. "Though I doubt their records go back that far."

"Paula Schutte at Island Realty," Liz said. "She sold me the house. The previous owner was a physician at the clinic, too."

Morgan looked at Dylan.

"Neal Emery," he said. "Here six months. Hated the winter, took off as soon as Grace was born."

"Not that one," Liz said. "The doctor before him. Donna something."

Silence thickened the air.

"Ah," Morgan said very softly.

Dylan nodded. "That would explain it."

Liz was tired of conversations going over her head. "Not to me."

"Donna Tomah, the previous inhabitant of this house, was possessed by a demon," Dylan said.

Liz swallowed. "Paula told me the owner couldn't come to the closing because she was in a rehabilitation facility."

"She is. In Portland," Dylan confirmed. He looked at Morgan. "Caleb's been keeping track of her since the attack last summer."

"Another attack?" Nerves lent an edge to Liz's voice. "What is this, open season on island doctors?"

Dylan would not meet her eyes. "The demon did not leave her willingly or gently."

Liz's stomach cramped. "So what happened?"

Dylan hesitated.

"When a demon will not exit its host," Morgan explained, "the only recourse is to render its victim's body uninhabitable."

"Meaning . . ."

His teeth flashed. "Regina bashed her head in with a table leg."

Liz winced. "Oh."

"The doctor is expected to make almost a full recovery," Dylan said. "Eventually."

"Am I supposed to find that reassuring?"

"Yes." Morgan's eyes met hers, not promising anything, but at least he didn't lie, she could trust him. "Because now you know Gau can be defeated if you have the will and the stomach. And now that I know how he gained access to your house, I can protect you."

"The island is warded," Dylan said again.

"The house must be cleansed," Morgan said. "And sealed."

"With what?" Liz demanded. "Holy water? Garlic?"

Morgan smiled and despite the general weirdness of her life and the awfulness of the situation, she felt better. He made her believe things could be . . . not normal, but okay.

"Nothing so exotic," he said.

"What, then?"

He gestured toward the bucket in the sink. "What do you use to clean up?"

"Water?" she guessed.

This time his smile warmed her clear to her toes. "Precisely. We are not so different, you and I."

17

MORGAN AND DYLAN WERE STILL OUTSIDE, PAC-
ing the yard, circling the house. Making magic, Liz thought,
suppressing a flutter of unease.

She watched them through her kitchen window. They
made quite a picture, Dylan with his dark, lean elegance
and brooding black eyes, Morgan with his brutal Viking
face and hair the color of sea foam, day and night, night
and day, every woman's fantasy brought to life.

Except she didn't want the fantasy. She wanted more
than fairy tales.

She poured the bucket of dirty water into the sink. She
had her own rituals to perform. Domestic ones, scrub the
wall and clean the stove and mop the floor, mundane, dirty
chores intended to return things to the way they were
before, to restore a bit of order, a layer of protection, a measure of control to her life.

"We are not so different, you and I."

She sighed. It wasn't that simple. Even if you believed.

She heard the slam of a car door as Dylan left. Morgan still stood in the front yard, eyeing the sky like a

man debating whether or not to mow the lawn before a rain. What was he doing out there alone? She glanced at the clock. Not even nine, the second feature hadn't even started, plenty of time to wash the smoke from her hair before Dylan brought her children home.

Shower, shampoo, condition, moisturize. More rituals, female and familiar.

By the time she padded from the bathroom, the light was fading, the night sliding in on a wave of clouds. Her skin felt scalded and tender from her shower. The towel rasped against her breasts. She cocked her head, listening to rain spatter against the glass, and walked to her bedroom window. Restless. Yearning. Confused.

He was there, Morgan, alone in the overgrown yard, his head flung back to the pouring rain, his palms turned open to the sky. Her lips parted in longing and in wonder. Power flashed around him like lightning, power and sex. Rain ran in rivulets down his strong face, plastered his hair to his skull, molded his wet white shirt to his body. He was beautiful, the most beautiful man she'd ever seen, his pale skin glowing in the dusk, a marble garden god come to life, primal, elemental.

Not-a-human, not-a-human, beat her heart.

She tightened her towel around her. She'd never liked the myths in school about the old gods descending to earth to satisfy their lusts with the daughters of men. She'd always felt slightly sorry for those women they had sex with, who got carried away by bulls or swans and ended up with wars and pregnancies and eternal punishment, got turned into trees or nightingales. No Disney studio transformations from Beast to Prince, no happy endings in those stories.

Nothing good ever came from sleeping with a god. She didn't need that kind of fantasy in her life. That kind of grief. She'd stick to reality, thank you very much, no matter how limited.

Or lonely.

He looked up and saw her, and her heart stumbled, and it was just the two of them, caught in the storm and the twilight, caught in the moment, her wet from her shower, him wet from the rain. His eyes darkened with everything she was feeling, desire and regret, surprise and confusion, and whatever else was the fairy tale, this was real, the emotion was real, she would never get over him this time.

This time, she vowed, he would never get over her.

Still holding his gaze through the window, she took a step back and dropped the towel.

* * *

Her image burned his retinas, Elizabeth naked with the light behind her, her strong calm face, her strong soft body, breasts, belly, thighs.

Her eyes, dark with invitation.

Morgan's blood surged. He lunged up the stairs, his heart pumping, his head swimming.

The door to her room was open. A yellow square of lamplight spilled onto the rug in the hall. He bared his teeth, electric pinpricks racing over his skin, the gale crackling, collecting, inside and out.

He stalked into her room. He had a vague impression of order and softness—tall, dark furniture, white, billowing curtains, a thick white comforter on the bed—but all he really saw was Elizabeth silhouetted against the rain, her damp hair dark against her bare shoulders, her towel crumpled at her feet. Need crashed through him bright as lightning. He wanted her. He had never wanted a woman so much.

And what he wanted, he took.

He strode across the room to her, ran his hands up her arms to her shoulders and lightly down to her breasts, watched the storm swirl in her face and in her eyes. The coolness of his palms made her skin prickle. She tilted her head back, exposing the strong, lovely line of her throat. He wanted to bite her right there, at the tender join of shoulder and neck, wanted to feel her tremble, hear her moan.

Her heart raced under his hand. She wanted this. Accepted him. Even knowing what he was, even after she'd been threatened and attacked, she welcomed him.

Unless . . .

The thought slid into his mind, disturbing and un-
wanted.

Unless she wanted him because she had been threatened. She was frightened. Who else could she turn to for
comfort, for relief?

For protection.

Cursing himself for six kinds of fool, he released her.

"Elizabeth." Only a breath separated her naked body
from his. He could feel his control slipping, seeping like
water through his fingers. "You do not know what you are
inviting. I am not . . ." Her scent was in his head, tangling
his thoughts, tripping up his tongue. "Fully in command
of myself."

"I don't want you in command." She smiled at him, making his blood pound. Tugging open his shirt, she trailed her
fingers down his chest, over his abdomen. "I'm seducing
you," she said, and followed her hands with her mouth.

*   *   *

He had the most amazing body, she thought, hard and
smooth and strong. She opened her mouth, breathing him
in, licking the cool moisture and hot salt dampness from
his skin, feeling him tense, absorbing his quiver. His stomach muscles contracted. He slid his hands over her torso,
cupped her breasts.

She allowed that—he had wonderful hands, big and
strong—but when his thumbs brushed her nipples, she
slipped out of his grasp. "Take off your clothes."

He lifted an eyebrow, surprised. Amused. Aroused, she
hoped.

Holding her gaze, he stripped out of his shirt and
shucked his pants. He stood before her, all clean lines and
heavy muscle, magnificently naked. Her eyes slid down his
broad torso, following the trail of dark blond hair that ran
from his navel to his thighs. Definitely aroused. Hers to
seduce and command.

Or not.

Her heart fluttered. She ran her tongue over her upper lip. "On the bed."

His eyes flickered. His shaft jerked. Tension throbbed in the air between them. She held her breath, testing the limits of his control and hers.

With a shrug, he stalked to her wide, white bed. He lay across her mattress, arms and legs slightly spread, his moonlight hair captured on her pillow, his body powerful even in repose.

Agitation surged from her breasts to her loins, a thrill of desire, a trickle of doubt. She squeezed her thighs together.

She was the thirty-seven-year-old mother of two with a limited sexual repertoire. How could she make him ache as she ached, yearn as she yearned?

His gaze met hers, hot, golden, intent. His mouth quirked. "I am in your hands."

His gentle taunt restored her confidence. Her skin bloomed. Her breath caught. Everything female in her rose to his challenge.

"Not yet." She smiled. "But you will be."

Her hair fell forward, a sleek waterfall sliding over her shoulders, against his skin. She flowed over him, restless and fluid as water, lapping, teasing, caressing, seeking the paths of least resistance, the points of greatest pleasure.

Morgan strained and quivered under her attentions, thrusting his hips forward, his cock jutting, demanding, pleading for her attention. She hummed low in her throat, a sound of pleasure and possession, and took him in.

Sensation sluiced through his limbs, blanketed his brain. Hot, wet suction. Her neat doctor's hands skimmed over him, her neat nails raked lightly up and down his ribs. He fisted his hands in her sheets as she fed, vulnerable in a way he had never been before, giving himself up for her pleasure, giving himself into her control, letting her take him with her small, smooth hands and avid mouth. His vision blurred. His breath tore in his lungs, fast and jagged. He felt his release building, gathering force in his balls and brain like a storm at sea, and choked out something, an imprecation, a plea.

One lick, and then she rose over him, powerful and hungry as the sea, her lips slick and swollen, her eyes hot and tender, bewitching in her beauty, irresistible in her greed.

His heart stopped.

Grabbing a packet from the bedside table, she sheathed him. Straddled him. "Now."

He growled, low and savage. "Yes."

Now.

Forever.

Elizabeth.

She rubbed herself over him like a cat, feeling his stiff cock prod and nudge apart her slick folds, delighting in his big hard body straining and shaking under hers, his hot strength, his leashed power. He gripped her hips to pull her down and she grabbed his arms, leaning over him to pin his thick, square wrists to her soft pillows, her breasts brushing his smooth, hot chest, his breath searing her lips, his body rearing under her.

Time shimmered and stood still as she lowered herself by increments, absorbing him by degrees, impaling herself on his rigid flesh, biting her lip at how full he felt, how good she felt, how powerful this was, how right. He arched, his thick shaft cleaving her, splitting her open, hard into soft, male into female, giving her what she wanted while she took everything he had. His arms flexed. His wrists twisted. His fingers turned and gripped hers as she rode him in a slow, rocking rhythm, their hands joined, their gazes locked, their breathing matched and ragged. She watched his eyes go blind and bright as her orgasm rolled through her like a wave, as he drove deep, held, and shuddered in his own release. Lowering her head to his shoulder, she let herself be swept away.

* * *

Morgan stared up at the flat white ceiling of Elizabeth's pretty bedchamber as she melted over him, their limbs tangled, her hair spread over his chest like a net drying in the sun, all warm, moist, fragrant woman. His woman. Sleepy. Satisfied.

She had taken him apart the way Emily's kitten would unravel a ball of yarn until his guts were strung out for her to play with and his heart rolled across the floor. He could not find strength to move or breath to speak, but his instincts, honed over centuries of survival, quivered in warning.

He was in very deep danger here.

She raised her head from his shoulder, the glow still on her cheeks and in her eyes. Her kiss-swollen lips curved. "That was nice."

His system was swamped, his world had been shaken to its foundation, and she thought it was "*nice*"?

He struggled to form words. "Yes."

She stretched against him, making his libido sit up and beg like a dog. "I feel wonderful."

He raised one hand, unsticking a strand of hair from her parted lips. "Yes."

She blushed, modest even after sex. "You're awfully agreeable all of a sudden."

"You have destroyed my brain," he told her truthfully. "I cannot think."

She grinned, pleased, and bounced a quick, affectionate kiss off his jaw. Another layer of his defenses swirled down like a sand castle assaulted by the tide. "I have a lot of lost time to make up for."

He cleared his throat. "How did you survive without a lover all these years?"

"Oh." She wiggled, distracting him. "I have a decent imagination. And some good memories."

Memories of him? Or of her husband?

An unfamiliar stab of possessiveness caught Morgan under the ribs. "The finfolk live in the moment. We are not bound by memories."

Elizabeth shook back her hair. "What about love?"

"We are not bound by love either." The words, practiced

for centuries, came easily. "Emotions are ephemeral. We are immortal. Nothing lasts forever but the sea."

She narrowed her eyes. "The sea and love."

He shrugged, uncomfortable with the conversation. "That's what my sister thought, and she died."

"You have a sister?"

"Had."

"What happened to her?"

He drew a quick, harsh breath, regretting he had ever introduced the subject. "She died. She took a mortal lover and gave up everything for him, the sea and her life."

Elizabeth's brow pleated. "Did she regret her decision?"

"I do not know. I never spoke to her again."

Not a decision he was proud of, upon reflection. But he was not much given to self-examination.

"How sad," Elizabeth said.

"I believe she was happy," he offered stiffly. "There were children. Five."

Tiny figures on the shore, playing by the sea that should have been their birthright. Morwenna had walked with them, her pale hair floating in the breeze, her husband at her side. The lady of Farness. A wave of yearning for what had been, for what never was, swept through him.

"The first year . . ." Elizabeth's voice faltered.

His attention sharpened. She was no more prone to faltering than he was to introspection. "Go on."

"After Ben died, I was angry with him for leaving me. Leaving us." Her throat moved as she swallowed. "Even though his death wasn't his fault, even though I knew my feelings were part of the grieving process, it took me a long time to forgive. But until I got past the anger, I couldn't get on with my life."

Her words struck him like stones. Were they still talking about his sister and her dead husband? *"I was angry with him for leaving me . . . It took me a long time to forgive."*

"And did you?" Morgan asked, braced for her answer. "Forgive?"

She nodded so that her hair brushed his collarbone. "I remembered how much I loved him, and how he loved each of us. I thought how much richer my life was because he was in it even for a little while." Compassionate and direct, her gaze sought his. "And I realized that I would rather have loved him and lost him than never to have had him in my life at all."

He lay beneath her, mute and stiff.

"You say you live in the moment. Maybe," she suggested softly, "you should let go of the past."

Could he? His emotions churned. His revelation earlier today must have turned her world upside down. But she had turned him inside out, leaving him uneasy, aching, raw.

"I never told her that I loved her," he said abruptly. "My sister. I gave her all the reasons in the world to stay but that."

Elizabeth cupped his jaw, her touch indescribably tender. "Maybe she knew without you telling her."

He met her steady dark eyes. "I cannot promise you a future, Elizabeth."

"Then I'll take now."

He covered her hand with one of his own, holding it to his cheek. "Take me."

"Yes," she said.

He wanted her again. He would always want her.

He pushed the fear aside. He dug in the drawer for another of the damn sheaths and put it on before he rolled with her, deliberately overwhelming her with his strength, shoving into her without foreplay or finesse. She was still silky, soft, wet. With a moan of welcome, she opened to him, wrapping her legs around his hips, her arms around his ribs.

"That feels so . . . Oh." Her tremor shook them both. Yet she craned her neck to look at the clock. "I don't think we have time."

No time, he thought.

Nothing lasts forever but the sea.

"I do not need long," he said and set out to prove it, stroking into her fast and hard, hammering into her over and over in a push toward forgetfulness, a rush toward release. But she met him, matched him, tilting her hips to take his thrusts, twining her fingers in his hair, her legs around his legs, *Elizabeth* in every pulse, push, breath. He felt her around him, inside him, part of him, and when she cried out and came, her orgasm took him like the sea, changed him in his heart and the marrow of his bones.

He lay on her, listening to the rain drum on the roof and drip through the trees.

Beached.

Bewildered.

Changed. He would never be the same, never be himself again.

Outside, a car crunched over gravel. Headlights sparked on the glass and arced away.

"I have to get dressed," Elizabeth kissed the side of his face, shoved at his shoulder. "It's getting late. You have to go."

He lay unmoving, his body as heavy as stone, her words trickling through him as cold and inescapable as water.

He had to go.

Sooner or later, whether he took the boy or not, he was warden of the northern deeps, with duties in the sea and on Sanctuary. He was lord of the finfolk, among the last blood born of his kind. He could not stay.

Could he?

Dylan had. But Dylan was both selkie and human, bound to land by his sealskin, anchored by a human life and human responsibilities.

"It is already too late," he said.

Elizabeth looked at him without understanding. "The children will be home soon."

The children. Zachary.

The reminder formed an icy ball in his gut. He disengaged slowly from Elizabeth's body, reluctant to part with her warmth, already anticipating in his heart and in his flesh the larger separation to come. "I must speak with him. Zachary."

Elizabeth's clouded eyes cleared. He watched the subtle shift from lover to mother as she marshaled her authority and defenses. "Not tonight. He's been through enough for one day."

So had she. But she did not make excuses for herself, he noticed. He admired her determination to protect their son. But he would not let admiration deter him from what must be said. What must be done.

"Zachary is old enough to make his own decisions."

She shook her head. "He doesn't know enough to decide anything. He needs time to adjust. To accept. We all need time."

The bitter echo of Conn's words played in his head. *"You need time to recover . . . Take as long as you need."*

"Time will not change what he is," Morgan said. "Or what I am."

A frown formed between Elizabeth's brows. "This isn't only about you. Or even about Zack. I have to consider Em."

He stared at her, perplexed, uneasy. "Emily already accepts me."

"Exactly. She's becoming attached."

Attached. Like a barb in his skin, a tiny hook in his heart.

The admission did not hurt as much as he thought it would.

"I am . . . attached to her, too," he said carefully.

Elizabeth did not appear impressed. "I've been very careful about limiting the children's contact with the men I've dated. I don't want Em to think that because we're involved, you're a father candidate."

The thought of Elizabeth with other men made him grit his teeth. Her rational tone drove him wild. She was still lying naked under him. How could she dismiss him so easily? "I was not aware you had come to this island to find a father for Emily."

Her eyes sparked. "I didn't. Any more than you came looking for a son. But here we are."

"In your bed," he reminded her.

"Yes." She sighed, releasing her anger with her breath, and touched his taut jaw. "I can accept you won't be around forever. I won't ask Emily to accept it. I think it would be better if you don't see her for a little while. You need to give us some space."

Her barriers were up again, he realized. And he was on the outside. Despite her gentle hands, her rueful tone, her complete and satisfying surrender to him moments ago, she would not compromise where her children were concerned.

Frustrated, he rolled from her to sit on the edge of her mattress. "And Zachary?"

"I won't stop him from seeing you. But if you care for him—if you care for me at all—you'll back off. Give us time."

Instinct and pride, primal, possessive, rose to refute her. Back off now? Leave her when she was vulnerable? When she was his? She would only use the opportunity to withdraw even further behind her formidable defenses.

And yet . . . She had no reason—he had no right—to expect otherwise. *"I can accept you won't be around forever . . ."*

He nodded stiffly, still with his back to her. "Very well. I will come back tomorrow."

"Tomorrow is Saturday. Zack's at the store all day."

"Sunday, then."

"We need one day together as a family."

A family he was not part of.

He cast a sardonic look over his shoulder. "Will one day make such a difference after fifteen years?"

Her smile trembled. "If it's the last day."

Ah, God.

He wanted to reassure her that he would not rip Zachary unwilling from this life and her arms. But he could say nothing until he had spoken to the boy. Zachary was finfolk. The choice must be his.

"How much time do you need?" he asked.

18

≈≈≈

FOR THREE DAYS, IT DID NOTHING BUT RAIN, a hard, cleansing downpour from clouds piled like oyster shells, thick white and luminous gray. The runoff penetrated every cranny of Liz's house and leaked under the duct tape holding her broken window together. The chill permeated her bones. The smell of loam and moss and pine was everywhere. Rain splashed in the road like a river, collecting in puddles on the saturated ground, driving the tourists to the mainland and the islanders to the clinic for every twinge and sniffle aggravated by the creeping damp.

Liz advised ibuprofen, saline rinses, and rest, and wished she had a home care remedy for the anarchy brewing in her heart and head.

"How much time do you need?"

She wished she knew. Morgan's absence ached like a bruise. She had made him promise to stay away from them until she had a chance to think, until she and Zack had a chance to talk, until she could figure out what was best for him and Emily.

But Zack seemed content to say nothing, to do nothing,

to slide through the days and nights with as little fuss as possible, as if ignoring the issue would make it go away.

Part of her was grateful for the respite after the stress of the past few years, the shock of the past few days. She found herself a silent coconspirator in avoidance, doing her best to recapture the rhythm of their earlier life, making pancakes, watching movies, playing Go Fish around the kitchen table as if everything were normal. As if Zack were normal. Hoping, selfishly, that the simple family pleasures, the familiar family routines, would be enough to hold him when the time came.

She knew they would not hold Morgan.

Something had changed the last time they'd made love. In him. In her. She felt it. But his words lay stark between them. *"I cannot promise you a future, Elizabeth."*

She didn't need guarantees, no longer believed in happily-ever-after. But her children deserved stability. Security.

"Are you sure you don't want a ride to work?" she asked Zack at lunchtime on Tuesday.

He grinned. "I don't think a little water will hurt me, Mom. Unless you're worried I'm going to grow gills on my way to Wiley's."

Her pulse bumped. "Very funny," she said dryly. "Don't forget your jacket. You want me to pick you up?"

He accepted the jacket, shrugging into it as he opened the door. "No, I'm good."

"Zack . . ."

"Mom, I've gotta go." His gaze met hers briefly. "I'll be fine."

Would he?

Her eyes blurred as she watched him jump down the porch steps and splash through the yard, a tall, skinny shadow in the silver rain. At the bottom of their driveway, he slid out of the jacket, bundling it under his arm, turning his face to the sky.

His wet profile looked like Morgan's. Her breathing hitched.

She returned to the clinic to see her afternoon patients, an ache in her throat that had nothing to do with the rain.

*   *   *

At the end of the day, the sky had lightened, even if her mood hadn't.

"Bobby Kincaid called," Nancy said as Liz retrieved her wet coat from the stand outside her office. "He should be able to get to your car next week."

"Did he tell you why it's taking so long to fix a simple broken window?"

Nancy shrugged. "We're on an island. It takes time to get parts. And the Kincaid boys were never worth a damn anyway."

Liz sighed. "Fine. I'll call and schedule an appointment."

At least the rain had stopped. She drove to the community center to pick up Emily.

Freed from the gym, the camp kids whooped and splashed on the playground. Em stood under the fort bridge with Nick, inspecting something he'd pulled from his pocket. A bead? A coin? The sight of her daughter's round, absorbed face sent a surge of protective love through Liz's chest.

Regina climbed out of the white catering van parked at the curb. Liz raised a hand in tentative greeting, still slightly embarrassed by the way she'd unloaded on Regina a few days ago. She badly wanted another woman's support. But despite their exclusive club membership, they hadn't known each other long.

Regina waved and hurried over, her brown eyes warm and concerned. "Dylan told me about the fire. You okay?"

"I'm fine." Liz summoned a smile. "Soggy."

"Safe. That's the important thing. And at least it's over now."

Her heart clutched, thinking of Morgan. "Over?"

"The rain," Regina explained. "Margred told the guys she wanted good weather for the baby shower tonight."

"They can do that?"

Regina nodded as if they were talking about changing the batteries in the remote. "They'd better. Nobody rains on Margred's parade. Or her party. She's been looking forward to it for weeks."

Liz blinked. "Wow."

"Yeah." Regina grinned. "Being married to a man who can control the weather is a definite advantage when I have a big catering job."

"I imagine it must be," Liz said faintly.

"You're coming, right?" Regina said. "Tonight?"

She hesitated. Would Morgan be there? She missed him with an almost physical ache, as if they had been lovers for years instead of one evening.

Yet this was a short separation compared to the one to come.

She had survived losing Ben to death. She would survive losing Morgan to the sea.

But she wasn't ready to give up Zack. Not yet. Their son still needed a chance to grow up before he made the most important choice of what could be a very long life. Emily deserved a better role model than a mother who accepted anything less than everything a man had to give.

"I don't want to intrude," she murmured.

"As if you could. You're Maggie's OB. If you don't belong at her baby's shower, I don't know who does. Anyway, half the island will show up, invited or not." Regina cocked her head. "You sure you're okay?"

Liz swallowed around the spiky lump in her throat. "Fine."

"Good." Regina pursed her lips. "Morgan looks like hell."

Liz gaped, flattered and distressed. "Excuse me?"

"He's been palling around with Dylan since you kicked him out. Holding the weather system in place—like it takes the two of them to make rain in Maine—and sulking. Poor guy."

"I thought you didn't like him."

"You mean because I called him a coldblooded son of a bitch?"

"That was a clue," Liz said dryly.

Regina grinned. "Okay, so he's the opposite of warm and fuzzy. But he's good with Nick. And . . . Well, you didn't ask for my opinion."

Ever since her parents cut off all financial support when she failed to follow their advice, Liz never asked for anyone's opinion. But she genuinely liked Regina. She hoped they could be friends. And she was both concerned and curious about Morgan.

"Tell me," she urged.

Regina met her gaze. "Dylan says you told Morgan you need time to think things through."

Liz nodded.

"That was smart," Regina said. "Maybe smarter than you realize."

She hid the pang at her heart. "You think things won't work out."

"I think they might," Regina said, surprising her. "Once Morgan has a chance to figure stuff out. You've got to remember they're no good at this emotional stuff."

"They." *Men?* Liz wondered.

"The children of the sea," Regina explained. "Maybe when you live forever, you can't afford too many attachments. You love a human, they die. You love another elemental, you have to sustain that relationship over centuries. Easier not to love at all."

"But Dylan loves you."

"Dylan had to learn to love me. To love anyone. And he's at least half-human. This is all new territory for Morgan. Whether he admits it or not, he needs time to adjust as much as you do. And the fact that he's at least trying to consider your feelings, to honor your request . . . That's big, coming from an elemental."

"I don't doubt that he cares for me," Liz said. His whisper seared her heart: *"For no other woman—for no other*

force on earth—would I have stayed." "But I have to think
about my kids. Would you get involved with someone who
didn't know how to love your children? Didn't love you
more than his life away from you?"

They both turned to look at the playground.

"No," Regina said quietly. "No way."

Emily dashed up, her halo of soft curls bouncing.
"Mommy, look what I got!"

She tipped back her head to show off the camp lanyard
around her neck. Hanging between with the red "caring
bead" and blue "responsibility bead" was a silver disk with
three interconnected spirals radiating from the center.

Liz bent for a closer look. "That's very . . ." Her breath
hitched. Something about the gleaming medal teased at
her memory. "Pretty."

"It's a triskelion," Regina said.

"A what?"

Regina turned over her wrist, exposing a simplified version of the same symbol tattooed against her pale skin. "It's
a sign of protection. A ward. Earth, sea, and sky—that's
the three curving lines, see?—around a common center."

Liz studied the flowing lines. "You got this for protection?"

Regina grinned. "Hell, no. I got it because I was drunk
and thought it was some kind of female empowerment
thing. It wasn't until I met Dylan that I knew the real meaning. It's a wardens' mark."

Recognition flashed through Liz. That's where she'd
seen that symbol before. The medal was a smaller replica
of the one around Morgan's neck.

"Honey," she asked gently, "where did you get this?"

Emily's gaze fell. "Nick gave it to me."

Liz looked at Regina for confirmation.

"I guess it's possible." Regina scanned the play equipment. "Nick!"

Her son came running, accompanied by a freckled
older boy.

"Did you give something to Emily?"

Nick rubbed the toe of one sneaker in the mud. "Yeah. Sort of."

His freckled friend grinned. "Nick's got a girlfriend, Nick's got a—"

Nick flushed. "Shut up, Danny."

"Which is it, kiddo?" Regina asked. "Yeah, or sort of?"

"Am I in trouble?"

"Not yet," his mother replied.

"Because he said it would be all right."

Liz's heart thumped. "Who said?"

"Morgan. He gave me the medal. To give to Em." Nick met his mother's eyes. "Can I go now?"

"Five more minutes," Regina said. "We need to get ready for Maggie's party tonight."

"Cool," Nick said and ran off.

Liz's mind churned. *Morgan* gave the medal to Em.

A sign of protection, Regina called it. A ward.

Liz looked from the engraved disk to her daughter's shining eyes, and her heart stumbled in her chest.

Even after she'd told him to back off, Morgan had been thinking of Emily. Had tried to protect her.

"*I am attached to her, too,*" he'd said, but so stiffly Liz hadn't understood.

Something constricted her lungs, as insubstantial and painful as hope.

"Mom." Emily tugged on her arm. "Are we going to the party?"

Margred's baby shower. Half the island would be there. Morgan would be there.

Liz took a deep breath, feeling her chest expand with possibilities. "Yes. We are."

*   *   *

Liz held Emily's small, warm hand as they strolled down the grassy slope from the parking lot toward the picnic shelter. Anticipation hummed through her. The saturated ground and the pink glow of the setting sun lent the air an enchanted shimmer, heightened by the fairy lights twined around the shelter's rafters and square wooden supports. Lanterns and rocks anchored red checkered tablecloths fluttering in the breeze. The air was alive with laughter and conversation, the clang of horseshoes, the cry of gulls, and the call of the surf.

It was a night to believe in magic.

In love.

Liz scanned the scene. Looking for Morgan, she admitted to herself. She was a little overdressed, she saw at once, in a blue wrap dress that hugged her waist and floated around her legs. Most of the guests wore jeans and windbreakers or khakis and sweaters. But she'd wanted to look pretty. She wanted to feel young. She'd left her hair loose on her shoulders and slicked an extra layer of mascara on her lashes, a deeper shade of rose on her mouth. She wanted Morgan to look at her and see the girl she'd been sixteen years ago, bright and fearless.

Blankets and camp chairs dotted the grass. A volleyball net stretched across the hard, damp sand. Zack had already joined the knot of teenagers around the cooler holding up one pole. Liz spotted a can in his hand and angled for a closer look. Catching her eye, he smiled crookedly and held it up.

Soda. She smiled back.

On the crescent of shale below the shelter, two huge steel washtubs balanced on rocks a foot above a roaring fire, the red flames competing with the radiance on the horizon. The scent of seaweed rode upward on the steam. The gray waves had the sheen of molten metal.

"Morgan!" Emily shouted as if she hadn't seen him in weeks.

Tugging away from Elizabeth's grasp, she darted to the lone, tall figure at the edge of the water. Liz followed more slowly, her heart beating in her throat.

He looked the same, her shadow rescuer, appearing out of the night. His face was angled, strong, and pale, his hair the color of moonlight. Her gaze slid up his powerful torso to his face, her pulse rioting.

His eyes were guarded and cold.

She put that look there, she realized with regret. When she sent him away. His pride—and her own—demanded she take the first step toward him.

She took a deep breath that did nothing to calm her racing heart. She wished she were as young and sure of her welcome as Em, so she could run, too, and throw her arms around him.

But she wasn't the girl she'd been in Copenhagen. Life and medicine had taught her caution, particularly when the stakes were high and the outcome unpredictable.

She stopped, her courage failing a few yards away.

"I did not know if you would come," Morgan said. "I am glad you did."

His words gave Liz hope.

"We came to see you." She cleared her throat. "To thank you. For, um, the necklace."

"I do not require thanks."

"We're supposed to say it anyway," Emily said.

He glanced down at the little girl attached to his leg like a barnacle to a ship's hull, his austere expression lightening. "Then you may."

"Not like that." She tugged at his arm until he bent over. "Like this," she said and smacked her puckered lips against his cheek.

Morgan looked as stunned as if a butterfly had landed on his knee or he'd been hit with a two-by-four.

Liz's heart swelled. Her eyes swam, blurring the picture they made, the pale, forbidding lord of the finfolk and her dark pixie daughter, so odd together, odd and right, his hand curled protectively over her shoulder, her weight resting against his thigh.

Morgan's gaze locked with hers. A tiny muscle beat at the corner of his mouth. "Are you going to thank me, too?"

Her pulse stuttered. They were attracting attention, she knew, curious and mostly friendly, from her neighbors, her patients, her children.

Her children.

For a moment she froze, nerves quivering in the pit of her stomach. She took two steps toward him, aware of taking a risk, of crossing a line she'd never crossed before.

Could she do it? Could she put the woman before the doctor, before the mother, in such a public way?

First steps, she told herself firmly. Sometimes the outcome was worth the gamble, in medicine and in life.

Standing on tiptoe, she leaned up to brush a kiss against his cheek. At the last moment, he turned his head, and their mouths met.

So soft, so tender, their lips seeking, claiming.

One, two, three long seconds, while her heart did a slow roll in her chest and her blood simmered. All the needs she'd tucked away, all the impulses she'd denied, swam to the surface.

He knew it, too. She felt it in his kiss.

He raised his head, a glint in his eyes.

She was dimly aware of some commotion behind her, scraping metal and billowing steam, shouts of caution and cries of appreciation, but her attention was on Morgan. She pressed her lips together as if she could hold the taste of him inside.

His eyes darkened. His nostrils flared. He wanted her. The knowledge made her giddy, lighthearted with hope, drunk with power.

"Mommy, look! The lobsters are done. See?"

Liz blinked and turned her head. Regina, swathed in a bright red apron, was ordering the transfer of dozens of lobsters and mountains of clams from washtubs draped in seaweed to long metal serving dishes. Volunteers heaped ears of corn in one tray and piles of red potatoes in another. Dylan, his hands in industrial-looking blue gloves, lifted a coffee can of melted butter from the rocks, swearing as the hot metal burnt his fingers.

She wanted this, to be part of this scene, not on the outskirts, an observer. She wanted to share in the joy and abundance. She wanted this life.

With Morgan.

The guests flowed toward the picnic shelter where the tables were set. Regina's lobster boil was augmented by the island potluck, Paula Schutte's tomato salad beside Edith Paine's blueberry cobbler, baked beans and corn bread and hot pepper jelly.

"We should join them," Morgan said. He took her hand, making her start with surprise and pleasure. Had he touched her like this before, so casually possessive? "Before the food is all gone."

She twined her fingers with his, determined to hold on to this moment as long as she could. "My thoughts exactly."

*   *   *

The fire had died to a red glow. The moon wove a silver web across the sea. Liz sat outside the wooden shelter with Morgan, her hand linked with his, her stomach and her heart both full enough to burst.

The teens had drifted away from the volleyball net to flirt in the shadows or sprawl by the fire. She didn't see Zack. But there was Emily, whispering secrets with Hannah Bly under the gift table. Nick rocked his baby sister in an infant carrier. Children ran around the shelter, faces shiny with butter and excitement, as their elders sat with cooling cups of coffee, chewing on brownies and the latest island gossip. Liz saw Dylan back his wife against one of the shelter's columns for a kiss. Margred tipped her head against her husband's shoulder, her eyes as full of dreams as the moon.

Something about the way she stood, her pelvis angled, one hand on her lower back, snagged Liz's attention.

"She didn't eat much," she murmured.

"Who?" Morgan asked.

"Margred."

"She must be the only one who did not."

Liz chuckled. "I may not eat again for a week. But it's nice the way everyone brought something. That's what I moved here hoping to find, that sense of community for Zack and Emily."

"And for yourself."

It was the opening she'd hoped for. Her insides jittered with nerves and anticipation.

"Yes," she admitted. "Of course, it's not easy, coming here as the doctor."

"But they need you."

"They need the medical care I can provide. There's always a distance, a deference, between doctor and patient. I can know the most intimate details of their lives—diet, depression, sexual dysfunction—and never be invited to their homes." She smiled ruefully. "Essentially, I'm an outsider here."

"Alone."

"Yes." She moistened dry lips. This was her moment. This was her chance. "You said once we weren't that different. Maybe we're more alike than either of us thought."

Morgan frowned, his gaze on the fire. "I have never sought to be part of a community. Or committed to anything but my duty."

Her hopes trembled. Her throat squeezed. "Is that a warning?" she asked with false lightness.

"An explanation, Elizabeth." He looked at her, his eyes dark in the light of the fire. "The finfolk are fluid by nature. It is our strength and our weakness. We are not bound by any form or by the land or by ties of family or affection. But . . ."

The water whispered and sighed. She waited, her pulse scrambling, hoping he would tell her, wishing he would ask her . . .

"Your children need me," he said finally. "You need me."

She did. Oh, she did.

She could live without him, had managed fine without him. But she wanted more in her life. She wanted passion. Joy. Magic.

"I have seen Dylan with his family," he continued heavily. "I will stay."

He took her breath away. He was offering her everything she dreamed of, everything she wanted.

Except the words she needed most to hear.

The scrape of pots, the clatter of serving dishes, seemed a world away. She heard a soft exclamation and a thump from one of the picnic tables, but all her attention was focused on the man beside her.

Her gaze searched his face. He didn't look like a man offering to share his life with the woman he loved. He looked like a soldier charged with a difficult mission.

Or a prisoner facing a jail sentence.

She sucked in air, letting it out slowly. "Is that what you want?"

He regarded her without speaking, his hard, beautiful face unreadable. Maybe he didn't know how to answer. As Regina said, this emotional stuff was all new to him.

Or maybe his silence was his answer. The thought slid into her chest like a knife.

"It's not that I don't appreciate the offer," she said gently. "I do. I know what you are and what you have to do. I can handle that. I wouldn't be the only woman to hold it together while her man was away at sea for long periods of time. As long as I knew that you missed us. As long as I knew you wanted to be with us."

His jaw set. "I have said I will stay."

Love and hurt and exasperation churned inside her. "I'm asking if you *want* us."

"I want you . . . to be safe," he said carefully. "I can make you happy."

Her heart was breaking. He was breaking her heart.

"That's such a wonderful thing to say." She swallowed hard. "Such a generous, wonderful, *wrong* thing to say."

"Then tell me," he snapped. "You want to control everything. Tell me what you want me to say."

Love and disappointment surged, breaking her control. "I want to know if you love me!" she shouted.

Her raised voice carried across the beach. The commotion from the picnic shelter stopped. Conversations died.

"Um, Liz?" Regina stood before them, twisting her hands in her red apron. "I'm sorry to interrupt this. But Margred needs you. Now."

*   *   *

Now. Zack's pulse pounded in his head. Throbbed against his fly. He squeezed his hand a half-inch farther between soft flesh and rough denim, *almost there, almost there, almost . . .*

Stephanie's breath caught. Her stomach muscles jumped against his wrist. "Zack, no."

He couldn't think. He could barely breathe. All the blood in his body had deserted his brain for his dick. "You're so . . ." *Warm. Soft.* "Pretty, Stephanie. Let me . . ."

She wriggled. "No."

No.

The word crashed and echoed in his empty skull. His body went rigid, all the parts of him that weren't stiff already.

"Please, Zack." She lay under him on the flat granite ledge, her eyes enormous, shiny in the moonlight.

Please.

Swallowing hard, he worked his hand out of her jeans, curling his fingers against the sense of loss. Rolling off her, he flung himself back, rapping his head hard against the rock.

Stars. Fireworks.

She gasped. Giggled. "Are you all right?"

"No. But I'll recover." He dragged air into his lungs. The granite was cool against his back, the air cool against his front. "Probably. In a couple of hours."

Stephanie shifted. Lifted. He saw a brief flash of white hip and blue thong before she zipped up her jeans.

He closed his eyes, frustrated. Aching. "Why?" The word burst out of him.

He heard a rustle as she settled beside him on the rock. "You mean, why not?"

"I mean . . ." Why did she have to think so much? "I guess."

"I like you, Zack. I really do. But I don't want to get pregnant, okay? I'm only sixteen. I don't want to get knocked up and have to take some dead-end job for my father and work on the island the rest of my life."

That was reasonable. Not that he felt very reasonable at the moment. But he opened his eyes. "I could use a condom."

"Do you have a condom?"

Hot blood swept his face. "No. But I could bring one. Next time."

His mother kept a box in the bedside table. *No.*

He could buy them from the grocery store. But then he'd have to worry about hiding his purchase from Mr. Wiley. And Dot. And every other fucking busybody on the whole fucking island.

But he would do it. For Stephanie.

"Zack, that's sweet. But it's not just about the condom. I don't want to get involved, not all the way involved, with anybody yet. I'm not ready to be part of a couple. I'm still all about me. I want to go to college. I want to travel. I want options."

Rejection was hot in his body, bitter in his mouth. "You want options more than you want me."

Her eyes widened slightly. "Well . . . Yeah. And so should you."

Options. *Jesus.*

His lungs hurt. His eyes burned. What options did he have? He was a kid, a freak, stuck in a body he couldn't control from a father he barely knew.

He wanted . . . Stephanie. Something.

His longing pushed and twisted inside him in great, slippery coils, fighting to bust out. He had to get out, get away, before he exploded.

"Fine." He pulled himself together, pushed himself to his feet, held out his hand to help her up. "Let me walk you back."

Hesitantly, she took his hand. "Zack . . ."

But he didn't want to talk anymore. He didn't want to

think. He stalked beside her without speaking until they could see the picnic shelter, the lights and the fire and people bustling under the roof. Something was going on. He didn't care. He waited until Stephanie had stumbled halfway down the slope before he took off, running, into the night.

Toward the sea.

19

❦

THE DOCTOR IN ELIZABETH TOOK OVER, PUSH-
ing all emotion, the regret and the pain, aside. She would
deal with Morgan and her feelings for him later.

Now she had a patient in active labor and an imminent
delivery on her hands.

"We need to transport," she ordered, her voice brisk
and professional. The doctor was confident even when the
woman inside wanted to crawl away and lick her wounds.

"She won't make it," Caleb said.

"Not to the hospital," Liz agreed.

Sixty minutes by lobster boat, twenty by LifeFlight.
Margred's contractions were less than three minutes apart
and over a minute long. If Liz hadn't been so focused on
her own conversation with Morgan . . .

She shook her head. No time for second-guessing or
guilt. "The clinic," she said.

Margred took a few short, careful steps from the shelter
toward the beach. "I am sitting now," she announced.

Sitting was good. The risk of infection made an internal

examination in the field impossible, but Liz still needed to check Margred's progress. A change of position might even slow labor. But Margred was heading in the wrong direction.

"Not in the sand," Liz said.

Caleb took his wife's arm. "You can sit in the Jeep."

"Here," Margred said. Gripping his muscled forearm, she lowered herself heavily to the beach.

His other arm came around her immediately for support. He knelt beside her. "Sweetheart . . ." His deep voice shook with nerves and laughter. "This wasn't in the birth plan."

She shook back her hair, smiling up at him. "Not your plan."

"Maggie . . ."

"Ah." She bit her lip, her face contracting in pain.

Liz dropped beside them, put an encouraging hand on Margred's knee. "All right, now you're down, let's see what that baby is up to."

She looked around, evaluating the crowded shelter, the dark beach. Dear God.

"What do you need?" Dylan asked.

"Light. Drapes. Pads. Those tablecloths? Clean ones, if you've got them. And my bag. In my car." She reached automatically for her keys, but the pretty blue dress lacked pockets. Half-rising, she craned her neck for her purse.

"Here." Her black medical bag appeared as if by magic, held in a strong, long-fingered hand. She looked up and met Morgan's eyes.

Her heart lurched. How did he . . .

He smiled thinly. "Your back window is broken."

Her mouth jarred open.

Margred grunted.

Liz's head snapped back around. She focused on her patient. "Don't push."

"I am having a baby," Margred said with some irritation. "I must push sometime."

"Not yet," Liz said firmly.

Not until, please God, they got to the clinic, where she had IVs. Oxygen. Clean sheets.

She scrubbed her hands and arms liberally with hand sanitizer, prepared to do a quick check and transport. A cursory examination, however, revealed Margred and her baby had no intention of waiting for sterile surroundings. The child was already crowning, each contraction forcing its damp, dark head to the entrance of the birth canal.

Liz's stomach rolled and then settled. She was trained for this. Not practiced, perhaps, but trained.

Margred panted, her hair sticking to her flushed face.

"The Jeep?" Caleb said.

Liz inhaled, her mind racing. This was an emergency, not a disaster. Margred was in good health. Excellent history. Normal fetal presentation. Women had babies away from the hospital all the time.

But Liz hadn't delivered one since her OB rotation more than ten years ago.

And she'd never delivered a selkie baby.

She gave herself a mental shake. She'd seen the ultrasound images. Margred's baby was human. As human as Zack.

She summoned a reassuring smile. "I think we'll all be fine here."

"Here," Caleb said sharply.

"Mm." Liz completed her examination, patted Margred's foot. They had a few minutes to prepare. "Dylan, can you move people . . . Thanks."

Under the swathing tablecloth, she adjusted Margred's clothing.

"Mommy?" Emily's voice was high and thin.

"Your mommy's busy right now, kiddo," Regina said. "Come wait with me and Nick over here. You've seen our baby, right? Grace, this is . . ."

Their voices faded away.

Thank God for Regina. Liz ran through the remembered birth protocol in her head while she sorted through her kit for the supplies she would need. *Gloves, alcohol, bulb syringe, scissors* . . . First pregnancy, she thought. No known problems, due date . . . Well, the date was irrelevant now.

Time slowed. Her world narrowed to the laboring woman on the beach, Caleb supporting her back. Lanterns cast pools of light on hard gray sand, the checkered tablecloths. Margred arched, strained, panted, pushed, her hands gripping her knees, her body rippling as contractions rolled through her.

"Good job," Liz murmured. Sweat rolled down her back and dampened her bra. Her skirt was smeared with blood and fluid. "Another push, now. Gently."

The crown, the brow, small, dark, scrunched . . . No cord. Good. Liz slipped her hand to support the baby's head, easing it to the side, remembering the pain of her own babies' births, the pain and the joy.

Margred groaned, deep and guttural. Her war-hardened husband turned pale.

Stroking her hair from her sweaty face, he pressed a kiss to her forehead. "You're doing great."

But she wasn't.

Tension seized Liz. The head was free, but the baby's shoulders hadn't cleared the birth canal. Margred's face was ashen, her lips cracked. Her blood pressure could be dropping. She needed fluids. She needed . . .

"Can you push?" Liz asked, keeping her voice steady. "Margred, you have to push now."

A great cry burst from her.

Liz winced. "Easy," she soothed.

God damn it, she wanted her equipment. Monitors, fluids, an operating room . . .

Caleb held his wife. "*Maggie.*"

She writhed. A long shadow fell across her swollen belly. Morgan, striding from the sea, water dripping from his cupped hands.

"Get out of my light," Liz snapped.

He ignored her, kneeling by Margred as she labored.

Her dark eyes were wide, her mouth open in distress. He dipped into his palm, laid his finger on her tongue, murmuring as he did so.

She gasped. Her bowed body suddenly sagged as she gripped her husband's hand. Her face flushed. And her child was delivered into Liz's hands, perfect, slippery. Beautiful.

Wonder shuddered through her. But her reaction was unimportant. Nothing mattered but the infant in her care. She concentrated on her job, *support, wipe, suction.*

Caleb met Morgan's eyes. "What did you say?"

Morgan shrugged. "Nothing. A blessing."

"'Born of water, for the water,'" Dylan translated. "'Drink deep and live.'"

"Congratulations, you have a son," Liz announced. Blinking tears from her eyes, she leaned forward to lay the wet, dusky infant, still attached to his cord, on Margred's tummy, skin to skin.

Holding her own breath, Liz listened for his first cry.

Waited, her heart racing. Her jaw tensed. Firmly, she stroked the infant's back.

Margred struggled to sit up. "What is it? What's wrong?"

Liz stroked again, harder, willing him to breathe. "Come on, little guy."

Caleb's big hand cupped the small, damp skull. "Born of water . . ." His voice cracked.

Liz reached for the baby to straighten his airway, to force air into his tiny lungs.

Margred's hand covered her husband's. She touched the baby's dark, pursed lips. "For the water," she whispered. "Drink deep and live."

Their son's wavering cry rose to the stars and the sea.

* * *

Morgan's arms flexed as he carried the washtub over his head from the beach to the catering van. Elizabeth was in the parking lot, leaning in the window of Caleb's Jeep, speaking to Margred in the back seat.

Elizabeth. Admiration for her moved him, for her calm in a crisis, her steady hands, her clear head, her warm heart. She was a remarkable woman.

His woman.

He slammed the van's doors.

"Nancy's getting your exam room all ready." Her voice carried across the gravel and under the trees. "I'll meet you there."

A murmur from Margred.

"As soon as we get you both checked out, you can go home," Elizabeth said, brisk and reassuring. "You drive carefully."

"I didn't think we'd be using the infant seat this soon," Caleb said. "Thanks, Liz."

"My pleasure. What are you going to name him?"

"Calder." Margred's voice came clearly from the back-seat.

From the wild water, Morgan translated silently.

"Nice," Elizabeth said. She stepped back with a wave as they drove away. Turning toward her own car, she saw Morgan.

She still wore her professional face, he saw, but behind her cool composure emotion flickered. He took a step closer for the simple pleasure of hearing her breath hitch, of seeing her eyes darken before she wrested her mask back into place.

"Nice job, Doctor."

Some of the wariness left her shoulders. She smiled, the lines digging deeper at the corners of her eyes. "Margred did the work."

"The bulk of it," he acknowledged. "But you helped."

"So did you."

He moved in, stalking her. "We were good together."

"Yes." She cleared her throat, edging toward her vehicle. "Thanks. You'll have to tell me sometime how that trick with the water works. But right now, I have to—"

He fingered a strand of her hair, cutting off her voice. He heard the quick intake of her breath. He knew her adrenaline was still high, her pulse still racing. She was ripe with sweat and salt and birth, earth and sea commingled.

He wanted her, craved her, the way he had never craved anything but the sea.

He had not seen their son born, his and Elizabeth's. He had not thought about it before, what it must have been like for her, what he had missed.

All he was missing.

He thought of Caleb tenderly supporting Margred's wracked body, of Dylan and Regina working instinctively as a team.

Elizabeth's words teased him. *"Is that what you want?"*

"Was he there with you when our son was born?" he asked. "Your husband."

"I, um . . ." It pleased him that it took her a moment to focus, to find her place in the conversation. "No. Ben and I weren't . . . We were just friends then. We got married about a year later."

She had told him once she was estranged from her parents. Did that mean . . .

"You were alone," he said.

Elizabeth's brows twitched together. She raised her chin, on the defensive. "The nurses were there for me. The doctor on call. I was a student there. I knew people."

His jaw set until it cracked. She would not admit to being vulnerable. She would not admit to needing him.

Her strength was laudable. Her pride was understandable. He had the same strength, the same pride. He must persuade her to lean on him, to trust in him.

He raised his arms, caging her against the side of her SUV. She stiffened. "I will be there for you," he murmured. He pressed his lips to her cheek, her brow. "I will stay with you." Remembering her words, he amended quickly. "I want to stay." He nuzzled her throat, delighting in the wild leap of her pulse, her involuntary tremble. "You need me."

Her hands tightened in his hair. "I need you."

He kissed the tender hollow under her ear, scenting her capitulation, tasting victory. "Yes."

She tugged, pulling back his head. "*I* need *you*."

He nodded cautiously, alerted by the shift in her emphasis, the spark in her eyes. "Yes. There is no harm, no shame, in needing someone."

Her gaze was pointed, her smile rueful. "Not unless he doesn't need you back."

Morgan gaped. She had played him. With one neat sentence, in one swift reversal, he was hooked. Reeled in. Eviscerated.

"I won't ask you to be anything less than what you are," Elizabeth continued, inexorable as the tide. "But I can't be less than who I am either. I'm not some coddled, weak woman in need of protection. I'm a woman who's made a career for herself, a life, and a home for her babies. I don't need you to take care of me. To take care of us. I need you to love me."

He floundered, out of his element. "I do not see you as weak. I want to care for you because you are . . . precious to me. You and your children."

"But do you love me? Can you love us?"

Fear and frustration churned inside him. His head was reeling, his heart in turmoil, his pride in tatters. "I want you. I trust you. I need you." He shot the words at her. "Is that love?"

Her breathing hitched.

She held his gaze, her brown eyes softening, glistening with tears. Morgan cursed silently. He had not meant to make her cry.

But slowly, her lips curved. "It'll do. Thank you. It will do wonderfully. For now."

He did not understand her. His heart banged in his chest as it did during battle.

One of them had won, he thought. But he didn't know who.

She sighed. "I have to go now. I promised to meet Margred and Caleb at the clinic. Can I drop you at the inn?"

He stared at her blindly, trying not to shake, trying not to panic, wanting her desperately, needing . . .

What?

Her. Only her. But she had no time for him, she was going to care for Margred and her baby. As she should, as she must. *"I can't be less than who I am either."*

He shook his head, disgusted with himself. There was no shame in needing someone.

Not unless she didn't need you back.

She did need him. She had said so.

"I will walk," he said. "To clear my head."

She smiled again, hesitantly. "Zack does that. I thought it was a boy thing, but maybe he gets it from you."

Zachary.

His mind cleared, sharpened.

"Where is he?"

Elizabeth blinked. "I don't know. I lost track of him during dinner, and after Margred started labor, I didn't have time to look." She bit her lip. "I should have. Regina and Dylan are watching Emily, but—"

"I will find him," he interrupted. "We will wait for you at home."

* * *

The water wrapped Zack like a fist, tight and comforting. Familiar. He shuddered in relief as it sheathed his sensitized skin, as the current yanked him along into cool, dark oblivion.

He didn't need Stephanie. He didn't need anybody. If she had places to go, so did he.

Places she would never go.

He didn't mean to swim so far. It just sort of happened, like staying out too late or drinking too much, the situation under control until you stopped paying attention and then, oops, there you were, staring at seven messages from home or puking vodka and Gatorade into the toilet of the Stoddards' basement powder room.

Or sliding through the liquid dark toward a crevice in the rock, heart thumping, blood pumping, the beat of the orb pulsing like the surge of the ocean.

He flicked his tail, and smaller fish scattered. Ha.

"You must not go into the water until you have learned to defend yourself."

He was fine. He could go back. Anytime. He would go back, as soon as he saw it again. That big shiny garden globe. The orb.

He could feel it vibrating like music, like heavy bass, in the cavities of his skull and along his skin. It drew him like a current closer to the roots of the island, closer to a fissure in the rock.

Closer.

Was that a glow? Pretty blue playing over the sandy bottom, exposing a litter of empty shells, a decaying skeleton. Caution brushed him like seaweed swaying in the dark.

Morgan didn't want him to be here.

Morgan could go fuck himself.

The thought slid into Zack's mind, not really his thought. Funny. Rude. Wrong.

He glided closer. The sand had drifted, exposing a slice of the glowing globe, like a sickle moon, like a dragon's half-shut eye. Colors swirled and throbbed in its depths, luring him on, luring him in. The rhythm of the orb grew stronger, catching up and overtaking the rhythm of his heart. Like he had two hearts. Two pulses. Two minds.

Who did Morgan think he was anyway?

My father, he thought.

Some father. Just because he's screwing your mother . . .

Zack thrashed and the pulse faltered, finding a subtly different rhythm, stirring up memories and resentment like sediment on the ocean floor. His emotions churned.

Ben was your father. The thought hooked him, drew him closer. *The fisherman, not the fish.*

Zack struggled, but the light of the orb was in his eyes, the throb of the orb was in his blood, the voice of the orb was in his head, implacable, inescapable.

Closer. *Touch me. You don't have to be alone.*

Closer. *Release me. I can give you what you want. Women. Stephanie.*

256   VIRGINIA KANTRA

He drifted, dazzled.

Caught.

A terrible jerk seized his body, immobilized his will. Pain lanced through him, pitiless, paralyzing. The orb drew him closer, reeled him in like a fish flailing on the end of a line.

He touched it and it shattered. The shock jolted through him, convulsing his body, stunning his mind. He fought, screaming inside his head. But the Thing that had him wouldn't let go.

*   *   *

Liz smiled as she locked the clinic doors. Despite her assurance that she would be fine, Caleb had insisted she leave with them.

"I'm a cop," he explained simply. "I don't want to get in a situation where I left you alone and something happened."

Liz tucked her keys into her purse. "No middle-of-the-night phone calls?" she teased.

His smile crinkled his warm green eyes. "I think we've had enough excitement for one night."

"And we will have our sleep interrupted enough as it is," Margred added, cuddling their newborn son against her shoulder.

"It'll take a little time to get in a routine," Liz said. "Just rest when he does, and you'll be fine. Tired, but fine. I'll drop by tomorrow and see how you're all doing."

They walked together to their cars. Observing the new family, Liz felt a lump rise in her throat. Their joy, warm and real and palpable, wrapped them as securely as the baby's receiving blanket. Love was so often in the details, she thought. In the tender touch of Caleb's hand on the small of Margred's back or the way she leaned her cheek against his arm. In their laughter as they fumbled with the new infant seat. In their tenderness with each other and with their baby.

She could have that, Liz thought as she drove through

the moon-washed night. A life, a home, a family, with Morgan. Maybe he didn't have all the right words yet to tell her that he loved her. But he needed her. He trusted her. He wanted to stay. It was enough, more than enough, for now.

Anticipation tingled through her. She was glad Regina had called to tell her Emily had fallen asleep watching a movie and could stay until morning. Not that Liz intended to, well, *do* anything with their fifteen-year-old son upstairs. She might want to rip Morgan's clothes off, but she still had to set an example. And Zack still needed time to adjust to Morgan's presence in their lives.

She smiled. Maybe she and Morgan could neck in the hammock. Assuming Zack was home and asleep, of course.

Oh, she hoped he was home and asleep.

But when she pulled into the driveway, all the windows were blazing. *All* the windows. Every light in the house must be on.

Liz frowned. Zack was definitely home. Only a teenager was that careless with utilities.

She climbed the porch steps, an odd misgiving squeezing her lungs, dragging at her feet. The front door was unlocked. Her heart thumped. Really, that was *too* careless. She'd told Zack and told him . . .

"Zachary?"

The living room was empty. The downstairs was quiet. If Zack were home, where was Morgan?

She set her medical bag in the hall, hanging her purse over the banister. The house was too warm, as if someone had fiddled with the thermostat.

"Zack!" She pitched her voice to carry up the stairs. "I want to talk to you."

No answer. He must be listening to his iPod.

Annoyed, she started up the stairs. He was fifteen and finfolk. He still had to follow the rules.

Sure, this was Maine. They had one of the lowest crime rates in the country. But he shouldn't be up in his room with the door unlocked. Anyone could walk right in.

His bedroom door was closed. She tapped. "Zack?"

"Don't come in." His voice was strained. Urgent.

What was he doing in there?

She grimaced. Okay, she could think of several things a fifteen-year-old could be doing alone in his room that he might not want his mother to see.

"Honey, we need to talk."

"No." He sounded really upset, almost as if he'd been crying.

She leaned closer to the door. "Are you all right?"

"No."

Maybe he was sick. Maybe . . . "I'm coming in," she warned and opened the door.

Zack huddled in the narrow space between his bed and the wall, curled in a tight ball, his arms wrapped around his knees. Concern clutched her heart. His face was flushed, his eyes fever bright and miserable.

She started across the room toward him. "Zack, what's wrong?"

"I don't know. Stay away."

She heard a sound—*the front door opening?*—from downstairs, but her attention was on her son.

"Do you have a fever?" She reached to brush a hand over his forehead the way she had a thousand times during his childhood.

He jerked his head away. *"Don't touch me!"*

"Zack." She stared at him, shocked, dismayed. "What's the matter with you? Did you take something? Did someone give you something?"

"He has been possessed," Morgan said grimly from the doorway. "By the demon Tan."

20

❧

ZACK WANTED TO HOWL. *IT WASN'T RIGHT, IT wasn't fair, Morgan wasn't supposed to be here, he would tell her everything, he was ruining everything . . .*

He gripped his head, fighting the pain, struggling for control of his own brain. No, that wasn't right, Morgan was his father, he was supposed to make things better, he was trying to help.

"What happened?" the woman—his mother—asked. "When did you get here?"

"I tracked them from the beach," Morgan said. "Zachary and the other."

Fishy bastard. The wave of rage burned Zack's throat until he nearly puked. *If Morgan hadn't shown up, none of this would have happened, everything would be all right.*

One heart. One pulse.

Two minds.

He struggled for control.

"What other?" The woman turned to him. "Zack? What's going on?"

She was killing him with her questions. She was wearing her fake, everything's-fine doctor face, but her eyes were wide and worried. *Scared. He liked that. He liked scaring her.*

Zack shuddered. No, he didn't.

"Don't want . . ." He choked the words past the constriction of his lungs, the searing in his throat. "To hurt."

"It's okay, honey. We'll take care of you," she said. "We'll take care of everything."

Stupid. She was stupid. She didn't understand.

Stop. Zack tried again, wresting another tiny victory from the demon. "Don't want to hurt . . . anybody."

Morgan said, "You won't."

Hate him. Hate him. Hate.

Zack hissed in pain.

Just for fun, the demon rolled his eyes back in his head and growled. "Fuck off, fish face. I'll suck your bones."

The woman gasped. Even Morgan, the big bad demon hunter of the deep, looked shaken. The demon laughed, hot energy spurting through him. It was *good* to be free. Three long years in the damp and the cold and the dark . . .

Tan wished he could stay long enough to enjoy himself, to feed on the pain of the human woman, to drink her despair. But his freedom was more important than his revenge. He must not underestimate his foe.

Margred, the sea bitch, had entrapped him.

Morgan, the warden, had the power to destroy him.

Tan forced the boy's reluctant limbs to uncurl, jerking his captive body to its feet like a marionette on wires. His borrowed eyes shifted from window to door and back again. He needed to be free. He needed to escape. Morgan would end him otherwise.

But . . .

Morgan would not be so quick to end his son. This body was Zack's body, the warden's seed, his legacy.

Tan's hostage.

The demon eyed the window again, balancing on his borrowed feet, gauging the distance and his chances.

Morgan slid forward into the room, putting the woman behind him. Seeing his opportunity, the demon sprang. But at the last second, the boy refused to cooperate, dragging his feet, throwing his arms wide, fingers scrabbling for the window frame, crying in fear.

"No! I'll fall!" Zack shouted.

Tan screamed in frustration, punishing the boy's disobedience, pouring fire along nerves and sinews, forcing him to release his grip. Too late.

He stumbled.

Morgan seized him from behind and whirled him around. Pain cracked Tan's jaw, knocked his head back.

He felt his host body sinking, felt unconsciousness reach and wrap him, trapping him in a useless shell.

Nononononooo . . .

It was so unfair.

* * *

Liz pleated her fingers together in her lap, trying to stop their shaking, struggling for calm in a situation in which she had no control.

Her son, her boy, her baby Zack, was in the grip of a demon. And she didn't know how to fight it. How to defeat it. How to fix this.

Morgan paced the kitchen, strong and vital and violent. Her eyes followed him.

She had faith in him. She had to have faith in him. The only alternative was despair.

"How long do we have?" she asked, fighting to keep her voice steady, to think past her terror.

Morgan's mouth compressed. "Perhaps five minutes until he regains consciousness. The bonds may buy us a little more time."

The bonds. She winced.

Morgan had tied up her son, their son, with latex tourniquets from her medical bag. Zack was lying trussed in the living room like a mental patient or a prisoner. Zack and Not Zack. She shivered.

Even bound, Morgan hadn't trusted him alone upstairs.
He didn't trust him in the same room either.

"The demon must not touch you," he had explained
when he carried Zack's prone body to the couch.

She'd looked at her son, helpless even to smooth the hair
that had fallen across his white face. A purpling shadow
rose on his jaw. "Why not?"

"Tan could possess you next."

She had flinched, her face stiff, her heart numb with
fear.

But her mind refused to rest.

"We can't leave him tied up indefinitely," she said.
Calm, when she felt like screaming. "What are you going
to do?"

Morgan turned to face her, every movement taut with
leashed frustration. "The demon is fire. He needs air to
survive. If the demon's air is cut off, he will die."

Shock held her still. Her heart pounded. "Then so will
Zack."

Morgan met her eyes. "Yes."

A single word, sharp and solid as an axe. It cleaved her
heart in two.

No. She was a doctor. Zack's mother, for God's sake.
Think. There had been that other doctor, the one who lived
here before. The possessed one. What had Morgan said?
*"When a demon will not exit its host, the only recourse is
to rend its victim's body uninhabitable . . . Regina bashed
her head in with a table leg."*

Liz drew a shaky breath. And realized what she had
to do.

*   *   *

The latex ties dug into his wrists. The damn things would
not tear. Tan was forced to dislocate the boy's shoulder
simply so he could reach the ties with his teeth. In a captive
corner of his mind, he heard Zack's guttural sobs, but pain
to his host did not bother the demon. He gnawed through
the bindings on one wrist and then, with his arms free,

snapped the joint back into place with a sickening crunch. Tan did not know how long he would inhabit this body, and he wanted to keep it functional. His to command, his own little finfolk lordling.

Wouldn't *that* annoy Morgan. The thought made Tan smile even as the one inside him fought his control.

But first they must get away.

Tan could hear the warden's voice through the white paneled door, and the woman, arguing. Deciding what to do about their precious son, no doubt.

Tan twitched sinew and muscle, forcing the boy's cooperation as he bent to release his ankles. The clumsiness of his injured arm made the demon hiss in irritation. Perhaps he would find another body after all. Plenty to choose from, once he was free. He would quite enjoy . . . sampling. The demon had old scores to settle on this island, if he could get around the pesky wards. And that girl, the one who occupied so many of the boy's thoughts, seemed appetizing. Tan would have her, one way or the other.

The door swung open. *Morgan.*

And the woman, but she was human. Female. No threat at all.

Tan jerked the boy to his feet. The warden worried Tan. But Morgan would be hampered by his concern for Zack. The demon had no such handicap. "You should have tied me tighter, fishface."

Morgan prowled forward without answering.

Tan frowned. He needed a distraction.

He saw the woman, scurrying behind Morgan, reaching for the soft black bag on the floor of the hall. She did not look at him. He did not want her in the hall. She was in his way.

The demon grinned and ran his tongue over his borrowed teeth, riffling quickly through his host's memories. "Mommy, he hurt me," he said in the voice of four-year-old Zack.

The woman stiffened. Morgan circled closer. Tan edged away.

"Help me," he called like a lost child. "Help me, Mommy."

For a moment, she squeezed her eyes shut, as if in pain. Stupid bitch. Taking advantage of her blindness, Tan sprang, quick as a fish in his borrowed body.

But Morgan rushed them, *whump*, hard, slamming Tan/Zack brutally to the floor. The demon overcame his shock, the pain, wresting control as they slithered, scrambled, rolled across the living room. Morgan grabbed him, wrapping them in his brute arms. Tan snapped at his wrist, spat in his face.

"You can't hurt me," he taunted. "Not without hurting your spawn."

"I do not intend to hurt you," Morgan said, curiously calm.

Tan exerted himself, wriggling furiously to get away. The body he inhabited was almost a match for the warden's. The boy had inherited his sire's height. But the warden had weight on his side.

"And you can't end me," Tan said breathlessly. "So you might as well let me go."

"No, I can't end you," Morgan said. "But she can."

"She . . ." Tan twisted the boy's head to see.

It was the damn woman, approaching with a syringe in her hand. Bitch, bitch, bitch.

Tan bucked and writhed. Betrayal burst from deep within him. "Mommy, no! Mommy, don't hurt me!"

Tears ran down her face. "I'm so sorry," she whispered. "But it's for the best."

The demon howled in disbelief as she leaned over them, jabbing the needle deep into his arm. "Murderer! Murderer! Bitch!"

She squeezed the plunger. Tan tried to reach her, to punish her, to possess her, but she stumbled back, weeping, and Morgan grabbed him tight. They rolled, thrashing, across the floor, crashing into the coffee table, Morgan on top. Morgan was crushing the boy's chest. He needed air.

Tan needed air.

Something was wrong. The body he inhabited was sluggish. Clumsy. Unresponsive. Tan felt dizzy. Weak. Horrified, he felt his host's breath begin to seize, his heart begin to slow.

"You have five minutes," Morgan said in the boy's ear. "For the drug to take full effect, before this body is useless to you. Will you stay with it and die?"

He was bluffing, Tan thought frantically. He must be bluffing. He would not sacrifice his own son.

"I hate this," the woman sobbed. "I hate . . ."

You.

Morgan raised his head to look at her, Hell in his eyes. "I should have kept you safe. I should have kept both of you safe."

Tan wavered. Was it possible? No, it couldn't be. But the boy's body was fading, failing him. He could not breathe. He needed air.

Morgan leaned harder. The boy's lungs compressed. Spots danced in the demon's blurring vision. His energy flickered.

"Will you come out, Tan?" Morgan taunted. "Will you come out and fight?"

* * *

Cold sweat beaded on Morgan's brow. Beneath him, the demon stared out of Zachary's eyes, a feverish, rabid glow.

Morgan increased his pressure on the boy's ribcage, praying he did not crack a rib, expelling a puff of breath that brushed his cheek like smoke.

And then Zack convulsed and vomited Tan out in a column of flame.

The demon erupted in a blaze of defiance, a fire of hate, leaping for the ceiling, reaching for the door.

Triumph seared Morgan. Heat singed his face, his chest, his arms.

He battled back with cold fury, calling the wind to seal the windows, to shut the door, containing the demon, closing him in. With grim purpose, Morgan summoned the smothering weight of magic. Power rose in him, smooth and high and hard as a wave, a great surge of power fueled by love and rage. It gathered inside him, churned inside him, towered inside him, taller than the demon's fire.

He directed the wall of magic down, crashing down on the cowering flame. *"Tan, I extinguish you!"*

And the demon snuffed out.

Morgan's heart pounded. Zachary lay abandoned, twisted on the floor. Fear wrenched Morgan's chest. This did not feel like victory. Elizabeth's protest seared his memory. *"Then Zack will die."*

But her use of the drug had deceived the demon. Zachary was heavily sedated. Unconscious, but alive. And Elizabeth was already scrambling forward, falling on her knees at their son's head, her black kit open by her side.

Morgan stood, watching helplessly, as she grabbed a pillow from the couch and bunched it under the boy's neck. She straightened his head, tilted his chin.

"It'll be okay," she crooned, promised, exhorted. To which one of them? "You'll be okay. You just need a little help breathing until this wears off."

She ripped an angled tube like a blade from its plastic sheath. Morgan winced as she wedged the boy's mouth open and slowly, smoothly slid the tube past his tongue and down his throat.

"Call Caleb," she ordered. Tears streaked her face, but her eyes never left their son. With deft, sure hands, she attached a bag to the tube protruding from Zachary's mouth. "He's going to need a stretcher."

* * *

Zack needed more than a stretcher. Phenobarbital caused a depression of the body's central and peripheral nervous systems, slowing the body's functions, including the electrical activity of the brain.

Elizabeth shivered, leaning her head against the back of

her chair, exhaustion pounding in her temples, guilt like a stone in her chest.

There was no antidote for barbiturate poisoning. Until Zack's body rid itself of the drug, his airway needed to be maintained by mechanical ventilation.

He lay motionless on a clinic bed, clear tubes in his arm and down his throat, machines monitoring his blood pressure, heart rate, oxygen, and respiration.

Dawn crept around the edges of the blinds, gray and cold.

He still hadn't regained consciousness.

"Regina is taking Emily to camp." Morgan spoke from the door of the examination room. "She will pick her up, too, if necessary."

If Zack didn't improve. If he didn't wake up.

Liz closed her eyes, sick at heart.

"That's quite a bump on his jaw," Morgan remarked. Liz opened her eyes. He stood over their son's bedside, surveying the damage. "Will he remember I hit him when he wakes up?"

Liz roused herself to answer. "He may. He might not. Phenobarbital can affect short-term memory." She shuddered, reliving the moment when she'd stuck him with the drug. *"Mommy, don't hurt me."* "I hope he forgets," she said passionately.

"You did what you must to deceive the demon," Morgan said, reading her thoughts with surprising accuracy. "Tan would have killed him and destroyed his soul in the process. You saved him. You saved our son. No one else could have done what you did."

Liz had stood vigil at many bedsides, comforting and reassuring. She was the doctor, the expert, the person patients and family could turn to for guidance. For answers.

But with Morgan, she could be the one to ask. She held his gaze, sharing her deepest fear. "What if he doesn't make it?"

Morgan took her hand. "He will make it. We will make it." He sat on the arm of her chair, holding their clasped hands together on his thigh, his touch warm. Reassuring. Strong. "I love you, Elizabeth."

His words seeped into her, rain to her parched and worried heart.

"I know," she said. "I love you, too."

They sat together quietly, hands joined, while the sun slowly suffused the room with gold and the machines whispered and beeped for the child on the bed.

Coming together.

Making it through.

Believing that somehow everything would be all right.

Believing in love.

*   *   *

After twelve hours, Zachary began breathing strongly on his own. Morgan gagged reflexively as Elizabeth removed the tube from their son's throat.

She looked up, her smile sympathetic, her eyes tired and strained. "I'm glad I can do this while he's still unconscious. He'll have a hell of a sore throat when he wakes up."

"*When*," not "*if.*" Progress, Morgan thought. His Elizabeth was getting her bearings again and her confidence. He was glad.

He nodded.

Throughout the morning, people came and went, Nancy from the front desk, the dour female mayor, the woman who sold Elizabeth her house. Morgan listened as Elizabeth offered explanations, reassurances, lies, watching each effort deplete her resources a little further, increasingly annoyed on her behalf.

". . . drug usually used to treat seizures . . . didn't realize until he fell and cracked his jaw on the coffee table . . . Thank you, I'm sure he'll be fine."

Dylan and Caleb pieced together a full report, augmented by their own suspicions and speculations.

"So this demon possessed Zack when he left the beach

last night," the police chief said. "Used the boy's energy to free himself."

Dylan nodded. "And used his body to get through the island's wards."

The brothers exchanged a look.

"We'll need to run by the island and check the orb," Caleb said. "Confirm the demon really was Tan."

"He could have been acting as an agent of Gau," Dylan said.

Caleb shook his head. "More likely, he saw an opportunity and took it."

"We don't know how well the demons communicate. If—"

"Enough," Morgan interrupted suddenly, roughly.

The Hunter brothers glanced at him, surprised.

"Elizabeth doesn't need to be bothered with this now, in our son's sickroom. I will speak with you tonight. Or tomorrow. Right now, Zachary needs quiet. And Elizabeth needs a break."

"Well." She studied him when they were gone, a smile tugging the corner of her mouth. "That was forceful."

Morgan scowled, aware she was about to scold him for treating her as the . . . what was it? Oh, yes, a weak and pampered woman in need of his protection.

"Thank you." She put her arms around him and held him, just held on. She sighed, her head fitting in the hollow of his chest, their bodies perfectly aligned.

It felt good.

It felt like home.

He stroked his hands lightly up and down her back, tipped back her head. She smiled up at him mistily.

"Go," he ordered gently. "Wash your face, catch your breath, get a cup of coffee."

Her smile trembled. "I do need to use the bathroom."

"Then go. I will stay."

He watched her leave the room, his heart so huge he thought it would burst the bounds of his chest.

I will always stay, he thought.

He turned and saw their son watching from beneath half-closed eyes.

"I really screwed up, didn't I." The boy's voice rasped. It wasn't a question.

Morgan was surprised. "You were unprepared. This is my fault, not yours."

"I let him take me."

So he did remember, Morgan thought with a flash of pity. "You fought."

"I didn't win."

Morgan chose his words with care. Zachary was still fragile. He needed reassurance. But he deserved the truth. "Sometimes the victory is in holding on." To a woman, he thought. Two children. A life. "You remembered who you are. You did not let Tan touch your mother. You resisted. You were strong." Morgan was forced to clear his throat. "I am proud of you."

Zachary's pale face colored to the roots of his hair. He smiled crookedly. "Gee, thanks, Dad."

Not a hook, Morgan thought dizzily. A harpoon, straight through the heart. *"Congratulations, you have a son."*

He went to the bed and awkwardly, for the first time, squeezed Zachary's hand. The boy turned his palm over and clung.

He heard a sound behind them. Elizabeth, standing in the doorway, her eyes shining with joy and tears.

"If you're both feeling better now," she said, "we should think about going home."

Epilogue

MORGAN OF THE FINFOLK STOOD BEFORE A PILLAR at the front of the small church, chafing against impatience and his suddenly tight collar. Zachary, beside him, wore the formal clothing with awkward dignity, the dark suit setting off the pale glitter of his newly shorn hair. Stephanie, sitting several rows back, kept glancing at Zachary as if she barely recognized him.

"The whole island must be here," Conn murmured on Morgan's other side.

Morgan stirred restively. As long as Elizabeth showed up soon, he hardly cared who was in attendance. But he was pleased for her sake that her parents had come, that the community she longed for had embraced her.

And he was glad, after all, to have their son standing with him. To feel the press of angels as even the children of air blessed this celebration. To see Dylan waiting with Nick in the front pew, daughter Grace gripping his thumbs as she practiced standing on his lap. Margred, Caleb, and their newborn son occupied the row behind with Lucy.

"We are honored by your presence, lord," he said to Conn.

"Lucy was glad for an excuse to see her family and meet her new nephew." Conn's gaze rested briefly on his consort, his silver eyes inscrutable. "She talks much of weddings these days."

To Morgan's knowledge, the selkie prince and the *targair inghean* had never wed. The children of the sea did not require the sacraments of men. But in this moment, waiting at the front of the church for Elizabeth, Morgan understood the importance of the promise made before God and witnesses.

He shifted his weight, his eyes still focused on the church doors. "I thought you might have come to remind me of my duty."

"Your duty is here," Conn said.

Morgan's attention was diverted from the back of the church. "Not on Sanctuary?"

"Griff has the work of rebuilding in hand. Lucy was able to use her power to relieve many of your people, and I have released others from my service."

Morgan felt as if a fist had been released in the center of his chest. "Then you have no objection if I stay."

"Hardly." Conn smiled thinly. "Why do you think I left you behind when Lucy and I returned to Sanctuary?"

Morgan frowned. "To recover from the crossing."

"I am not so tenderhearted," Conn said. "Dylan needs you here. I want you here. One warden is not enough to guard the next generation."

The next generation. *"Hope for the future,"* Conn had called them. Dylan's child. Margred's child.

Zack.

Whatever future Zachary chose for himself, he needed to be trained in survival and in magic. In the past few months, he had proven himself a focused and determined pupil.

"I want options," the boy had explained seriously when his father had complimented his progress.

Morgan looked at Conn and raised his eyebrows. "I could hardly have been your first choice. Given my prejudice against humankind."

Conn smiled coolly. "It was my hope that World's End would provide an opportunity for you to change your mind."

"Or an opportunity to rid yourself of a troublesome rival?"

Conn met his eyes in acknowledgment. "Either way, my strategy worked."

Morgan flashed his teeth. "Indeed."

But it wasn't his mind that had changed.

It was his heart.

Still, he forced himself to ask, "What of the northern deeps?"

Conn's expression was bleak. "The deeps are wounded almost beyond repair. On our return, Lucy and I go north to seal the seas around Yn Eslynn. After that . . . Any thoughts on who might replace you there?"

Morgan considered the wardens who sat on the council. "Enya."

"She is not finfolk."

"But she is fierce."

"Yes." The sea lord's gaze strayed to his consort in the second row. "Enya, too, might benefit from time away from Sanctuary."

Music rolled from the organ. Conn took his place beside Lucy as the congregation stirred and the air quivered in anticipation.

Morgan's heart raced. Yet his face remained calm, his gaze fixed on the door. He had not let himself feel anything, even hope, for such a long time. And now . . .

Light spilled from the back of the church. Emily appeared in the widening crack, dressed in seashell pink, a crown of flowers pinned securely to her halo of dark curls. Bodies shifted. Necks craned. A murmur rose. For a second, the child froze, rehearsal forgotten.

Morgan caught her anxious gaze and slowly winked.

Her stiff little face relaxed. Clutching her posy, she tripped forward.

Morgan's gaze moved beyond her to a grinning Regina, vivid in a deep rose sheath that hugged her post-baby curves.

The music changed, flowed, sure and triumphant. Morgan was aware of Zachary beside him, compulsively patting his pocket for the rings. The doors flung wide.

And framed against the light was his heart, his hope, his love.

Elizabeth.

She walked alone, a vision in silk the color of sea foam, its shades shifting from gray to pink to pearl. But it was the glow in her eyes that stilled his breath, that warmed his blood.

So beautiful she was, strong and beautiful.

He would love her as long as he lived, until the seas ran dry.

*   *   *

Liz was glad now she had let Regina and Margred talk her out of the sensible suit she'd first selected for her wedding.

Walking toward Morgan, she felt beautiful. Like a bride. She felt loved.

She held her bouquet—lavender and wild beach roses— a little more tightly. Her misty gaze flickered over her friends and family in the pews to find Zack beside Morgan, tall and assured, a younger version of his father. Emily had forgotten where she was supposed to stand and was clinging to Morgan's pant leg.

Liz's eyes met Morgan's. Her heart leaped. He smiled at her crookedly, his face transformed by trust and tenderness, companionship and commitment.

By love.

Elizabeth smiled back and stepped forward into her future.

TURN THE PAGE FOR A SPECIAL PREVIEW
OF THE NEXT CHILDREN OF THE SEA NOVEL

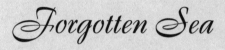

Forgotten Sea

BY VIRGINIA KANTRA

COMING SOON FROM BERKLEY SENSATION!

1

THE MAN ON THE BOAT STRIPPED HALF-NAKED, exposing a lean golden chest and muscled arms.

In the parking lot across the street from the dock, Lara Rho sucked in her breath. Held it as he dropped his shirt to the deck and began to climb.

The top of the mast swayed, stark against the bold blue sky. Her stomach fluttered. Nerves? she wondered. Recognition? Or simple female appreciation?

The sun beat down, forging the water of the bay to a sheet of hammered gold. The air inside the car heated like an oven.

Beside her in the driver's seat, Gideon stirred, chafing in the heat. His corn silk hair was pulled into a ponytail, his blue eyes narrowed against the glare. "Is he the one?"

Lara leaned forward to peer through the windshield of their nondescript gray car, testing the pull of the internal compass that had woken her at dawn. They'd driven all morning from the rolling hills of Pennsylvania through the flat Virginia tidewater, wasting precious minutes in

the traffic around Norfolk before they found this place.
This man.

Are you the one?

She exhaled slowly, willing herself to focus on the
climber. He certainly looked like an angel, hanging in the
rigging against the bold blue sky, his bronze hair tipped
with gold like a halo.

"I think so." She bit her lip. She should *know*. "Yes."

"He's too old," Gideon said.

Lara swallowed her own misgivings. She was the des-
ignated Seeker on this mission. Gideon was along merely
to support and defend. She wanted her instincts to be right,
wanted to justify their masters' faith in her. "Late twen-
ties," she said. "Not much older than you."

"He should have been found before this."

"Maybe he wasn't meant to be found before." Her
heartbeat quickened. Maybe she was the one meant to
find him.

"Then he should be dead," Gideon said.

The brutal truth made her shiver despite the heat. Survival depended on banding together under the Rule. She
was only eleven when they brought her to Rockhaven, but
she remembered being alone. Hunted. If Simon Axton had
not found her . . .

She pushed the memories away to study her subject. He
must be forty feet above the gleaming white deck. Snag-
ging a rope at the top of the mast, he fed it to the two men
waiting below, one old, one young, both wearing faded
navy polo shirts. Some kind of uniform?

"He's been at sea," she murmured. "The water could
have protected him."

It could do that, couldn't it? Protect against fire. Even if
the water wasn't blessed.

"I don't like it," Gideon said bluntly. "You're sure he's
one of us?"

She had felt him more with every mile, a tug on her
attention, a prickle in her fingertips. Now that she could
actually see him, the hum in her blood had become a buzz.

But it was all vibration, like listening to a vacuum cleaner in the dark, without shape or color. Not only human, not wholly elemental . . .

"What else could he be?" she asked.

"He could be possessed."

"No."

She would know; she would feel that. She was attracted, not repelled, by his energy. And yet . . . Uncertainty ate at her. She had not been a Seeker very long. The gift was rough and raw inside her, despite Hanna's careful teaching. What if she were wrong? What if he wasn't one of them? At best she and Gideon would have a wasted trip and she'd look like a fool. At worst, she could betray them to their enemy.

She watched the man begin his descent, his long limbs fluid in the sun, sheened with sweat and sunlight.

And if she were right, his life would depend on her.

She shook her head in frustration. "We're too far away. If I could touch him . . ."

"What are you going to do?" Gideon asked dryly. "Walk up and ask to feel his muscles?"

There was an idea. She gave a small, decisive nod. "If I have to."

She opened her door. Gideon opened his.

"No," she said again. She needed to assert herself. Gideon was five years older, in the cohort ahead of hers, but she was technically in charge. "I can get closer if you're not standing next to me."

A frown formed between his straight blond brows. "It could be dangerous."

She had chosen their watch post. They both had scanned the area. It was safe. For now. "There's no taint."

"That's not the kind of danger I'm talking about," Gideon muttered.

She disregarded him. For twelve years, she had trained to handle herself. She could handle this.

She swung out of the car, lowering her sunglasses onto her nose like a knight adjusting his helm, considering her strategy. Her usual approach was unlikely to work here. This subject was no confused and frightened child or even a dazed, distrustful adolescent.

After a moment's thought, she undid another button on her blouse. Ignoring Gideon's scowl—after all, *he* was not the one responsible for the success of their mission—she crossed the street to the marina.

It was a long, uneven walk along sun-bleached boards to the end of the dock.

The man descending the mast had stopped halfway down, balanced on some sort of narrow crossbeam, staring out at the open sea on the other side of the boat.

She tipped back her head. Her nerves jittered. Surely he wasn't going to . . .

He jumped. Dived, rather, a blinding arc of grace and danger, sending up a plume of white water and a shout from the younger man on deck.

She must have cried out, too. The two men on the boat turned to look at her, the young one with a nudge and the old one with a nod.

The one in the water surfaced with an explosion of breath, tossing his wet hair back from his face.

Cooling off? Or showing off? It didn't matter.

He stroked cleanly through the water, making for the swimming platform at the back of the boat.

Show time, she thought.

Pasting a smile on her face, she walked to the edge of the dock. "Eight point six."

He angled his head, meeting her gaze. She felt the jolt clear to her stomach, threatening her detachment. His eyes were the same hammered gold as the water, with shadows beneath the surface.

"Ten."

She pushed her sunglasses up on her head. "I deducted a point for recklessness. You shouldn't dive this close to the dock."

He grinned and grabbed the ladder. "I wasn't talking about my dive."

Heat rose in her cheeks. No one under the Rule would speak to her that way. But that was what she wanted, wasn't it? For him to respond to her while she figured out what to do with him.

"Thanks." This close, she could feel his energy pulsing inside him like a second heart. She tried again to identify it, but her probing thought slid off him like a finger on wet glass. He was remarkably well shielded. Well, he would have to be, to survive this long on his own.

She cast about for a subject. "Nice boat."

He shot her a measuring glance; hauled himself out of the sea, water streaming from his arms and chest. "Yeah, she is."

She tried not to goggle at the way his wet shorts drooped on his hips, clung to his thighs. "How long have you had her?"

"She's not mine. Four of us crewed her up from the Caribbean for her owners."

"So you're staying here? In town."

He shook his head. "As soon as she's serviced, I'm on to the next one."

Apprehension gripped her. She arched her brows. "You're still referring to the boat, I hope."

He flashed another grin, quick and crooked as lightning. "Just making it clear. Once I line up another berth, another job, I'm gone."

"Then we don't have much time," she said with more truth than he knew.

He stood there, shirtless, dripping, regarding her with glinting golden eyes. "How much time do you need?"

Her heart beat in her throat. Her mouth was dry. He thought her interest was sexual. Of course he did. That's what she had led him to think.

"Why don't we start with coffee," she suggested, "and see what happens."

He glanced at his companions, bundling sails on deck. "Drinks, and you've got yourself a date."

Lara swallowed. She had hoped to be back in Rock-haven by nightfall. But a few hours wouldn't make that much difference to their safety. She wanted desperately to succeed in their mission, to prove herself to the school council. She rubbed her tingling fingertips together. If only she could touch him . . . But they were separated by more than four feet of water. "Five o'clock?"

"Seven. Where?"

She scrambled to cull a name from their frustrating foray along the waterfront earlier in the day. Someplace close, she thought. Someplace dark. "The Galaxy?"

His eyes narrowed before he nodded. "I'll be there."

Relief rushed through her. "I'll be waiting."

* * *

Justin watched her walk away, slim legs, trim waist, snug skirt, nice ass, a shining fall of dark hair to the middle of her back. Definitely a ten.

"Hot." Rick Scott, the captain, offered his opinion.

"Very," Justin agreed.

Her face was as glossy and perfect as a picture in a magazine, her eyes large and gray beneath dark winged brows, her nose straight, her mouth full-lipped. Unsmiling.

Why a woman like that would choose a dive like the Galaxy was beyond him. Unless she was slumming. He picked his way through the collapsed sails and coiled ropes on deck. Which explained her interest in him even after she'd learned he wasn't a rich yacht owner.

The stink of mineral spirits competed with the scent of brine and the smells of the bay: fish and fuel and mudflats.

"The hot chicks always go for Justin," Ted said. "Lucky bastard."

Rick spat with precision over the side. He was tidy that way, an ex-military man with close-cropped graying hair and squinting blue eyes. "Next time you send the halyard up the mast, you can climb after it. Maybe some girl will hit on you."

A red stain crept under the younger crewman's tan. "It was an accident."

Justin felt a flash of sympathy. He remembered—didn't

he?—when he was that young. That dumb. That eager to please. "Could have happened to anybody."

He'd made enough mistakes himself his first few months and years at sea. Worse ones than tugging on an unsecured line.

He wondered if the girl would be another one.

Dredging the disassembled winch out of the bucket of mineral spirits, he laid out the gears to dry. He was working his way north again like a migrating seabird, following the coast and an instinct he did not try to understand. The last thing he needed was to get tangled up onshore.

"*I'll be waiting*," she'd said in that smooth, low voice.

He reached for the can of marine grease. Maybe she could slake the ache inside him, provide a few hours of distraction, a few minutes of release.

Mistake or not, he would be there.

* * *

This bar was a mistake, Lara thought.

The Galaxy was four blocks from the waterfront, off the tourist path, in a rundown neighborhood of shaded windows, sagging porches, and chain fences.

She perched in one of the dingy booths, trying to watch the room without making eye contact with the sailors and construction types straddling the stools at the bar.

Or maybe not.

Certainly no one would question if she and Gideon helped one slurring, stumbling patron out to their car later that night.

Over the bottles, a TV flickered, competing with the glow of the neon signs. Miller. Bud. Pabst Blue Ribbon. The air stank of bodies and beer, a trace of heavy cologne, a whiff from the men's room down the hall. She folded her hands in her lap, her untouched diet Coke leaving another ring on the cloudy table.

"Is it hot in here, or is it you?"

She looked up to find two sailors flanking her table. "Excuse me?"

The larger sailor shifted closer, trapping her into the booth. "You're too pretty to be sitting here alone. Mind if we join you?"

She wasn't alone. Gideon watched from an ill-lit corner, his attention divided between her and the door.

She straightened on the sticky vinyl seat. "I'm waiting for someone."

"I don't see anybody." The sailor—hovering drunkenly between cheerful and offensive—nudged his companion. "You see anybody, T.J.?"

T.J.'s blurred gaze remained focused on Lara's breasts. "Nope."

"Let me buy you a drink," the first guy said.

"No, thanks," Lara said firmly.

"There you are." A male voice, deep and smooth, broke through the noise of the bar and the wail of the jukebox. Somehow the sailors shifted, and there *he* was, tall and lean and attractively unshaven, looking perfectly at ease among the Galaxy's rough clientele.

It was him. Her quarry from the boat.

Her heart, her breath, her whole body reacted. Her fingertips tingled. Well, they would. She was attuned to him, to his energy.

He grinned at her. "Miss me?"

"You're late," she said.

Twelve minutes. Not enough to abandon her mission, but enough to pinch her ego.

"Come on, baby, don't be mad. You know I had to work." The newcomer's eyes danced, and she realized abruptly he was acting, playing a part for the sailors who still hemmed her into the booth. He lowered his voice confidingly. "Thanks for keeping an eye on her. She gets . . . restless if I leave her alone too long. If you know what I mean."

Lara kept her mouth shut with an effort. The shorter sailor guffawed. His companion shifted his weight like a bull, hunching his shoulders.

"I should spot you back," the newcomer continued easily. Man-to-man, she thought, making them like him, make them side with him, diffusing the tension. He moved again, angling his body so smoothly she almost didn't see him slide his wallet from his front pocket.

Feet shuffled. Something passed hands. The sailors nodded to her and then ambled back to the bar.

Lara narrowed her eyes. "Did you just give them money?"

"I bought them a round." His grin flashed. "Why not?"

"You *paid* them to go away," she said, torn between outrage and admiration. She couldn't imagine Gideon—or Zayin or any of the Guardians—dispatching an opponent by buying him a drink.

"Think of it as supporting our troops." He met her gaze, his own wickedly amused. "Unless you'd rather we pound each other for the privilege of plying you with alcohol."

"Of course not. Anyway, I already have a drink, thank you."

He eyed her glass and shook his head. "Place like this, you order beer. In a bottle. Unless you want to wake up with something a hell of a lot worse than a headache."

He turned to signal the waitress.

Lara appreciated his concern. But his caution would make her task more difficult. Her fingers curled around the handle of her bag on the seat beside her. Maybe it wouldn't be necessary to drug his drink, she thought. Explanations were out of the question. He wouldn't believe her, and they might be overheard. But surely she could rouse something in him, a response, a spark, a memory.

Assuming he was one of them.

Perhaps she should offer to feel his muscles after all.

The thought made her flush. "I don't even know your name."

"Justin." No last name.

"Lara. Lara Rho."

She started to extend her hand, but at that moment he caught the waitress's eye and the opportunity to touch him was lost.

Lara swallowed her disappointment.

The waitress, a hard-edged, hard-eyed blonde who

looked like she'd rather be somewhere else, left the knot of locals absorbed by the game on TV. "What can I get you?"

"Two Buds," Justin said.

The waitress looked at Lara. "ID?"

"Of course," she said, reaching for her purse.

Axton insisted they do their best to abide by human laws, to blend in with their human neighbors. She pulled out her perfectly valid Pennsylvania driver's license, hoping Justin would do the same, eager for any hint to his identity, any clue why he hadn't been found before now.

He smiled at the waitress. "Thanks."

The blonde cocked her hip, pulled a pen from her stack of hair. "Anything else?"

His grin was quick and charming. "I'll let you know."

Oh, he was smooth, Lara thought, as the waitress sashayed away.

"So, Lara Rho." He stretched his arms along the back of the booth, his knees almost-not-quite brushing Lara's under the table. "What brings you to Norfolk?"

You.

Bad answer.

"Um." She inched her foot closer to his across the sticky floor, hoping that small, surreptitious contact would give her the answers she needed. "Just visiting."

"For work? Or pleasure?"

Her toe nudged his. A buzz radiated up her leg, as if her foot had fallen asleep.

Deliberately, she met his gaze. "That depends on you."

His tawny eyes locked with hers. The tingling spread to her thighs and the pit of her stomach.

"I'm done working," he said.

Her mouth dried at the lazy intent in his eyes. "Won't they be expecting you? Back at the boat?"

"Boat's been delivered and I got paid. Nobody will care if I jump ship." He smiled at her winningly. "I'm a free man."

She moistened her lips. "Isn't that convenient."

No one would miss him if he disappeared tonight.

Her heart thudded in her chest. All she had to do was identify him as one of her own kind, the nephilim, the fallen children of air.

From his corner, Gideon glowered, no doubt wondering what was taking her so long.

If only she were more experienced . . .

The waitress returned with their beer, two bottles, no glasses.

Lara gripped the slick surface and gulped, drinking to ease the constriction of her throat.

"Let's get out of here," Justin invited suddenly.

"What?"

He reached across the table and took her hand, wet from the bottle. An almost visible spark arced between them, a snap of connection, a burst of power. Shock ripped through her.

His eyes flickered. "You pack quite a punch."

So he felt it, too. Felt something. Hope and confusion churned inside her. She dampened her own reaction, feeling as though her circuits had all been scrambled. The air between them crackled, too charged to breathe.

"I . . . You too."

Her heart thudded. *He was not human.*

Or only partly human. His elemental energy beat inside his mortal flesh.

But he was not nephilim, either. She didn't know what he was.

His energy was not light, but movement, swirling, thick, turbulent as storm. It swamped her. Flooded her. She clung to his hand like a lifeline, focusing with difficulty on his face.

". . . find someplace quiet," he was saying. "Let me take you out to dinner. Or for a walk along the waterfront."

"What are you doing?" Gideon demanded.

Lara flinched.

"Who the hell are you?" Justin asked.

Gideon ignored him. "Are you *trying* to call attention to yourself?" he asked Lara.

Lara tugged her hand from Justin's, her mind still stunned, her senses reeling from the force of their connection. "You felt that?"

"They could feel you in Philadelphia," Gideon said grimly. "Shield, before you get us both killed."

Justin's eyes narrowed. "Look, buddy, I don't know who the fuck you think you are, but—"

Gideon gripped Lara's elbow. "We're getting out of here."

Justin rose from the booth. "Take your hands off her."

"It's all right," Lara said quickly. She struggled to pull herself together. "I know him."

Justin's mouth tightened. "That doesn't mean you have to go with him."

"Try and stop her," Gideon invited.

Lara shook her arm from his grasp. "That's enough," she said, her voice sharp as a slap.

Gideon met her gaze. "Your little energy flare just gave away our location. This place will be crawling in an hour. We need to leave before they get here."

Lara's throat constricted. "What about him?"

"Is he one of us?"

Not human. Not nephilim, either.

"No," she admitted.

"Then lose him. He's not our responsibility."

He was right. She was still new to her duties as Seeker, but the Rule was clear about their obligations to their own kind. And the dangers of getting involved with those who were not their kind.

Yet . . .

"Give us a minute," she said.

Gideon's face set, cold and rigid as marble. "Five minutes," he acceded. "I'll wait for you outside."

Where he could guard the entrance and scan for danger. She nodded.

With another glare at Justin, he left.

"Are you okay?" Justin asked.

"Fine," she said firmly, whether it was true or not. Why had she felt the pull of his presence if she wasn't meant to find him?

"Listen, it's none of my business," he said. "But if this guy is giving you a hard time . . ."

His willingness to look out for a stranger shamed her. Especially since she was about to abandon him to his fate.

"Nothing like that. We work together," she explained.

He looked unconvinced.

"What about you?" she asked.

He frowned. "What about me?"

Who are you?

What are you?

"Will you be all right?" she asked.

"I think my ego will survive being ditched for another guy." The glint in his eye almost wrung a smile from her.

She bit her lip. Their enemies would be circling, drawn by that unexpected snap of energy. She already had to account for one mistake. She couldn't afford another.

Besides, he was not one of them.

He would be safe. He had to be.

"Right. Well." She slipped her purse strap onto her shoulder. At least now she didn't have to drug his beer.

"Take care of yourself."

As she slid out of the booth, he stepped back, lean and bronzed and just beyond her reach. "You too."

She walked away, reluctance dogging her steps and dragging at her heart.

*   *   *

Justin watched his plans for the evening walk out the door with more regret than he had a right to. Her tight butt in that slim skirt attracted more than a few glances. Her fall of dark brown hair swung between her shoulders. The woman sure knew how to move.

He shook his head. He'd known she was slumming when she came on to him this afternoon. Presumably she was going back where she belonged, with Mr. Tall, Blond, and Uptight.

He hadn't lost anything more than half an hour of his time. So why was there this ache in the center of his chest, this sense of missed opportunity?

He took a long, cold pull at his bottle, his gaze drifting over the bar. He'd been in worse watering holes over the past nine years, before he got his bearings and some control over his life. Worse situations, in Porto Parangua and Montevideo, in Newark and Miami. He drank more beer. He fit in with the surly locals and tattooed sea rats better than pretty Lara Rho and her upscale boyfriend ever could. But he didn't belong here. He belonged . . . The beer tasted suddenly flat in his mouth. He didn't know where he belonged.

He set down his bottle. He didn't want to drink alone tonight. And he didn't want to drink with the company the Galaxy had to offer.

Careful not to flash his roll, he dropped a couple of bills on the table and walked out.

Nobody followed.

Outside, the sky was stained with sunset and a chemical haze, orange, purple, gray. The day's heat lingered, radiating from the crumbling asphalt, sparking off the broken glass. He headed instinctively for the water, free as a bird thanks to the coworker boyfriend with the ponytail, trying to figure out what to do with the rest of his evening.

Or maybe his life.

Beyond the jumbled rooftops at the end of the street, he could see the flat shimmer of the sea. He passed a homeless guy huddled in a doorway, clutching a bottle, watching the street with flat, dead eyes. Something wrong there. He kept his arms loose and at his sides as the pawn shops and tattoo parlors gave way to warehouses and razed lots.

His neck crawled. Alley ahead. Empty. Good.

He lengthened his stride, taking note of blank windows and deserted doorways. Good place to get jumped, he thought, and angled to avoid the dirty white van blocking a side street.

He heard a thump. A grunt.

Not his problem, he reminded himself. None of his business.

A woman's cry, sharp with anger and alarm.

Shit.

He circled the van, shot a quick look down the street.

And saw Lara Rho backed against the brick wall of an empty lot with a couple of rough guys circling her like dogs.

Penguin Group (USA) Online

What will you be reading tomorrow?

Patricia Cornwell, Nora Roberts, Catherine Coulter,
Ken Follett, John Sandford, Clive Cussler,
Tom Clancy, Laurell K. Hamilton, Charlaine Harris,
J. R. Ward, W.E.B. Griffin, William Gibson,
Robin Cook, Brian Jacques, Stephen King,
Dean Koontz, Eric Jerome Dickey, Terry McMillan,
Sue Monk Kidd, Amy Tan, Jayne Ann Krentz,
Daniel Silva, Kate Jacobs...

You'll find them all at
penguin.com

*Read excerpts and newsletters,
find tour schedules and reading group guides,
and enter contests.*

Subscribe to Penguin Group (USA) newsletters
and get an exclusive inside look
at exciting new titles and the authors you love
long before everyone else does.

PENGUIN GROUP (USA)
penguin.com

M224G0909

continued . . .

Sea Fever

"An especially fine paranormal with strong characters, logical plotting, and a *great* sense of place. Don't go to the shore without this bit of selkie romance."
—*Romantic Times* (4 ½ stars)

"An exciting and spellbinding addition to this phenomenal paranormal series." —*Fresh Fiction*

"There's no second-novel slump for this trilogy . . . Moving, heartbreaking, and beautiful."
—*Errant Dreams Reviews* (5 stars)

Sea Witch

"A paranormal world that moves with the rhythm of the waves and the tide . . . Kantra tells Margred and Caleb's story with a lyric, haunting, poetic voice."
—Suzanne Brockmann, *New York Times* bestselling author

"Full of excitement, humor, suspense, and loads of hot, hot sex. Anyone who enjoys a good paranormal should *not* miss this one!" —*Fresh Fiction*

"An absolutely fantastic paranormal/fantasy read . . . Gorgeous, complex, and fascinating."
—*Errant Dreams Reviews* (5 stars)

"What a refreshing and unique world Virginia Kantra has created for Children of the Sea! Full of sensual magic, intrigue, and compelling characters, *Sea Witch* is a book to be savored." —*CK²S Kwips and Kritiques* (4 ½ clovers)

"A bestseller arises from the depths of the sea and floats to the top of the romance/paranormal list! *Sea Witch* is enthralling!" —*A Romance Review* (5 roses)